# RENÉE MAUPERIN

# LECTOR HOUSE PUBLIC DOMAIN WORKS

# RENÉE MAUPERIN

**EDMOND DE GONCOURT,
JULES DE GONCOURT,
ALYS HALLARD,
JAMES FITZMAURICE-KELLY,
OCTAVE UZANNE**

ISBN: 978-93-89582-63-5

Published:                    -

LECTOR HOUSE LLP
E-MAIL: lectorpublishing@gmail.com

DE GONCOURT


# RENÉE MAUPERIN

BY

## EDMOND DE GONCOURT
## AND
## JULES DE GONCOURT


TRANSLATED FROM THE FRENCH BY
ALYS HALLARD


WITH A CRITICAL INTRODUCTION BY
JAMES FITZMAURICE-KELLY


A FRONTISPIECE AND NUMEROUS OTHER PORTRAITS
WITH DESCRIPTIVE NOTES BY
OCTAVE UZANNE

# EDMOND AND JULES DE GONCOURT

## I

The partnership of Edmond and Jules de Goncourt is probably the most curious and perfect example of collaboration recorded in literary history. The brothers worked together for twenty-two years, and the amalgam of their diverse talents was so complete that, were it not for the information given by the survivor, it would be difficult to guess what each brought to the work which bears their names. Even in the light of these confidences, it is no easy matter to attempt to separate or disengage their literary personalities. The two are practically one. Jamais âme pareille n'a été mise en deux corps. This testimony is their own, and their testimony is true. The result is the more perplexing when we remember that these two brothers were, so to say, men of different races. The elder was a German from Lorraine, the younger was an inveterate Latin Parisian: "the most absolute difference of temperaments, tastes, and characters—and absolutely the same ideas, the same personal likes and dislikes, the same intellectual vision." There may be, as there probably always will be, two opinions as to the value of their writings; there can be no difference of view concerning their intense devotion to literature, their unhesitating rejection of all that might distract them from their vocation. They spent a small fortune in collecting materials for works that were not to find two hundred readers; they passed months, and more months, in tedious researches the results of which were condensed into a single page; they resigned most of life's pleasures and all its joys to dedicate themselves totally to the office of their election. So they lived—toiling, endeavouring, undismayed, confident in their integrity and genius, unrewarded by one accepted triumph, uncheered by a single frank success or even by any considerable recognition. The younger Goncourt died of his failure before he was forty; the elder underwent almost the same monotony of defeat during nearly thirty years of life that remained to him. But both continued undaunted, and, if we consider what manner of men they were and how dear fame was to them, the constancy of their ambition becomes all the more admirable.

## EDMOND DE GONCOURT

Despising, or affecting to despise, the general verdict of their contemporaries, they loved to declare that they wrote for their own personal pleasure, for an audience of a dozen friends, or for the delight of a distant posterity; and, when the absence of all appreciation momentarily weighed them down, they vainly imagined that the acquisition of a new *bibelot* consoled them. No doubt the passion of the collector was strong in them: so strong that Edmond half forgot his grief for his brother and his terror of the Commune in the pursuit of first editions: so strong that the chances of a Prussian bomb shattering his storehouse of treasures—the *Maison d'un artiste*—at Auteuil saddened him more than the dismemberment of France. But, even so, the idea that the Goncourts could in any circumstances subordinate literature to any other interest was the merest illusion. Nothing in the world pleased them half so well as the sight of their own words in print. The arrival of a set of proof-sheets on the 1st of January was to them the best possible augury for the new year; the sight of their names on the placards outside the theatres and the booksellers' shops enraptured them; and Edmond, then well on in years, confesses that he thrice stole downstairs, half-clad, in the March dawn, to make sure that the opening chapters of *Chérie* were really inserted in the *Gaulois*. These were their few rewards, their only victories. They were fain to be content with such small things—*la petite monnaie de la gloire*. Still they were persuaded that time was on their side, and, assured as they were of their literary immortality, they chafed at the suggestion that the most splendid renown must grow dim within a hundred thousand years. Was so poor a laurel worth the struggle? This was the whole extent of their misgiving.

Baffled at every point, the Goncourts were unable to account for the unbroken series of disasters which befell them; yet the explanation is not far to seek. For one thing, they attempted so much, so continuously, in so many directions, and in such quick succession, that their very versatility and diligence laid them under suspicion. They were not content to be historians, or philosophers, or novelists, or dramatists, or art critics: they would be all and each of these at once. In every branch of intellectual effort they asserted their claims to be regarded as innovators, and therefore as leaders. Within a month they published *Germinie Lacerteux* and an elaborate study on Fragonard; and, while they plumed themselves (as they very well might) on their feat, the average intelligent reader joined with the average intelligent critic in concluding that such various accomplishment must needs be superficial. It was not credible that one and the same pair—*par nobile fratrum*—could be not only close observers of contemporary life, but also authorities on Watteau and Outamaro, on Marie Antoinette and Mlle. Clairon. To admit this would be to emphasize the limitations of all other men of letters. Again, the uncanny element of chance which enters into every enterprise was constantly hostile to the Goncourts. They not only published incessantly: they somehow contrived to publish at inopportune moments—at times when the public interest was turned from letters to politics. Their first novel appeared on the very day of Napoleon III's *Coup d'état*, and their publisher even refused to advertise the book lest the new authorities should see in the title of *En 18*—a covert allusion to the 18th Brumaire. It would have been a pleasing stroke of irony had the Ministry of the 16th of May been supported by the country as it was supported by Edmond de Goncourt, for that Ministry intended to prosecute him as the author of *La Fille Élisa*. *La Faustin* was issued on the morning of Gambetta's downfall; and the seventh volume of the *Journal des Goncourt* had barely been published a few hours when the news of Carnot's assassination reached Paris. Lastly, the personal qualities of the brothers—their ostentation of independence, their attitude of supercilious superiority, and, most of all, their fatal gift of irony—raised up innumerable enemies and alienated both actual and possible friends. They gave no quarter and they received none. All this is extremely human and natural; but the Goncourts, being nervous invalids as well as born fighters, suffered acutely from what they regarded as the universal disloyalty of their comrades.

They could not realize that their writings contained much to displease men of all parties, and, living at war with literary society, they sullenly cultivated their morbid sensibility. The simplest trifle stung them into frenzies of inconsistency and hallucination. To-day they denounced the liberty of the press; to-morrow they raged at finding themselves the victims of a Government prosecution. Withal their ferocious wit, there was not a ray of sunshine in their humour, and, instead of smiling at the discomfiture of a dull official, they brooded till their imaginations magnified these petty police-court proceedings into the tragedy of a supreme martyrdom. Years afterward they continually return to the subject, noting with exasperated complacency that the only four men in France who were seriously concerned with letters and art—Baudelaire, Flaubert, and themselves—had been dragged before the courts; and they ended by considering their little lawsuit as one of the historic state trials of the world. Henceforth, in every personal matter— and their art was intensely personal—they lost all sense of proportion, believing that there was a vast Semitic plot to stifle *Manette Salomon* and that the President had brought pressure on the censor to forbid an adaptation of one of their novels being put upon the boards. Monarchy, Empire, Republic, Right, Centre, Left—no shade of political thought, no public man, no legislative measure, ever chanced to please them. They sought for the causes of their failure in others: it never occurred to them that the fault lay in themselves. Their minds were twin whirlpools of chaotic opinions. Revolutionaries in arts and letters as they claimed to be, they detested novelties in religion, politics, medicine, science, abstract speculation. It never struck them that it was incongruous, not to say absurd, to claim complete liberty for themselves and to denounce ministers for attempting to extend the far more restricted liberty of others. And as with the ordering of their lives, so with their art and all that touched it. Unable to conciliate or to compromise, they were conspicuously successful in stimulating the general prejudice against themselves. They paraded their self-contradictions with a childish pride of paradox. In one breath they deplored the ignorance of a public too uncultivated to appreciate them; in another breath they proclaimed that every government which strives to diminish illiteracy is digging its own grave. Priding themselves on the thoroughness of their own investigations, they belittled the results of learning in others, mocked at the superficial labour of the Benedictines, ridiculed the inartistic surroundings of Sainte-Beuve and Renan, and protested that antiquity was nothing but an inept invention to enable professors to earn their daily bread. Not content with asserting the superiority of Diderot to Voltaire, they pronounced the Abbé Trublet to be the acutest critic who flourished during that eighteenth century which they had come to consider as their exclusive property. Resolute conservatives in theory, piquing themselves on their descent, their personal elegance, their tact and refinement, these worshippers of Marie Antoinette admired the talent shown by Hébert in his infamous *Père Duchêne,* and then went on to lament the influence of socialism on literature. They were *papalini* who sympathized with Garibaldi; they looked forward to a repetition of '93, and almost welcomed it as a deliverance from the respectable uniformity of their own time; they trusted to the working men—masons, house-painters, carpenters, navvies—to regenerate an effete civilization and to save society as the barbarians had saved it in earlier centuries. Whatever the value of these views, they can scarcely have found favour among those who rallied to the Second Empire and who imagined that the Goncourts were a pair of firebrands: whereas, in fact, they were petulant, impulsive men of talent, smarting under neglect.

If we were so ingenuous as to take their statements seriously, we might refuse to admit their right to find any place in French literature. For, though it would be easy to quote passages in which they contemn the cosmopolitan spirit, it would be no less easy to set against these their assertions that they are ashamed of being French; that they are no more French than the Abbé Galiani, the Prince de Ligne, or Heine; that they will renounce their nationality, settle in Holland or Belgium, and there found a journal in which they can speak their minds. These are wild, whirling words: the politics of literary men are on a level with the literature of politicians. On their own showing, it does not appear that the Goncourts were in any way fettered. The sum of their achievement, as they saw it, is recorded in a celebrated passage of the preface to *Chérie*: "*La recherche du vrai en littérature, la résurrection de l'art du XVIII<sup>e</sup> siècle, la victoire du japonisme.*" These words are the words of Jules de Goncourt, but Edmond makes them his own. If the brothers were entitled to claim—as they repeatedly claimed—to be held for the leaders of these "three great literary and artistic movements of the second half of the nineteenth century," it is clear that they were justified in thinking that the future must reckon with them. It is equally clear that, if their title proves good, their environment was much less unfavourable than they assumed it to be.

The conclusion is that their sublime egotism disabled them from forming a judicial judgment on any question in which they were personally concerned. They never attempted to reason, to compare, to balance; their minds were filled with the vapour of tumultuous impressions which condensed at different periods into dogmas, and were succeeded by fresh condensations from the same source. But, amid all changes, their self-esteem was constant. They had no hesitation in setting Dunant's *Souvenir de Solférino* above the *Iliad*; but when Taine implied that he was somewhat less interested in *Madame Gervaisais* than in the writings of Santa Teresa, they were startled at his boldness. And, to define their position more precisely, Edmond confidently declares (among many other strange sayings) that the fifth act of *La Patrie en Danger* contains scenes more dramatically poignant than anything in Shakespeare, and that in *La Maison d'un Artiste au XIX<sup>e</sup> Siècle* he takes under his control—though he candidly avows that none but himself suspects it—a capital movement in the history of mankind. These are extremely high pretensions, repeatedly renewed in one form or another—in prefaces, manifestos, articles, letters, conversation, and, above all, in nine invaluable volumes which consist of extracts from a diary covering a period of over forty years. This extraordinary record incidentally embodies the rough sketches of the Goncourts' finished work, but its interest is far wider and more essentially characteristic. Other men have written confessions, memoirs, reminiscences, by the score: mostly books composed long after the events which they relate, recollections revised, reviewed in the light of after events. The Goncourts are perhaps alone in daring to unbosom themselves with an absolute sincerity of their emotions, intentions, aims. If they come forth damaged from such a trial, it is fair to remember that the test is unique, and that no other writers have ever approached them in courage and in what they most valued—truth: *la recherche du vrai en littérature.*

## II

A most authoritative critic, M. Brunetière, has laid it down that there is more truth, more fidelity to the facts of actual life, in any single romance by Ponson du Terrail or by Gaboriau than in all the works of the Goncourts put together, and so long as we leave truth undefined, this opinion may be as tenable as any other. But it may be well to observe at the outset that the creative work of the Goncourts is not to be condemned or praised *en bloc,* for the simple reason that it is not a spontaneous, uniform product, but the resultant of diverse forces varying in direction and intensity from time to time. They themselves have recorded that there are three distinct stages in their intellectual evolution. Beginning, under the influence of Heine and Poe, with purely imaginative conceptions, they rebounded to the extremest point of realism before determining on the intermediate method of presenting realistic pictures in a poetic light. Pure imagination in the domain of contemporary fiction seemed to them defective, inasmuch as its processes are austerely logical, while life itself is compact of contradictions; and their first re-action from it was entirely natural, on their own principles. It remains to be seen what sense should be attached to the formula—*la recherche du vrai en littérature*—in which they summarized their position as regards their predecessors.

Obviously we have to deal with a question of interpretation. The Goncourts did not—could not—pretend that they were the first to introduce truth into litera-ture: they merely professed to have attained it by a different route. The innovation for which they claimed credit is a matter of method, of technique. Their deliberate purpose is to surprise us by the fidelity of their studies, to captivate and convince us by an accumulation of exact minutiæ: in a word, to prove that truth is more in-teresting than fiction. So history should be written, and so they wrote it. First and last, whatever form they chose, they remained historians. Alleging the example set by Plutarch and Saint-Simon, they make their histories of the eighteenth cen-tury a mine of anecdote, a pageant of picturesque situations. State-papers, blue-books, ministerial despatches, are in their view the conventional means used for hoodwinking simpletons and forwarding the interests of a triumphant faction. The most valuable historical material is, as they believed, to be sought in the au-tograph letter. They held that the secret of the craftiest intriguer will escape him, despite himself, in the expansion of confidential correspondence. The research for such correspondence is to be supplemented by the study of sculpture, paintings, engravings, furniture, broadsides, bills—all of them indispensable for the recon-struction of a past age and for the right understanding of its psychology. But these means are simply complementary. The chief vehicle of authentic truth is the au-tograph letter, and, though they professed to hold the historical novel in abhorrence, they applied their historical methods to their records of contemporary life. Thus we inevitably arrive at the famous theory of the *document humain*—a phrase received with much derision when first publicly used in the preface to *La Faustin*, and a theory conscientiously adopted by many later novelists. And here, again, it is important to realize the restricted extent of the authors' claim.

The Goncourts draw a broad, primary distinction between ancient and modern literature: the first deals mainly with generalities, the second with details. They then proceed to establish an analogous distinction between novels written before and after Balzac's time, the modern novel being based on *des documents racontés, ou relevés d'après nature*, precisely as formal history is based on *des documents écrits*. But they make no pretence of having initiated the revolution; their share was limited to continuing Balzac's tradition, to enlarging the field of observation, and especially to multiplying the instruments of research. They declared that Gautier had, so to say, endowed literature with vision; that Fromentin, in describing the silence of the desert, had revealed the literary value of hearing; that with Zola, Loti—and they might surely have added Maupassant—a fresh sense was brought into play: *c'est le nez qui entre en scène*. Their personal contribution was their nervous sensibility: *les premiers nous avons été les écrivains des nerfs*. And they were prouder of this morbid quality than of their talent. They were ever on the watch for fragments of talk caught up in drawing-rooms, in restaurants, on omnibuses: ever ready to take notes at death-beds, church, or taverns. Their life was one long pursuit of *l'imprévu, le décousu, l'illogique du vrai*. These observations they transcribed at night while the impression was still acute, and these they utilized more or less deftly as they advanced towards what they rightly thought to be the goal of art: the perfect adjustment of proportion between the real and the imagined.

It would seem that we are now in a position to judge the Goncourts by their own standard. *Le dosage juste de la littérature et de la vie*—this formula recurs in one shape or another as a leading principle, and it is supplemented by other still more emphatic indications which should serve to supply a test. Unhappily, with the Goncourts these indications are unsystematic and even contradictory. The elder brother has naturally no hesitation in saying that the highest gift of any writer is his power of creating on paper real beings—*comme des êtres créés par Dieu, et comme ayant eu une vraie vie sur la terre*—and he is bold enough to add that Shakespeare himself has failed to create more than two or three personages. He protests energetically against the academic virtues, and insists on the importance of forming a personal style which shall reproduce the vivacity, brio, and feverish activity of the best talk. It is, then, all the more disconcerting to learn from another passage in the *Journal* that the creation of characters and the discovery of an original form of expression are matters of secondary moment. The truth is that if the Goncourts had, as they believed, something new to say, it was inevitable that they should seek to invent a new manner of utterance. Renan was doubtless right in thinking that they were absolutely without ideas on abstract subjects; but they were exquisitely susceptible to every shade and tone of concrete objects, and the endeavour to convey their innumerable impressions taxed the resources of that French vocabulary on whose relative poverty they so often insist. The reproaches brought against them in the matter of verbal audacities by every prominent critic, from Sainte-Beuve in one camp to Pontmartin in the other, are so many testimonies to the fact that they were innovators—*apporteurs du neuf*—and that their intrepidity cost them dear. Still their boldness in this respect has been generally exaggerated. Setting out as imitators of two such different models as Gautier and Jules Janin, they slowly acquired an individual manner—the manner, say, of *Germinie Lacerteux* or *Manette Salomon*—but they never attained the formula which they had conceived as final. It was not given to them to realize their ambition—to write novels which should not contain a single bookish expression, plays which should reveal that hitherto undiscoverable quantity—colloquial speech, raised to the level of consummate art. The famous *écriture artiste* remained an unfulfilled ideal. The expression, first used in the preface to *Les Frères Zemganno*, merely foreshadows a possible development of style which shall come into being when realism or naturalism, ceasing to describe the ignoble, shall occupy itself with the attempt to render refinements, reticences, subtleties, and half-tones of a more elusive order. It is an aspiration, a counsel of perfection offered to a younger school by an artist in experiment, who declares the quest to be beyond his powers. It is nothing more.

Leaving on one side these questions of style and manner, it may safely be said that in the novels of the Goncourts the characters are less memorable, less interesting as individuals than as illustrations of an epoch or types of a given social sphere. Charles Demailly, Madame Gervaisais, Manette Salomon, Renée Mauperin, Sœur Philomène, are not so much dramatic creations as figures around which is constituted the life of a special *milieu*—the world of journalism, of Catholicism seen from two opposite points of view, of artists, of the *bourgeoisie*, as the case may be. There are in the best work of the Goncourts astonishingly brilliant scenes; there is dialogue vivacious, witty, sparkling, to an extraordinary degree. And this dialogue, as in *Charles Demailly*, is not only supremely interesting, but intrinsically true to nature. It could not well be otherwise, for the speeches assigned to Masson, Lampérière, Remontville, Boisroger, and Montbaillard are, as often as not, verbatim reports of paradoxes and epigrams thrown off a few hours earlier by Théophile Gautier, Flaubert, Saint-Victor, Banville, and Villemessant. But these flights, true and well worth preserving as they are, fail to impress for the simple reason that they are mere exercises in bravura delivered by men much less concerned with life than with phrases, that they are allotted to subordinate characters, and that they rather serve to diminish than to increase the interest in the central figures. The Goncourts themselves are much less absorbed in life than in writing about it: just as landscapes reminded them of pictures, so did every other manifestation of existence present itself as a possible subject for artistic treatment. They had been called the detectives of history; they became detectives, inquisitors in real life, and, much as they loathed the occupation, they never rested from their task of spying and prying and "documentation." As with *Charles Demailly*, so with their other books: each character is studied after nature with a grim, revolting persistence. Their aunt, Mlle. de Courmont, is the model of Mlle. de Varandeuil in *Germinie Lacerteux*; Germinie herself is drawn from their old servant Rose, who had loved them, cheated them, blinded them for half a lifetime; the Victor Chevassier who figures in *Quelques créatures de ce temps* is sketched from their father's old political ally, Colardez, at Breuvannes; the original of the Abbé Blampoix in *Renée Mauperin* was the Abbé Caron; the painter Beaulieu and that strange Bohemian Pouthier are both worked into *Manette Salomon.* And the novel entitled *Madame Gervaisais* is an almost exact transcription or record of the life of the authors' aunt, Mme. Nephthalie de Courmont: a report so literal that in three hundred pages there are but two trifling departures from the strictest historical truth.

Mommsen himself has not excelled the Goncourts in conscientious "documentation"; and yet, for all their care, their personages do not abide in the memory as living beings. We do not see them as individuals, but as types; and, strangely enough, the authors, despite the remarkable skill with which they materialize many of their impressions, are content to deliver their characters to us as so many illustrations of a species. Thus Marthe Mance in *Charles Demailly* is *un type, l'incarnation d'un âge, de son sexe et d'un rôle de son temps;* Langibout is *le type pur de l'ancienne école;* Madame Gervaisais, too, is *un exemple et un type* of the intellectual *bourgeoise* of Louis-Philippe's time; Madame Mauperin is *le type* of the modern *bourgeoise* mother; Renée is the type of the modern *bourgeoise* girl; the Bourjots "represent" wealth; Denoisel is a Parisian—*ou plutôt c'était le Parisien.* The Goncourts, in their endeavour to be more precise, resort to odd combinations of conflicting elements. Within some twenty pages Renée Mauperin is *une mélancolique tintamarresque;* the adjectives *bourgeoise* and *diabolique* are used to characterize the same thing; the Abbé Blampoix is at once "priest and lawyer, apostle and diplomatist, Fénelon and M. de Foy." And the same types constantly reappear. The physician Monterone in *Madame Gervaisais* is simply an Italian version of Denoisel in *Renée Mauperin;* the Abbé Blampoix has his counter-part in Father Giansanti; Honorine is Germinie, before the fall; Nachette and Gautruche might be brothers. The procedure, too, is almost invariable. The antecedents of each personage are given with abundant detail. We have minute information as to the family history of the Mauperins, the Villacourts, Germinie, Couturat, and the rest; and the mention of Father Sibilla involves a brief account of the order of Barefooted Trinitarians from January, 1198, to the spring of 1853! There is a frequent repetition of the same idea with scarcely any verbal change: *un dos d'amateur* in *Renée Mauperin* and *le dos du cocher* in *Germinie Lacerteux.* And the possibilities of the human back were evidently not exhausted, for at Christmas, 1882, Edmond de Goncourt makes a careful note of the *dos de jeune fille du peuple.*

It is by no means an accident that the most frequent theme of the brothers is illness: the insanity of Demailly, the tortures of Germinie, the consumption of Madame Gervaisais, the decay of Renée Mauperin, the record of pain in *Sœur Philomène,* in *Les Frères Zemganno,* and in other works of the Goncourts. Emotion in less tragic circumstances they rarely convey; and when they attempt it they are prone to stumble into an unimpressive sentimentalism. Their strength lay in pure observation, not in the philosophic or psychological presentment of nature. For their fine powers to have full play, it was necessary that they should deal with things seen: in other words, that feeling should take a concrete shape. Once this condition is fulfilled, they can focus their own impressions and render them with unsurpassable skill. We shall find in them nothing epic, nothing inventive on a grand scale: the transfiguring, ennobling vision of the greatest creators was denied them. But they remain consummate masters in their own restricted province: delicate observers of externals, noting and remembering with unmatched exactitude every detail of gesture, attitude, intonation, and expression. The description of landscape—of the Bois de Vincennes in *Germinie Lacerteux*, the Forest of Fontainebleau in *Manette Salomon*, or of the Trastevere quarter in *Madame Gervaisais*—commonly affords them an occasion for a triumph; but the description of prolonged malady gives them a still greater opportunity. Nor is this due simply to the fact that they, who had never known what it was to enjoy a day of perfect health, spoke from an intimate knowledge of the subject. Each landscape preserves at least its abstract idiosyncrasy; illness is an essentially "typical" state in which individual characteristics diminish till they finally disappear. And it is especially in the portraiture of types, rather than of individuals, that the genius of the Goncourts excels.

In their own opinion, their initiative extended over a vast field and in all directions. They seriously maintained that they were the first to introduce the poor into French fiction, the first to awaken the sentiment of pity for the wretched; they admitted the priority of Dickens, but they apparently forgot that they had likewise been anticipated by George Sand—that George Sand whose merits it took them twenty years to recognise. They forgot, too, that compassion is precisely the quality in which they were most lacking. Gavarni had killed the sentiment of pity in them, and had communicated to them his own mocking, sardonic spirit of inhumanity, his sinister delight in every manifestation of cruelty, baseness, and pain. In their most candid moods they confessed that they were all brain and no heart, that they were without real affections; and their writings naturally suffer from this unsympathetic attitude. But when every deduction is made, it is impossible to deny their importance and significance. For they represent a distinct stage in an organized movement—the reaction against romanticism in the novel and lyrism in the theatre. And there is some basis for their bold assertion that they led the way in every other development of the modern French novel. They believed that they had founded the naturalistic school in *Germinie Lacerteux*, the psychological in *Madame Gervaisais*, the symbolic in *Les Frères Zemganno*, and the satanic in *La Faustin*. It is unnecessary to recognise all these claims in full: to discuss them at all, even if we deny them, is to admit that the Goncourts were men of striking intellectual force, of singular ambition, of exceptionally rich and diverse gifts amounting, at times, to unquestionable genius. If they were unsuccessful in their attempt to create an entire race of beings as real as any on the planet, their superlative talent produced, in the form of novels, invaluable studies of manners and customs, a brilliant series of monographs on the social history of the nineteenth century. And Daudet and M. Zola, and a dozen others whom it would be invidious to name, may be accounted as in some sort their literary descendants.

It is not unnatural that Edmond de Goncourt should have ended by disliking the form of the novel, which he came to regard as an exhausted convention. His pessimism was universal. Art was dying, literature was perishing daily. The almost universal acceptance of Ibsen and of Tolstoi was in itself a convincing symptom of degeneration, if the vogue of the latter writer were not indeed the result of a cosmopolitan plot against the native realistic school. It was some consolation to reflect that, after all, there was more "philosophy" in Beaumarchais than in Ibsen; that the name of Goncourt was held in honour by Scandinavians and Slavs. Yet it could not be denied that, the world over, aristocracy of every kind was breaking down. To the eyes of the surviving Goncourt all the signs of a last great catastrophe grew visible. Mankind was ill, half-mad, and on the road to become completely insane. There were countless indications of intellectual and physical decadence. Sloping shoulders were disappearing; the physique of the peasant was not what it had been; good food was practically unattainable; in a hundred years a man who had once tasted genuine meat would be pointed out as a curiosity. The probability was, that within half a century there would not be a man of letters in the world; the reporter, the interviewer, would have taken possession. As it was, the younger generation of readers no longer rallied to the Goncourts as it had rallied when *Henriette Maréchal* was first replayed. The weary old man buried himself in memoirs, biographies, books of travel; then turned to his first loves—to Poe and Heine—and found that "we are all commercial travellers compared to them." But, threatened as he was by blindness, despairing as were his presentiments of what the future concealed, his confidence in the durability of his fame and his brother's fame was undimmed. There would always be the select few interested in two such examples of the *littérateur bien né.* There would always be the official historians of literature to take account of them as new, perplexing, elemental forces. There would always be the curious who must turn to the Goncourts for positive information. "Our romances," as the brothers had noted forty years earlier, "will supply the greatest number of facts and absolute truths to the moral history of this century." And Edmond de Goncourt clung to the belief, ending, happily and characteristically enough, by conceiving himself and his brother to be "types," and the best of all types: *le type de l'honnête homme littéraire, du persévérant dans ses convictions, et du contempteur de l'argent.* The praise is deserved. It is a distinction of which greater men might well be proud.

JAMES FITZMAURICE-KELLY.

# BIOGRAPHICAL NOTE - LIVES OF EDMOND AND JULES DE GONCOURT

*The Goncourts were the sons of a cavalry officer, commander of a squadron in the Imperial army. EDMOND was born at Nancy, on the 26th of May, 1822, and his brother JULES in Paris, on the 17th of December, 1830. They were the grandsons of the deputy of the National Assembly of 1789, Huot de Goncourt. A very close friendship united the brothers from their earliest youth, but it appears to have been in the younger that the irresistible tendency to literature first displayed itself. They were originally drawn almost exclusively to the study of the history of art. They devoted themselves particularly to the close of the eighteenth century, and in their earliest important volumes, "La Révolution dans les Mœurs" (1854), "Histoire de la Société Française pendant la Révolution" (1854), and "Pendant le Directoire" (1855), they invented a new thing, the evolution of the history of an age from the objects and articles of its social existence. They were encouraged to continue these studies further, more definitely concentrating their observations around individuals, and some very curious monographs—made up, as some one said, of the detritus of history—were the result, "Une Voiture de Masques," 1856; "Les Actrices (Armande)," 1856; "Sophie Arnauld," 1857. The most ingenious efforts of the brothers in this direction were, however, concentrated upon "Portraits Intimes du XVIII<sup>e</sup> Siècle," 1857-'58, and upon the "Histoire de Marie Antoinette," 1858.*

*Towards 1860 the Goncourts closed their exclusively historical work, and transferred their minute observation and excessively meticulous treatment of small aspects of life to realistic romance. Their first novel, "Les Hommes de Lettres," 1860 (now known as "Charles Demailly"), showed some lack of ease in using the new medium, but it was followed by "Sœur Philomène," 1861, one of the most finished of their fictions, and this by "Renée Mauperin," 1864; "Germinie Lacerteux," 1864; "Manette Salomon," 1867; and "Madame Gervaisais," 1869. Meanwhile, numerous studies of the art of the bibelot appeared under the name of the two Goncourts, and in particular their great work on "L'Art du XVIII<sup>e</sup> Siècle," which began to be published in 1859, although not completed until 1882. All this while, moreover, they were secretly composing their splenetic "Journal." On the 20th of June, 1870, the fair companionship was broken by the death of Jules de Goncourt, and for some years Edmond did no more than complete and publish certain artistic works which had been left unfinished. Of these, the most remarkable were, a monograph on the life and work of Gavarni, 1873; a compilation called "L'Amour au XVIII<sup>e</sup> Siècle," 1875; studies of the Du Barry, the Pompadour, and the Duchess of Châteauroux, 1878-'79 (these three afterward united in one volume as "Les Maîtresses de Louis XV"); and notes of a tour in Italy, 1894.*

*Edmond de Goncourt, however, after several years of silence, returned alone to the composition of prose romance. He published in 1877 "La Fille Élisa," an ultra-realistic tragedy of low life. In 1878, in the very curious story of two mountebanks, "Les Frères Zemganno," he betrayed the secret of his own perennial sorrow. Two more novels, "La Faustin," 1882, and "Chérie," the pathetic portrait of a spoiled child, close the series of his works in fiction. He returned to a close examination of the history of art, and published cat-* alogues raisonnés *of the entire work of Watteau (1875) and of Prud'hon (1876). His latest interests were centred around the classical Japanese designers, and he published elaborate monographs on Outamaro (1891) and Hokousaï (1896). In 1885 he collected the Letters of his brother Jules, and issued from 1887 to 1896, in nine volumes, as much as has hitherto been published of the celebrated "Journal des Goncourts."*

*Edmond de Goncourt died while on a visit to Alphonse Daudet, at Champrosay, the country-house of the latter, on the 16th of July, 1896. He left his considerable fortune, which included valuable collections of bibelots, mainly for the purpose of endowing an Academy of Prose Literature, in opposition to the French Academy. In spite of extreme hostility from the members of his family, and innumerable legal difficulties, this "Académie des Goncourts" was formed, on what seems to be a secure basis, in 1901, and M. Joris Karl Huysmans was elected its first president.*

EDMUND GOSSE

# CONTENTS

# RENÉE MAUPERIN

## I

"You don't care about society, then, mademoiselle?"

"You won't tell any one, will you?—but I always feel as though I've swallowed my tongue when I go out. That's the effect society has on me. Perhaps it is that I've had no luck. The young men I have met are all very serious, they are my brother's friends—quotation young men, I call them. As to the girls, one can only talk to them about the last sermon they have heard, the last piece of music they have learned, or their last new dress. Conversation with my contemporaries is somewhat restricted."

"And you live in the country all the year round, do you not?"

"Yes, but we are so near to Paris. Is the piece good they have just been playing at the Opéra Comique? Have you seen it?"

"Yes, it's charming—the music is very fine. All Paris was at the first night—I never go to the theatre except on first nights."

"Just fancy, they never take me to any theatre except the Opéra Comique and the Français, and only to the Français when there is a classical piece on. I think they are terribly dull, classical pieces. Only to think that they won't let me go to the Palais Royal! I read the pieces though. I spent a long time learning 'The Mountebanks' by heart. You are very lucky, for you can go anywhere. The other evening my sister and my brother-in-law had a great discussion about the Opera Ball. Is it true that it is quite impossible to go to it?"

"Impossible? Well— —"

"I mean—for instance, if you were married, would you take your wife, just once, to see it?"

"If I were married I would not even take— —"

"Your mother-in-law. Is that what you were going to say? Is it so dreadful—really?"

"Well, in the first place, the company is— —"

"Variegated? I know what that's like. But then it's the same everywhere. Every one goes to the Marche and the company is mixed enough there. One sees ladies, who are rather queer, drinking champagne in their carriages. Then, too, the Bois de Boulogne! How dull it is to be a *young person*, don't you think so?"

"What an idea! Why should it be? On the contrary, it seems to me— —"

"I should like to see you in my place. You would soon find out what a bore it is to be always proper. We are allowed to dance, but do you imagine that we can talk to our partner? We may say 'Yes,' 'No,' 'No,' 'Yes,' and that's all! We must always keep to monosyllables, as that is considered proper. You see how delightful our existence is. And for everything it is just the same. If we want to be very proper we have to act like simpletons; and for my part I cannot do it. Then we are supposed to stop and prattle to persons of our own sex. And if we go off and leave them and are seen talking to men instead—oh, well, I've had lectures enough from mamma about that! Reading is another thing that is not at all proper. Until two years ago I was not allowed to read the serials in the newspaper, and now I have to skip the crimes in the news of the day, as they are not quite proper.

"Then, too, with the accomplishments we are allowed to learn, we must not go beyond a certain average. We may learn duets and pencil drawing, but if we want anything more, why, it's affectation on our part. I go in for oil-painting, for instance, and that is the despair of my family. I ought only to paint roses and in water-colours. There's quite a current here, though, isn't there? I can scarcely stand."

This was said in an arm of the Seine just between Briche and the Île Saint Denis. The girl and the young man who were conversing were in the water. They had been swimming until they were tired, and now, carried along by the current, they had caught hold of a rope which was fastened to one of the large boats stationed along the banks of the island. The force of the water rocked them both gently at the end of the tight, quivering rope. They kept sinking and then rising again. The water was beating against the young girl's breast; it filled out her woollen bathing-dress right up to the neck, while from behind little waves kept dashing over her which a moment later were nothing but dewdrops hanging from her ears.

She was rather higher up than the young man and had her arms out of the water, her wrists turned round in order to hold the rope more firmly, and her back against the black wood of the boat. Instinctively she kept drawing back as the young man, swayed by the strong current, approached her. Her whole attitude, as she shrank back, suspended from the rope, reminded one of those sea goddesses which sculptors carve upon galleys. A slight tremor, caused partly by the cold and partly by the movement of the river, gave her something of the undulation of the water.

"Ah, now this, for instance," she continued, "cannot be at all proper—to be swimming here with you. If we were at the seaside it would be quite different. We should have just the same bathing costumes as these, and we should come out of a bathing-van just as we have come out of the house. We should have walked across the beach just as we have walked along the river bank, and we should be in the water to the same depth, absolutely like this. The waves would roll us about as this current does, but it would not be the same thing at all; simply because the Seine water is not proper! Oh, dear! I'm getting so hungry—are you?"

"Well, I fancy I shall do justice to dinner."

"Ah! I warn you that I eat."

"Really, mademoiselle?"

"Yes, there is nothing poetical about me at meal-times. If you imagine that I have no appetite you are quite mistaken. You are in the same club as my brother-in-law, are you not?"

"Yes, I am in M. Davarande's club."

"Are there many married men in it?"

"Yes, a great many."

"How odd! I cannot understand why a man marries. If I had been a man it seems to me that I should never have thought of marrying."

"Fortunately you are a woman."

"Ah, yes, that's another of our misfortunes, we women cannot stay unmarried. But will you tell me why a man joins a club when he is married?"

"Oh, one has to be in a club—especially in Paris. Every man of any standing—if only for the sake of going in there for a smoke."

"What! do you mean to say that there are any wives nowadays without smoking-rooms? Why, I would allow—yes, I would allow a halfpenny pipe!"

"Have you any neighbours?"

"Oh, we don't visit much. There are the Bourjots at Sannois, we go there sometimes."

"Ah, the Bourjots! But, here, there cannot be any one to visit."

"Oh, there's the curé. Ha! ha! the first time he dined with us he drank the water in his finger-bowl! Oh, I ought not to tell you that, it's too bad of me—and he's so kind. He's always bringing me flowers."

"You ride, don't you, mademoiselle? That must be a delightful recreation for you."

"Yes, I love riding. It is my one pleasure. It seems to me that I could not do without that. What I like above everything is hunting. I was brought up to that in the part of the world where papa used to live. I'm desperately fond of it. I was seven hours one day in my saddle without dismounting."

"Oh, I know what it is—I go hunting every year in the Perche with M. de Beaulieu's hounds. You've heard of his pack, perhaps; he had them over from England. Last year we had three splendid runs. By-the-bye, you have the Chantilly meets near here."

"Yes, I go with papa, and we never miss one. When we were all together at the last meet there were quite forty horses, and you know how it excites them to be together. We started off at a gallop, and you can imagine how delightful it was. It was the day we had such a magnificent sunset in the pool. Oh, the fresh air, and the wind blowing through my hair, and the dogs and the bugles and the trees flying along before you—it makes you feel quite intoxicated! At such moments I'm so brave, oh, so brave!"

"Only at such moments, mademoiselle?"

"Well—yes—only on horseback. On foot, I own, I am very frightened at night; then, too, I don't like thunder at all—and—well, I'm very delighted that we shall be three persons short for dinner this evening."

"But why, mademoiselle?"

"We should have been thirteen! I should have done the meanest things for the sake of getting a fourteenth—as you would have seen. Ah, here comes my brother with Denoisel; they'll bring us the boat. Do look how beautiful it all is from here, just at this time!"

She glanced round, as she spoke, at the Seine, the river banks on each side, and the sky. Small clouds were sporting and rolling along in the horizon. They were violet, gray, and silvery, just tipped with flashes of white, which looked like the foam of the sea touching the lower part of the sky.

Above them rose the heavens infinite and blue, profound and clear, magnificent and just turning paler as they do at the hour when the stars are beginning to kindle behind the daylight. Higher up than all hung two or three clouds stretching over the landscape, heavy-looking and motionless.

An immense light fell over the water, lying dormant here, flashing there, making the silvery streaks in the shadow of the boats tremble, touching up a mast or a rudder, or resting on the orange-coloured handkerchief or pink jacket of a washerwoman. The country, the outskirts of the town, and the suburbs all met together on both sides of the river. There were rows of poplar trees to be seen between the houses, which were few and far between, as at the extreme limit of a town.

Then there were small, tumble-down cottages, inclosure's planked round, gardens, green shutters, wine-trade signs painted in red letters, acacia trees in front of the doors, old summer arbors giving way on one side, bits of walls dazzlingly white, then some straight rows of manufactories, brick buildings with tile and zinc-covered roofs, and factory bells. Smoke from the various workshops mounted straight upward and the shadow of it fell in the water like the shadows of so many columns.

On one stack was written "Tobacco," and on a plaster façade could be read "Doremus Labiche, Boats for Hire."

Over a canal which was blocked up with barges, a swing-bridge lifted its two black arms in the air. Fishermen were throwing and drawing in their lines. The sound of wheels could be heard, carts were coming and going. Towing-ropes scraped along the road, which was hard, rough, black, and dyed all colours by the unloading of coal, mineral refuse, and chemicals.

From the candle, glucose, and fecula manufactories and sugar-refining works which were scattered along the quay, surrounded by patches of verdure, there was a vague odour of tallow and sugar which was carried away by the emanations from the water and the smell of tar. The noise from the foundries and the whistle of steam engines kept breaking the silence of the river.

It was like Asnières, Saardam, and Puteaux combined, one of those Parisian landscapes on the banks of the Seine such as Hervier paints, foul and yet radiant, wretched yet gay, popular and full of life, where Nature peeps out here and there between the buildings, the work and the commerce, like a blade of grass held between a man's fingers.

"Isn't it beautiful?"

"Well, to tell the truth, I am not in raptures about it. It's beautiful—in a certain degree."

"Oh, yes, it is beautiful. I assure you that it is very beautiful indeed. About two years ago at the Exhibition there was an effect of this kind. I don't remember the picture exactly, but it was just this. There are certain things that I feel——"

"Ah, you have an artistic temperament, mademoiselle."

"Oh!" exclaimed the young girl, with a comic intonation, plunging forthwith into the water. When she appeared again she began to swim towards the boat which was advancing to meet her. Her hair had come down, and was all wet and floating behind her. She shook it, sprinkling the drops of water all round.

Evening was drawing near and rosy streaks were coming gradually into the sky. A breath was stirring over the river, and at the tops of the trees the leaves were quivering. A small windmill, which served for a sign over the door of a tavern, began to turn round.

"Well, Renée, how have you enjoyed the water?" asked one of the rowers as the young girl reached the steps placed at the back of the boat.

"Oh, very much, thanks, Denoisel," she answered.

"You are a nice one," said the other man, "you swim out so far—I began to get uneasy. And what about Reverchon? Ah, yes, here he is."

# II

Charles Louis Mauperin was born in 1787. He was the son of a barrister who was well known and highly respected throughout Lorraine and Barrois, and at the age of sixteen he entered the military school at Fontainebleau. He became sublieutenant in the Thirty-fifth Regiment of infantry, and afterward, as lieutenant in the same corps, he signalized himself in Italy by a courage which was proof against everything. At Pordenone, although wounded, surrounded by a troop of the enemy's cavalry and challenged to lay down arms, he replied to the challenge by giving the command to charge the enemy, by killing with his own hand one of the horsemen who was threatening him and opening a passage with his men, until, overcome by numbers and wounded on the head by two more sword-thrusts, he fell down covered with blood and was left on the field for dead.

After being captain in the Second Regiment of the Mediterranean, he became captain aide-de-camp to General Roussel d'Hurbal, went through the Russian campaign with him, and was shot through the right shoulder the day after the battle of Moscow.

In 1813, at the age of twenty-six, he was an officer of the Legion of Honour and major in the army. He was looked upon as one of the commanding officers with the most brilliant prospects, when the battle of Waterloo broke his sword for him and dashed his hopes to the ground.

He was put on half-pay, and, with Colonel Sauset and Colonel Maziau, he entered into the Bonapartist conspiracy of the *Bazar français*.

Condemned to death by default, as a member of the managing committee, by the Chamber of Peers, constituted into a court of justice, he was concealed by his friends and shipped off to America.

On the voyage, not knowing how to occupy his active mind, he studied medicine with one of his fellow-passengers who intended taking his degree in America, and on arriving, Mauperin passed the necessary examinations with him. After spending two years in the United States, thanks to the friendship and influence of some of his former comrades, who had been taken again into active service, he obtained pardon and was allowed to return to France.

He went back to the little town of Bourmont, to the old home where his mother was still living. This mother was one of those excellent old ladies so frequently met with in the provincial France of the eighteenth century. She was gay, witty, and fond of her glass of wine. Her son adored her, and on finding her ill and under doctor's orders to avoid all stimulants, he at once gave up wine, liqueurs, and coffee for her sake, thinking that it would be easier for her to abstain if he shared her privations. It was in compliance with her request, and by way of humouring her sick fancies, that he married a cousin for whom he had no especial liking. His mother had selected this wife for her son on account of a joint claim to certain land, fields which touched each other, and all the various considerations which tend to unite families and blend together fortunes in the provinces.

After the death of his mother, the narrow life in the little town, which had no further attraction for him, seemed irksome, and, as he was not allowed to dwell in Paris, M. Mauperin sold his house and land in Bourmont, with the exception of a farm at Villacourt, and went to live with his young wife on a large estate which he bought in the heart of Bassigny, at Morimond. There were the remains of a large abbey, a piece of land worthy of the name which the monks had given it—"*Mort-au-monde*"—a wild, magnificent bit of Nature with a pool of some hundred acres or more and a forest of venerable oak trees; meadows with canals of freestone where the spring-tide flowed along under bowers of trees, a veritable wilderness where the vegetation had been left to itself since the Revolution; springs babbling along in the shade; wild flowers, cattle-tracks, the remains of a garden and the ruins of buildings. Here and there a few stones had survived. The door was still to be seen, and the benches were there on which the beggars used to sit while taking their soup; here the apse of a roofless chapel and there the seven foundations of walls *à la Montreuil*. The pavilion at the entrance, built at the beginning of the last century, was all that was still standing; it was complete and almost intact.

M. Mauperin took up his abode in this and lived there until 1830, solitary and entirely absorbed in his studies. He gave himself up to reading, educating himself on all subjects, and reaping knowledge in every direction. He was familiar with all the great historians, philosophers, and politicians, and was thoroughly master of the industrial sciences. He only left his books when he felt the need of fresh air, and then he would rest his brain and tire his body with long walks of some fifteen miles across the fields and through the woods.

Every one was accustomed to see him walk like this, and the country people recognised him in the distance by his step, his long frock-coat, all buttoned up, his officer's gait, his head always slightly bent, and the stick, made from a vine-stalk, which he used as a cane. The only break in his secluded and laborious life was at election time. M. Mauperin then put in an appearance everywhere from one end of the department to the other. He drove about the country in a trap, and his soldierly voice could be heard rousing the electors to enthusiasm at all their meetings; he gave the word of command for the charge on the Government candidates, and to him all this was like war once more.

When the election was over he left Chaumont and returned to his regular routine and to the obscure tranquility of his studies.

Two children had come to him—a boy in 1826 and a girl in 1827. After the Revolution of 1830 he was elected deputy. When he took his seat in the chamber, his American ideas and theories were very much like those of Armand Carrel. His animated speeches—brusque, martial, and full of feeling—made quite a sensation.

He became one of the inspirers of the *National* after being one of its first shareholders, and he suggested articles attacking the budget and the finances.

The Tuileries made advances to him; some of his former comrades, who were now aides-de-camp under the new king, sounded him with the promise of a high military position, a generalship in the army, or some honour for which he was still young enough. He refused everything point-blank. In 1832 he signed the protestation of the deputies of the Opposition against the words "Subjects of the King," which had been pronounced by M. de Montalivet, and he fought against this system until 1835.

That year his wife presented him with a child, a little girl whose arrival stirred him to the depths of his being. His other two children had merely given him a calm joy, a happiness without any gaiety. Something had always seemed wanting—just that something which brightens a father's life and makes the home ring with laughter.

M. Mauperin loved his two children, but he did not adore them. The fond father had hoped to delight in them, and he had been disappointed. Instead of the son he had dreamed of—a regular boy, a mischievous little urchin, one of those handsome little dare-devils with whom an old soldier could live over again his own youth and hear once more, as it were, the sound of gunpowder—M. Mauperin had to do with a most rational sort of a child, a little boy who was always good, "quite a young lady," as he said himself. This had been a great trouble to him, as he felt almost ashamed to have, as his son and heir, this miniature man who did not even break his toys.

With his daughter, M. Mauperin had had the same disappointment. She was one of those little girls who are women when they are born, and who play with their parents merely to amuse them. She scarcely had any childhood, and at the age of five, if a gentleman called to see her father, she always ran away to wash her hands. She would be kissed on certain spots, and she seemed to dread being ruffled or inconvenienced by a father's caresses and love.

Thus repelled, M. Mauperin's affection, so long hoarded up, went out to the cradle of the little newcomer whom he had named Renée after his mother. He spent whole days with his little baby-girl in divine nonsense. He would keep taking off her little cap to look at her silky hair, and he taught her to make grimaces which charmed him. He would lie down beside her on the floor when she was rolling about half naked with all a child's delightful unconsciousness. In the night he would get up to look at her asleep, and would pass hours listening to this first breath of life, so like the respiration of a flower. When she woke up he would be there to have her first smile—that smile of little girl-babies which comes from out of the night as though from Paradise. His happiness kept changing into perfect bliss; it seemed to him that the child he loved so much was a little angel from heaven.

What joy he had with her at Morimond! He would wheel her all round the house in a little carriage, and at every few steps turn round to look at her screaming with laughter, with the sunshine playing on her cheeks, and her little supple, pink foot curled up in her hand. Or he would take her with him when he went for a walk, and would go as far as a village and let the child throw kisses to the people who bowed to him, or he would enter one of the farm-houses and show his daughter's teeth with great pride. On the way, the child would often go to sleep in his arms, as she did with her nurse. At other times he would take her into the forest, and there, under the trees full of robin-redbreasts and nightingales, towards the end of the day when there are voices overhead in the woods, he would experience the most unutterable joy on hearing the child, impressed by the noises around, try to imitate the sounds, and to murmur and prattle as though she were answering the birds and speaking to the singing heavens.

Mme. Mauperin had not given this last daughter so hearty a welcome. She was a good wife and mother, but Mme. Mauperin was eaten up with that pride peculiar to the provinces—namely, the pride of money. She had made all her arrangements for two children, but the third one was not welcome, as it would interfere with the pecuniary affairs of the other two, and, above all, would infringe on her son's share. The division of land which was now one estate, the partition of wealth which had accumulated, and in consequence the lowering of social position in the future and of the importance of the family—all this was what the second little daughter represented to her mother.

M. Mauperin very soon had no more peace. The mother was constantly attacking the politician, and reminding the father that it was his duty to sacrifice himself to the interests of his children. She endeavoured to separate him from his friends and to make him forsake his party and his fidelity to his ideas. She made fun of what she called his tomfoolery, which prevented him from turning his position to account. Every day there were fresh attacks and reproaches until he was fairly haunted by them; it was the terrible battle of all that is most prosaic against the conscience of a Deputy of the Opposition. Finally, M. Mauperin asked his wife for two months' truce for reflection, as he, too, would have liked his beloved Renée to be rich. At the end of the two months he sent his resignation in to the Chamber and opened a sugar-refinery at Briche.

That had been twenty years ago. The children had grown up and the business was thriving. M. Mauperin had done very well with his refinery. His son was a barrister, his elder daughter married, and Renée's dowry was waiting for her.

# III

Every one had gone into the house, and in a corner of the drawing-room, with its chintz hangings gay with bunches of wild flowers, Henri Mauperin, Denoisel, and Reverchon were talking. Near to the chimney-piece, Mme. Mauperin, with great demonstrations of affection, was greeting her son-in-law and daughter, M. and Mme. Davarande, who had just arrived. She felt obliged on this occasion to make a display of family feeling and to exhibit her motherly love.

The greeting between Mme. Mauperin and Mme. Davarande was scarcely over when a little old gentleman entered the drawing-room quietly, wished Mme. Mauperin good-evening with his eyes as he passed, and walked straight across to the group where Denoisel was.

This little gentleman wore a dress-coat and had white whiskers. He was carrying a portfolio under his arm.

"Do you know that?" he asked Denoisel, taking him into a window recess and half opening his folio.

"That? I should just think I do. It's the 'Mysterious Swing,' an engraving after Lavrience's."

The little old gentleman smiled.

"Yes, but look," he said, and he half opened his portfolio again, but in such a way that Denoisel could only just see inside.

"'Before letters.' It's a proof before letters! Can you see?"

"Perfectly."

"And margins!—a gem, isn't it? They didn't give it me, I can tell you, the thieves! It was run up—and by a woman, too!"

"Oh, of course!"

"A *cocotte*, who asked to see it every time I went any higher. The rascal of an auctioneer kept saying, 'Pass it to the lady.' At last I got it for five pounds eight. Oh, I wouldn't have paid one halfpenny more."

"I should think not! If I had only known—why, there's a proof like that, exactly like it, at Spindler's, the artist's—and with larger margins, too. He does not care about Louis Seize things, Spindler. If I had only asked him!"

"Good heavens!—and before letters, like mine? Are you quite sure?"

"Before letters—before—Oh, yes, it's an earlier one than yours. It's before—"

and Denoisel whispered something to the old man which brought a flush of pleasure to his face and a moisture to his lips.

Just at this moment M. Mauperin entered the drawing-room with his daughter. She was leaning on his arm, her head slightly thrown back in an indolent way, rubbing her hair against the sleeve of her father's coat as a child does when it is being carried.

"How are you?" she said as she kissed her sister. She then held her forehead to her mother's lips, shook hands with her brother-in-law, and ran across to the little man with the portfolio.

"Can I see, god-papa?"

"No, little girl, you are not grown-up enough yet," he replied, patting her cheek in an affectionate way.

"Ah, it's always like that with the things you buy!" said Renée, turning her back on the old man, who tied up the ribbon of his portfolio with the special little bow so familiar to the fingers of print collectors.

"Well, what's this I hear?" suddenly exclaimed Mme. Mauperin, turning to her daughter.

Reverchon was sitting next her, so near that her dress touched him every time she moved.

"You were both carried away by the current," she continued. "It was dangerous, I am sure! Oh, that river! I really cannot understand how M. Mauperin allows——"

"Mme. Mauperin," replied her husband, who was by the table looking through an album with his daughter, "I do not allow anything—I tolerate——"

"Coward!" whispered Renée to her father.

"I assure you, mamma, there was no danger," put in Henri Mauperin. "There was no danger at all. They were just slightly carried along by the current, and they preferred holding on to a boat to going half a mile or so lower down the river. That was all! You see——"

"Ah, you comfort me," said Mme. Mauperin, the serenity of her expression gradually returning at her son's words. "I know you are so prudent, but, you see, M. Reverchon, our dear Renée is so foolish that I am always afraid. Oh, dear, there are drops of water on her hair now. Come here and let me brush them off."

"M. Dardouillet!" announced a servant.

"A neighbour of ours," said Mme. Mauperin in a low voice to Reverchon.

"Well, and where are you now?" asked M. Mauperin, as he shook hands with the new arrival.

"Oh, we are getting on—we are getting on—three hundred stakes done to-day."

"Three hundred?"

"Three hundred—I fancy it won't be bad. From the green-house, you see, I am going straight along as far as the water, on account of the view. Fourteen or sixteen inches of slope—not more. If we were on the spot I shouldn't have to explain. On the other side, you know, I shall raise the path about three feet. When all that's done, M. Mauperin, do you know that there won't be an inch of my land that will not have been turned over?"

"But when shall you plant anything, M. Dardouillet?" asked Mlle. Mauperin. "For the last three years you have only had workmen in your garden; sha'n't you have a few trees in some day?"

"Oh, as to trees, mademoiselle, that's nothing. There's plenty of time for all that. The most important thing is the plan of the ground, the hills and slopes, and then afterward trees—if we want them."

Some one had just come in by a door leading from another room. He had bowed as he entered, but no one had seen him, and he was there now without any one noticing him. He had an honest-looking face and a head of hair like a pen-wiper. It was M. Mauperin's cashier, M. Bernard.

"We are all here; has M. Bernard come down? Ah, that's right!" said M. Mauperin on seeing him. "Suppose we have dinner, Mme. Mauperin, these young people must be hungry."

The solemnity of the first few moments when the appetite is keen had worn off, and the buzz of conversation could be heard in place of the silence with which a dinner usually commences, and which is followed by the noise of spoons in the soup plates.

"M. Reverchon," began Mme. Mauperin. She had placed the young man by her, in the seat of honour, and she was amiability itself, as far as he was concerned. She was most attentive to him and most anxious to please. Her smile covered her whole face, and even her voice was not her every-day voice, but a high-pitched one which she assumed on state occasions. She kept glancing from the young man to his plate and from his plate to a servant. It was a case of a mother angling for a son-in-law. "M. Reverchon, we met a lady just recently whom you know—Mme. de Bonnières. She spoke so highly of you—oh, so highly!"

"I had the honour of meeting Mme. de Bonnières in Italy—I was even fortunate enough to be able to render her a little service."

"Did you save her from brigands?" exclaimed Renée.

"No, it was much less romantic than that. Mme. de Bonnières had some difficulty about the bill at her hotel. She was alone and I prevented her from being robbed."

"It was a case of robbers, anyhow, then," said Renée.

"One might write a play on the subject," put in Denoisel, "and it would be quite a new plot—the reduction of a bill leading to a marriage. What a good title, too, 'The Romance of an Awkward Moment, *à la* Rabelais!'"

"Mme. de Bonnières is a very nice woman," continued Mme. Mauperin. "I like her face. Do you know her, M. Barousse?" she asked, turning to Renée's godfather.

"Yes, she is very pleasant."

"Oh! why, god-papa, she's like a satyr!" exclaimed Renée.

When the word was out some of the guests smiled, and the young girl, turning red, hastened to add: "I only mean she has a face like one."

"That's what I call mending matters!" said Denoisel.

"Did you stay long in Italy, monsieur?" asked M. Mauperin, by way of changing the subject.

"Six months."

"And what did you think of it?"

"It's very interesting, but one has so much discomfort there. I never could get used to drinking coffee out of glasses."

"Italy is the most wretched place to go to; it is the least practical of all places," said Henri Mauperin. "What a state agriculture is in there—and trade, too! One day in Florence at a masked ball I asked the waiter at a restaurant if they would be open all night. 'Oh, no, sir,' he said, 'we should have too many people here.' That's a fact, I heard it myself, and that shows you what the country is. When one thinks of England, of that wonderful initiative power of individuals and of the whole nation, too; when one has seen the business genius of the London citizen and the produce of a Yorkshire farm—Oh, a fine nation that!"

"I agree with Henri," said Mme. Davarande, "there is something so distinguished about England. I like the politeness of the English people, and I approve of their way of always introducing people. Then, too, they wrap your change up in paper—and some of their dress materials have quite a style of their own. My husband bought me a poplin dress at the Exposition—Oh, mamma, I have quite decided about my cloak. I was at Alberic's—it's most amusing. He lets one of the girls put a cloak over your shoulders and then he walks round you and just marks with an ebony ruler the places where it does not fit; he scarcely touches you with it, but just gives little taps—like that—and the girl marks each tap with chalk. Oh, he certainly has a lot of character, that Alberic! And then he's the only one—there isn't another place—he has such good style for cloaks. I recognised two of his yesterday at the races. He is very expensive though."

"Oh, those people get what they like to ask," said Reverchon. "My tailor, Edouard, has just retired—he's made over a hundred thousand pounds."

"Oh, well, quite right," remarked M. Barousse. "I'm always very glad when I see things like that. The workers get the money nowadays—that's just what it is. It's the greatest revolution since the beginning of the world."

"Yes," said Denoisel, "a revolution that makes one think of the words of Chapon, the celebrated thief: 'Robbery, Monsieur le Président, is the principal trade of the world!'"

"Were the races good?" asked Renée.

"Well, there were plenty of people," answered Mme. Davarande.

"Very good, mademoiselle," said Reverchon. "The Diana prize especially was very well run. Plume de coq, that they reckoned at thirty-five, was beaten by Basilicate by two lengths. It was very exciting. The hacks was a very good race, too, although the ground was rather hard."

"Who is the Russian lady who drives four-in-hand, M. Reverchon?" asked Mme. Davarande.

"Mme. de Rissleff. She has some splendid horses, some thoroughbred Orloffs."

"You ought to join the Jockey Club, Jules, for the races," said Mme. Davarande, turning to her husband. "I think it is so common to be with everybody. Really if one has any respect for one's self—a woman I mean—there is no place but the jockey stand."

"Ah, a mushroom patty!" exclaimed M. Barousse. "Your cook is surpassing herself, she really is a veritable *cordon-bleu*. I shall have to pay her my compliments before leaving."

"I thought you never eat that dish," said Mme. Mauperin.

"I did not eat it in 1848—and I did not eat it up to the second of December. Do you think the police had time then to inspect mushrooms? But now that there is order again."

"Henriette," said Mme. Mauperin to Mme. Davarande, "I must scold your husband. He neglects us. We have not seen you for three weeks, M. Davarande."

"Oh, my dear mother, if you only knew all I have had to do! You know I am on very good terms with Georges. His father has his time taken up at the Chamber and the business falls on Georges as principal. There are hundreds of things that he can only trust to people in whom he has confidence—friends, in fact. There was that big affair—that *début* at the Opéra. There was no end of interviews and parleyings and journeys backward and forward. It would not have done to have had any strife between the two ministries. Oh, we have been very busy lately. He is so considerate that I could not——"

"So considerate?" put in Denoisel. "He might pay your cab-fares at least. It's more than two years since he promised you a sub-prefectship."

"My dear Denoisel, it's more difficult than you imagine. And then, too, when one does not care about going too far from Paris. Besides, between ourselves, I can tell you that it's almost arranged. In about a month from now I have every reason to believe——"

"What *début* were you speaking of?" asked Barousse.

"Bradizzi's," answered Davarande.

"Ah, Bradizzi! Isn't she astounding!" said Reverchon. "She has some runs that are wonderfully light. The other day I was in the manager's box on the stage and we couldn't hear her touch the ground when she was dancing."

"We expected to see you yesterday evening, Henri," said Mme. Davarande to her brother.

"Yesterday I was at my lecture," he answered.

"Henri has been appointed reporter," said Mme. Mauperin proudly.

"Ah," put in Denoisel, "the d'Aguesseau lecture? That's still going on then, your speechifying affair? How many are there in it?"

"Two hundred."

"And all statesmen? It's quite alarming. What were you to report on?"

"A law that was proposed with reference to the National Guard."

"You go in for everything," said Denoisel.

"I am sure you do not belong to the National Guard, Denoisel?" observed M. Barousse.

"No, indeed!"

"And yet it is an institution."

"The drums affirm that it is that, M. Barousse."

"And you do not vote either, I would wager?"

"I would not vote under any pretext."

"Denoisel, I am sorry to say so, but you are a bad citizen. You were born as you are, I am not blaming you, but the fact remains— —"

"A bad citizen—what do you mean?"

"Well, you are always in opposition to the laws."

"I am?"

"Yes, you are. Without going any farther back, take for instance the money you came into from your Uncle Frédéric. You handed it over to his illegitimate children— —"

"What of that?"

"Well, that is what I call an illegal action, most deplorable and blameworthy. What does the law mean? It is quite clear—the law means that children not born in wedlock should not be able to inherit their father's money. You were not ignorant of this, for I told you that it was so; your lawyer told you and the code told you. What did you do? Why, you let the children have the money. You ignored the code, the spirit of the law, everything. To give up your uncle's fortune in that way, Denoisel, was rendering homage to low morals. It was simply encouraging— —"

"I know your principles in the matter, M. Barousse. But what was I to do? When I saw those three poor lads I said to myself that I should never enjoy the cigars I smoked with their bread-money. No one is perfect— —"

"All that is not law. When there is a law there is some reason for it, is there not? The law is against immorality. Suppose others imitated you— —"

"You need not fear that, Barousse," said M. Mauperin, smiling.

"We ought never to set a bad example," answered Barousse, sententiously. "Do not misunderstand me," he continued, turning to Denoisel. "I do not respect you any the less for it, on the contrary, I appreciate your disinterestedness, but as to saying that you were right—no, I cannot say that. It's the same with your way of living—that is not as it should be. You ought to have your time occupied—hang it all! You ought to do something, go in for something, take up some work, pay your debt to your country. If you had begun in good time, with your intelligence, you would perhaps have had a post bringing you in a thousand or more——"

"I have had a better thing than that offered me, M. Barousse."

"More money?" asked Barousse.

"More money," answered Denoisel tranquilly.

Barousse looked at him in astonishment.

"Seriously," continued Denoisel, "I had the most brilliant prospects—just for five minutes. It was on the twenty-fourth of February, 1848. I did not know what to do with myself, for when one has done the Tuileries in the morning it rather un-settles one for the rest of the day. It occurred to me that I would go and call on one of my friends who has a Government appointment—a Government appointment, you know, on the other side of the water. I arrived, and there was no one there. I went upstairs into the minister's office where my friend worked—no friend there. I lighted a cigarette, intending to wait for him. A gentleman came in while I was smoking, and seeing me seated, imagined I belonged to the place. He had no hat on, so that I thought he also did. He asked me very politely to show him the way about the house. I took him round and then we came back. He gave me something to write down, just telling me the sense of it. I took my friend's pen and wrote. He then read it and was delighted. We talked; he admired my orthography. He shook hands with me and found I had gloves on. To cut it short, at the end of a quarter of an hour he was pressing me to be his secretary. It was the new minister."

"And you did not accept?"

"My friend arrived and I accepted for him. He is at present quite a high func-tionary in the Council of State. It was lucky for him to be supernumerary only half a day."

They were having dessert, and M. Mauperin had pulled one of the dishes nearer and was just helping himself in an absent-minded way.

"M. Mauperin!" exclaimed his wife, looking steadily at him.

"I beg pardon, my dear—symmetry—you are quite right. I wasn't thinking," and he pushed the dish back to its place.

"You always do disarrange things——"

"I'm sorry, my dear, I'm very sorry. My wife is an excellent woman, you know, gentlemen, but if you disarrange her symmetry for her—It's quite a religion with my wife—symmetry is."

"How ridiculous you are, M. Mauperin!" said Mme. Mauperin, blushing at being convicted of the most flagrant provincialism; and then, turning upon her daughter, she exclaimed, "Oh, dear, Renée, how you stoop! Do sit up, my child — —"

"That's always the way," murmured the young girl, speaking to herself. "Mamma avenges herself on me."

"Gentlemen," said M. Mauperin, when they had returned to the drawing-room, "you can smoke here, you know. We owe that liberty to my son. He has been lucky enough to obtain his mother's— —"

"Coffee, god-papa?" asked Renée.

"No," answered M. Barousse, "I shouldn't be able to go to sleep— —"

"Here," put in Renée, finishing his sentence for him.

"M. Reverchon?"

"I never take it, thank you very much."

She went backward and forward, the steam from the cup of hot coffee she was carrying rising to her face and flushing it.

"Is every one served?" she asked, and without waiting for any reply she sat down to the piano and struck the first notes of a polka.

"Are we going to dance?" she asked, breaking off. "Let us dance—oh, do let us dance!"

"Let us smoke in peace!" said M. Mauperin.

"Yes, daddy," and going on with her polka she danced it herself on her music-stool, only touching the floor with her tip-toes. She played without looking at her notes, her face turned towards the drawing-room, smiling and animated, her eyes lighted up and her cheeks flushed with the excitement of the dance; like a little girl playing dance music for other people and moving about herself as she watches them. She swung her shoulders, her form swayed as though she were being guided along, while her whole body marked the rhythm and her attitude seemed to indicate the step she was dancing. Then she turned towards the piano again and her eyes followed her hands over the black and white keys. Bending over the music she was playing, she seemed to be striking the notes, then caressing them, speaking to them, scolding them or smiling on them, and then lulling them to sleep. She would sustain the loud parts, then linger over the melody; there were movements that she would play with tenderness and others with little bursts of passion. She bent over the piano, then rose again, the light playing on the top of her tortoise-shell comb one moment, while the next moment it could scarcely be seen in her black hair. The two candles on the piano flickered to the noise, throwing a light over her profile or sending their flame over her forehead, her cheeks, and her chin. The shadow from her ear-rings—two coral balls—trembled all the time on the delicate skin of her throat, and her fingers ran so quickly over the keyboard that one could only see something pink flying backward and forward.

"And it's her own composition," said M. Mauperin to Reverchon.

"She has had lessons from Quidant," added Mme. Mauperin.

"There—I've finished!" exclaimed Renée, suddenly leaving the piano and planting herself in front of Denoisel. "Tell me a story now, Denoisel, to amuse me—anything you like."

She was standing before him, her arms crossed and her head slightly thrown back, the weight of her body supported on one leg, and a mischievous, daring look on her face which lent additional grace to her slightly masculine dress. She was wearing a high collar of piqué with a cravat of black ribbon, and the revers of her white front turned back over her jacket bodice of cloth. There were pockets on the front of her skirt.

"When shall you cut your wisdom teeth, Renée?" asked Denoisel.

"Never!" she answered, laughing. "Well, what about my story?"

Denoisel looked round to see that no one was listening, and then lowering his voice began:

"Once upon a time a papa and a mamma had a little daughter. The papa and mamma wished her to marry, and they sent for some very nice-looking gentlemen; but the little daughter, who was very nice-looking, too——"

"Oh, how stupid you are!—I'll get my work, there—" and taking her work out of a basket on the table she went and sat down by her mother.

"Are we not going to have any whist to-night?" asked M. Mauperin.

"Yes, of course, my dear," answered Mme. Mauperin. "The table is ready—you see there are only the candles to light."

"Going, going, gone!" called out Denoisel in M. Barousse's ear.

The old gentleman was just beginning to doze in a corner by the chimney-piece and his head was nodding like a passenger's in a stage-coach. M. Barousse started up and Denoisel handed him a card:

"The King of Spades! *before the letter!* You are wanted at whist."

"You are not over-tired this evening, mademoiselle?" asked Reverchon, approaching Renée.

"I? I could dance all night. That's how I feel."

"You are making something—very pretty——"

"This?—oh, yes, very pretty! It is a stocking—I am knitting for my little poor children. It's warm, that's all it is. I am not very clever with my needle, you know. With embroidery and wool-work you have to think about what you are doing, but with this, you see, your fingers go; it just makes itself when once you start, and you can think about anything—the Grand Turk if you like——"

"I say, Renée," observed M. Mauperin, "it's odd; it's no good my losing, I can't catch up again."

"Oh, that's clever — I shall remember that for my collection," answered Renée. "Denoisel, come here," she called out, suddenly, "come here a minute — nearer — nearer still. Will you come here at once — there now — kneel down — —"

"Are you mad, child?" exclaimed Mme. Mauperin.

"Renée," said Denoisel, "I believe you have made up your mind to prevent my getting married."

"Come, come, Renée!" said M. Mauperin paternally from the card-table.

"Well — what is it?" asked Renée threatening Denoisel playfully with a pair of scissors. "Now if you move! Denoisel's head always looks untidy — his hair is badly cut — he always has a great, ugly lock that falls over his forehead. It makes people squint when they look at him. I want to cut that lock. There — he's afraid. Why, I cut hair very well — you ask papa," and forthwith she gave two or three clips with her scissors, and then crossing over to the fireplace, shook the hair into the grate. "If you fancy it was for the sake of getting a lock of your hair — " she said, turning round as she spoke.

She had paid no attention to the nudge her brother had given her as she passed. Her mother, who an instant before was perfectly crimson, was now pale, but Renée had not noticed that. Her father left the whist-table and came across to her with an embarrassed expression, looking as though he were vexed with her. She took the cigarette which he had lighted from him, put it between her own lips, and drawing a puff of smoke, blew it away again quickly, turning her head away, coughing and blinking. "Ugh! — how horrid it is!"

"Well, really, Renée!" exclaimed Mme. Mauperin severely, and evidently in great distress, "I really don't know — I have never seen you like this — —"

"Bring the tea in," said M. Mauperin to a servant who had entered in answer to his peal at the bell.

# IV

"A quarter past ten already!" said Mme. Davarande. "We shall only just have time to get to the station. Renée, tell them to bring me my hat."

Every one rose. Barousse woke up from his nap with the noise, and the little band of guests from Paris set out for Saint-Denis.

"I'll come with you," said Denoisel. "I should like a breath of air."

Barousse was in front, arm-in-arm with Reverchon. The Davarandes followed, and Henri Mauperin and Denoisel brought up the rear.

"Why don't you stay all night? You could go back to Paris to-morrow," Denoisel began.

"No," answered Henri, "I won't do that. I have some work to do to-morrow morning. I should get to Paris late and my day would be wasted."

They were silent, and every now and then a few words from Barousse to Reverchon in praise of Renée came to them through the silence of the night.

"I say, Denoisel, I'm afraid it is all up with that, don't you think so?"

"Yes, I think it is."

"Oh, dear! Will you tell me, my dear fellow, what made you humour Renée in all the nonsense that came into her head this evening? You have a great deal of influence over her and ——"

"My dear boy," answered Denoisel, puffing at his cigar, "you must let me give you a social, philosophical, and historical parenthesis. We have quite finished, have we not, and when I say we, I mean the majority of the French people, with the pretty little young ladies who used to talk like mechanical dolls. They could say 'papa' and 'mamma,' and when they went to a dance they never lost sight of their parents. The little childlike young lady who was always so timid and bashful and who used to blush and stammer, brought up to be ignorant of everything, neither knowing how to stand up on her legs nor how to sit down on a chair—all that sort of thing's done with, old-fashioned, worn out. That was the marriageable young lady of the days of the Gymnase Theatre. There is nothing of that kind nowadays. The process of culture has changed; it used to be a case of the fruit-wall, but at present the young person grows in the open. We ask a girl now about her impressions and we expect her to say what she thinks naturally and originally. She is allowed to talk, and indeed is expected to talk, about everything, as that is the accepted thing now. She need no longer act sweet simplicity, but native intelligence. If only she can shine in society her parents are delighted. Her mother takes her to classes. If she should have any talent it is encouraged and cultivated. Instead of ordinary governesses she must have good masters, professors from the Conservatoire, or artists whose pictures have been hung. She goes in for being an artist and every one is delighted. Come, now, isn't that the way girls are being educated now in middle-class society?'

"And the result?"

"Now, then," continued Denoisel without answering the question, "in the midst of this education, which I am not criticising, remember—in the midst of all this, let us imagine a father who is an excellent sort of man, goodness and kindness personified, encouraging his daughter in her new freedom by his weakness and his worship of her. Let us suppose, for instance, that this father has countenanced all the daring and all the mischievousness of a boy in a woman, that he has allowed his daughter little by little to cultivate manly accomplishments, which he sees with pride and which are after his own heart——"

"And you, my dear fellow, who know my sister so well and the way she has been brought up, the style she has gone in for, authorized as she considers herself (thanks to father's indulgence), you, knowing how difficult it is to get her married, allowed her to do all kinds of unseemly things this evening when you might have stopped her short with just a few words such as you always find to say and which you alone can say to her?"

The friend to whom Henri Mauperin was speaking, Denoisel, was the son of a compatriot, and old school friend and brother-in-arms of M. Mauperin. The two men had been in the same battles, they had shed their blood in the same places, and during the retreat from Russia they had eaten the same horse-flesh.

A year after his return to France, M. Mauperin had lost this friend, who on his death-bed had left him guardian to his son. The boy had found a second father in his guardian. When at college, he had spent all his holidays at Morimond, and he looked upon the Mauperins as his own family.

When M. Mauperin's children came it seemed to the young man that a brother and sister had been just what he had wanted; he felt as though he were their elder brother, and he became a child again in order to be one with them.

His favourite was, of course, Renée, who when quite little began to adore him. She was very lively and self-willed and he alone could make her listen to reason and obey. As she grew up he had been the moulder of her character, the confessor of her intellect, and the director of her tastes. His influence over the young girl had increased day by day as they grew more and more familiar. A room was always kept ready for Denoisel in the house, his place was always kept for him at table, and he came whenever he liked to spend a week with the Mauperins.

"There are days," continued Henri, "when Renée's nonsense does not matter, but this evening—before that man. It will be all off with that marriage, I'm sure! It would have been an excellent match—he has such good prospects. He's just the man in every respect—charming, too, and distinguished."

"Do you think so? For my part, I should have been afraid of him for your sister. That is really the reason why I behaved as I did this evening. That man has a sort of common distinction about him—a distinction made up of the vulgarity of all kinds of elegancies. He's a fashion poster, a tailor's model, morally and physically. There's nothing, absolutely nothing, in a little fellow like that. A husband for your sister—that man? Why, how in the world do you suppose he could ever understand her? How is he ever to discover all the warmth of feeling and the elevation and nobility of character hidden under her eccentricities? Can you imagine them having a thought in common? Good heavens! if your sister married, no matter whom, so long as the man were intelligent and had some character and individuality, as long as there were something in him that would either govern or appeal to a nature like hers—why, I would say nothing. A man has often great faults which appeal to a woman's heart. He may be a bad lot, and there is the chance that she will go on loving him through sheer jealousy. With a busy, ambitious man like you she would have all the thought and excitement and all the dreams about his career to occupy her mind. But a dandy like that for life! Why, your sister would be absolutely wretched; she would die of misery. She isn't like other girls, you know, your sister—one must take that into consideration. She is high-minded, untrammelled by conventionalities, very fond of fun, and very affectionate. At bottom she is a *mélancolique tintamarresque*."

"A *mélancolique tintamarresque*? What does that mean?"

"I'll explain. She——"

"Henri, hurry up!" called out Davarande from the platform. "They are getting into the train. I have your ticket."

# V

M. and Mme. Mauperin were in their bed-room. The clock had just struck midnight, gravely and slowly, as though to emphasize the solemnity of that confidential and conjugal moment which is both the *tête-à-tête* of wedded life and the secret council of the household — that moment of transformation and magic which is both *bourgeois* and diabolic, and which reminds one of that story of the woman metamorphosed into a cat. The shadow of the bed falls mysteriously over the wife, and as she lies down there is a sort of charm about her. Something of the bewitchments of a mistress come to her at this instant. Her will seems to be roused there by the side of the marital will which is dormant. She sits up, scolds, sulks, teases, struggles. She has caresses and scratches for the man. The pillow confers on her its force, her strength comes to her with the night.

Mme. Mauperin was putting her hair in papers in front of the glass, which was lighted by a single candle. She was in her skirt and dressing-jacket. Her stout figure, above which her little arms kept moving as if she were crowning herself, threw on the wall a fantastic outline of a woman of fifty in deshabille, and on the paper at the end of the room could be seen wavering about one of those corpulent shadows which one could imagine Hoffman and Daumier sketching from the back of the beds of old married couples. M. Mauperin was already lying down.

"Louis!" said Mme. Mauperin.

"Well?" answered M. Mauperin, with that accent of indifference, regret, and weariness of a man who, with his eyes still open, is beginning to enjoy the delight of the horizontal position.

"Oh, if you are asleep——"

"I am not asleep. What is it?"

"Oh, nothing. I think Renée behaved most improperly this evening; that's all. Did you notice?"

"No, I wasn't paying any attention."

"It's just a whim. There isn't the least reason in it. Hasn't she said anything to you? Do you know anything? I'm nowhere — with all your mysteries and secrets. I'm always the last to know about things. It's quite different with you — you are told everything. It's very fortunate that I was not born jealous, don't you think so?"

M. Mauperin pulled the sheet up over his shoulder without answering.

"You certainly are asleep," continued Mme. Mauperin in the sharp, disappointed tone of a woman who is expecting a parry for her attack.

"I told you I wasn't asleep."

"Then you surely don't understand. Oh, these intelligent men—it's curious. It concerns you though, too; it's your business quite as much as mine. This is another marriage fallen through—do you understand? A marriage that was most suitable—money—good family—everything. I know what these hesitations mean. We may as well give up all idea of it. Henri was talking to me about it this evening; the young man hadn't said anything to him; of course, he's too well-bred for that. But Henri is quite persuaded that he's drawing out of it. One can always tell in matters of this kind; people have a way of——"

"Well, let him draw out of it then; what do you want me to say?" M. Mauperin sat straight up and put his two hands on his thighs. "Let him go. There are plenty of young men like Reverchon; he is not unique, we can find others; while girls like my daughter——"

"Good heavens! Your daughter—your daughter!"

"You don't do her justice, Thérèse."

"I? Oh, yes, I do; but I see her as she is and not with your eyes. She has her faults, and great faults, too, which you have encouraged—yes, you. She is as heedless and full of freaks as a child of ten. If you imagine that it doesn't worry me—her unreasonableness, her uncertain moods, and so many other absurdities ever since we have been trying to get her married! And then her way of criticising every one to whom we introduce her. She is terrible at interviews of this kind. This makes about the tenth man she has sent about his business."

At Mme. Mauperin's last words a gleam of paternal vanity lighted up M. Mauperin's face.

"Yes, yes," he said, smiling at the remembrance, "the fact is she is diabolically witty. Do you recollect her words about that poor Prefect: 'Oh, he's a regular old cock!' I remember how she said it directly she saw him."

"It really is very funny, and above all very fit and proper. Jokes of this kind will help her to get married, take my word for it. Such things will induce other men to come forward, don't you think so? I am quite certain that Renée must have a reputation for being a terror. A little more of her precious wit and you will see what proposals you will get for your daughter! I married Henriette so easily! Renée is my cross."

M. Mauperin had picked up his snuff-box from the table by the side of the bed and appeared to be intent on turning it round between his thumb and first finger.

"Well," continued Mme. Mauperin, "it's her own lookout. When she is thirty, when she has refused every one, and there is no one left who wants her, in spite of all her wit, her good qualities and everything else, she will have time to reflect a little—and you will, too."

There was a pause. Mme. Mauperin gave M. Mauperin time enough to imagine that she had finished, and then changing her tone she began again:

"I want to speak to you, too, about your son——"

Hereupon M. Mauperin, whose head had been bent while his wife was talking, looked up, and there was a half smile of mischievous humour on his face. In the upper as well as the lower middle class there is a certain maternal love capable of rising to the height of passion and of sinking to mere idolatry. There are mothers who in their affection and love will fall down and worship their son. Theirs is not that maternal love which veils its own weaknesses, which defends its rights, is jealous of its duties, which is careful about the hierarchy and discipline of the family, and which commands respect and consideration. The child, brought near to his mother by all kinds of familiarity, receives from her attentions which are more like homage, and caresses in which there is a certain amount of servility. All the mother's dreams are centred in him, for he is not only the heir but the whole future of the family. Through him the family will reap the benefits of wealth, of all the improvements and progressive rise of the *bourgeoisie* from one generation to another. The mother revels in the thought of what he is and what he will be. She loves him and is glorified herself in him. She dedicates all her ambitions to him and worships him. This son appears to her a superior being, and she is amazed that he should have been born of her; she seems to feel the mingled pride and humility of the mother of a god.

Mme. Mauperin was a typical example of one of these mothers of modern middle-class life. The merits, the features, the intellect of her son were for her those of a divinity. His whole person, his accomplishments, everything he said and everything he did, all was sacred to her. She would spend her time in contemplation of him; she saw no one else when he was there. It seemed to her as though the whole world began and ended in her son. He was in her eyes perfection itself, the most intelligent, the handsomest, and, above all, the most distinguished of men. He was short-sighted and wore an eye-glass, but she would not even own that he was near-sighted.

When he was there she watched him talk, sit down or walk about, and she would smile at him when his back was turned. She liked the very creases of his coat. When he was not there she would lean back for a few minutes in her armchair and some reminiscence of infinite sweetness would gradually brighten and soften her face. It was as though light, restfulness, and peace had suddenly come to her; her expression was joyous at such times, her eyes were looking at something in the past, her heart was living over again some happy moment, and if any one spoke to her she seemed to wake up out of a dream.

It was in a certain measure hereditary, this intense maternal love. Mme. Mauperin came of a race which had always loved its sons with a warm, violent, and almost frenzied love. The mothers in her family had been mothers with a vengeance. There was a story told of her grandmother in the Haute-Marne. It was said that she had disfigured a child with a burning coal who had been considered handsomer than her own boy.

At the time of her son's first ailments Mme. Mauperin had almost lost her reason; she had hated all children who were well, and had hoped that God would kill them if her son died. Once when he had been seriously ill she had been forty-eight nights without going to bed, and her legs had swelled with fatigue. When he was about again he had been allowed anything and everything. If any one came to complain to her that he had been fighting with the village children she would say feelingly: "Poor little dear!" As the boy grew up his mother's spirit preceded him on his walk through life, strewing his pathway with hope as he emerged into manhood. She thought of all the heiresses in the neighbourhood whose age would be suitable to his. She used to imagine him visiting at all the country-houses, and she saw him on horseback, riding to the meet in a red coat. She used to be fairly dazzled by all her dreams of the future.

Then came the time when he went away to college, the time when she had to separate from him. Mme. Mauperin struggled for three months to keep her son, to have him educated at home by a tutor, but M. Mauperin was resolute on this score. All that Mme. Mauperin could obtain from him was the permission to select the college for her son. She chose one with the mildest discipline possible, one of those colleges for the children of wealthy parents, where there is no severity, where the boys are allowed to eat pastry when they are taking their walks, and where the professors believe in more theatrical rehearsals than punishments. During the seven years he was there, Mme. Mauperin never missed a single day going from Saint-Denis to see him during the recreation hour. Rain, cold, fatigue, illness, nothing prevented her. In the parlour or in the courtyard the other mothers pointed her out to each other. The boy would kiss her, take the cakes she had brought him, and then, telling her he had a lesson to finish learning, he would hurry back to his games. It was quite enough for his mother, though, for she had seen him and he was well. She was always thinking about his health. He was weighed down with flannel, and in the holidays she fed him well with meat, giving him all the gravy from underdone beef so that he should grow strong and tall. She bought him a small mat to sit on at school because the forms were so hard. There were separate bed-rooms for the pupils, and Mme. Mauperin furnished her son's like a man's room. At twelve years of age he had a rosewood dressing-table and chest of drawers of his own. The boy became a young man, the young man left college, and Mme. Mauperin's passion for him increased with all that satisfaction which a mother feels in a tall son when his looks begin to change and his beard makes its first appearance. Forgetting all about the tradespeople whose bills she had paid, she was amazed at the style in which her son dressed, at his boots, and the way in which he did his hair. There was a certain elegance of taste in everything that he liked, in his luxurious habits, in his ways, and in his whole life, to which she bowed down in astonishment and delight, as though she herself were not the mainspring of it all and his cashier. Her son's valet did not seem to her like an ordinary domestic; his horse was not merely a horse, it was her son's horse. When her son went out she gave orders that she should be told so that she might have the satisfaction of seeing him get into the carriage and drive away.

Every day she was more and more taken up with this son. She had no diversions, nothing to occupy her imagination; she did not read, and had grown old living with a husband who had brought her no love and whom she had always felt to be quite apart from her, engrossed as he had ever been in his studies, politics, and business. She had no one left with her but a daughter to whom she had never given her whole heart, and so she had ended by devoting her life to Henri's interests and putting all her vanity into his future. And her one thought—the thought which occupied every hour of her days and nights, her fixed idea—was the marriage of this adored son. She wanted him to marry well, to make a match which should be rich enough and brilliant enough to make up to her and repay her for all the dulness and obscurity of her own existence, for her life of economy and solitude, for all her own privations as wife and mother.

"Do you even know your son's age, M. Mauperin?" continued Mme. Mauperin.

"Henri, why, my dear, Henri must be—He was born in 1826, wasn't he?"

"Oh, that's just like a father to ask! Yes, 1826, the 12th of July, 1826."

"Well, then, he is twenty-nine. Fancy that now, he is twenty-nine!"

"And you fold your arms and take things easily! You don't trouble in the least about his future! You say, 'Fancy that now, he's twenty-nine'—just like that, quite calmly! Any other man would stir himself and look round. Henri isn't like his sister, he wants to marry. Have you ever thought of finding a suitable match for him—a wife? Oh, dear, no, not any more than for the King of Prussia, of course not! It's just the same as it was for your elder daughter. I should like to know what you did towards that marriage? Whether she found any one or not, it appeared to be all the same to you. How I did have to urge you on to do anything in the matter! Oh, you can wipe your hands of that marriage; your daughter's happiness can't weigh much on your conscience, I should think! If I had not been there you would have found a husband like M. Davarande, shouldn't you? A model husband, who adores Henriette—and such a gentleman!"

Mme. Mauperin blew out the candle and got into bed by the side of M. Mauperin, who had turned over with his face towards the wall.

"Yes," she went on, stretching herself out full length under the sheets, "a model husband! Do you imagine that there are many sons-in-law who would be so attentive to us? He would do anything to give us pleasure. You invite him to dinner and give him meat on fasting-days and he never says a word. Then, too, he is so obliging. I wanted to match some wools for my tapestry-work the other day— —"

"My dear, what is it we were talking about? I must tell you that I should like to get a bit of sleep to-night. You began with your daughter, and now you've started the chapter of M. Davarande's perfections. I know that chapter—there's enough to last till to-morrow morning. Come now, you want your son to marry, don't you? That's it, isn't it? Well, I'm quite willing—let's get him married."

"Just as though I could count on you for getting him married! A lot of trouble you'll go to about it; you are the right sort of man to inconvenience yourself for anything."

"Oh, come, come, my dear, that's unjust. It seems to me that about a fortnight ago I showed you what I was capable of. To go and listen to the dullest of operas, to eat ices at night, which is a thing I detest, and to talk about the weather with a provincial man who shouted about his daughter's dowry on the boulevards. If you don't call that inconveniencing myself! I suppose you'll say it didn't come to anything? Was it my fault, though, if the gentleman wanted '*a handsome, manly husband*,' as he put it, for his daughter? Is it my fault and mine only if our son has not the frame of a Hercules?"

"M. Mauperin— —"

"Oh, yes, it is, of course. I am to blame for everything, according to you. You would make me pass everywhere for a selfish— —"

"Oh, you are like all men!"

"Thank you on behalf of them all."

"No, it's in your character—it's no good blaming you. It's only the mothers who worry. Ah, if you were only like I am; if at every instant you were thinking of what might happen to a young man. I know Henri is sensible; but a young man's fancy is so quickly caught. It might be some worthless creature—some bad lot—one never knows—such things happen every day. I should go mad! What do you say to sounding Mme. Rosières? Shall we?"

There was no reply, and Mme. Mauperin was obliged to resign herself to silence. She turned over and over, but could not sleep until daylight appeared.

# VI

"Ah, what's that mean? Where in the world are you going?" asked M. Mauperin in the morning as Mme. Mauperin stood at the glass putting on a black lace cape.

"Where am I going?" said Mme. Mauperin, fastening the cape to her shoulder with one of the two pins she was holding in her mouth. "Is my cape too low down? Just look."

"No."

"Pull it a little."

"How fine you are!" said M. Mauperin, stepping back and examining his wife's dress.

She was wearing a black dress of the most elegant style, in excellent taste though somewhat severe looking.

"I am going to Paris."

"Oh! you are going to Paris? What are you going to do in Paris?"

"Oh, dear, how you do worry always with your questions: 'Where are you going? What are you going to do?' You really want to know, do you?"

"Well, I was only asking you— —"

"My dear, I am going to confession," said Mme. Mauperin, looking down.

M. Mauperin was speechless. His wife in the early days of her married life had gone regularly on Sundays to church. Later she had accompanied her daughters to their catechism class, and these were all the religious duties he had ever known her to accomplish. For the last ten years it seemed to him that she had been as indifferent as he was about such things—naturally and frankly indifferent. When the first moment of stupefaction had passed, he opened his mouth to speak, looked at her, said nothing, and, turning suddenly on his heels, went out of the room humming a kind of air to which music and words were about all that were missing.

On arriving at a handsome, cheerful-looking house in the Rue de la Madeleine, Mme. Mauperin went upstairs to the fourth story and rang at a door where there was no attempt at any style. It was opened promptly.

"M. l'Abbé Blampoix?"

"Yes, madame," answered a servant-man in black livery.

He spoke with a Belgian accent and bowed as he spoke. He took Mme. Mauperin across the entrance-hall, where a faint odour was just dying away, and through a dining-room flooded with sunshine, where the cloth was simply laid for one person. Mme. Mauperin then found herself in a drawing-room decorated and scented with flowers. Above a harmonium with rich inlaid work was a copy of Correggio's "Night." On another panel, framed in black, was the Communion of Marie Antoinette and of her gendarmes at the Conciergerie, lithographed according to a story that was told about her. Keepsakes, a hundred little things that might have been New Year's gifts, filled the brackets. A small bronze statue of Canova's "Madeleine" was on a table in the middle of the room.

The tapestry chairs, each one of a different design and piously worked by hand, were evidently presents which devoted women had done for the abbé.

There were men and women waiting there, and each by turn went into the abbé's room, stayed a few minutes, then came out again and went away. The last person waiting, a woman, stayed a long time, and when she came out of the room Mme. Mauperin could not see her face through her double veil.

The abbé was standing by his chimney-piece when Mme. Mauperin entered. He was holding apart the flaps of his cassock like the tails of a coat.

The Abbé Blampoix had neither benefice nor parish. He had a large connection and a specialty: he was the priest of society people, of the fashionable world, and of the aristocracy. He confessed the frequenters of drawing-rooms, he was the spiritual director of well-born consciences, and he comforted those souls that were worth the trouble of comforting. He brought Jesus Christ within reach of the wealthy. "Every one has his work to do in the Lord's vineyard," he used often to say, appearing to groan and bend beneath the burden of saving the Faubourg Saint-Germain, the Faubourg Saint-Honoré, and the Chaussée-d'Antin.

He was a man of common sense and intellect, an obliging sort of priest who adapted everything to the precept, "*The letter killeth, and the spirit maketh alive.*" He was tolerant and intelligent, could comprehend things and could smile. He measured faith out according to the temperament of the people and only gave it in small doses. He made the penances light, he loosened the bonds of the cross and sprinkled the way of salvation with sand. From the hard, unlovely, stern religion of the poor he had evolved a pleasant religion for the rich; it was easy, charming, elastic, adapting itself to things and to people, to all the ways and manners of society, to its customs and habits, and even to its prejudices. Of the idea of God he had made something quite comfortable and elegant.

The Abbé Blampoix had all the fascination of the priest who is well educated, talented, and accomplished. He could talk well during confession, and could put some wit into his exhortations and a certain graciousness into his unction. He knew how to move and interest his hearers. He was well versed in words that touch the heart and in speeches that are flattering and pleasing to the ear. His voice was musical and his style flowery. He called the devil "*the Prince of evil,*" and the eucharist "*the Divine aliment*"! He abounded in periphrases as highly coloured as sacred pictures. He talked of Rossini, quoted Racine, and spoke of "*the Bois*" for the Bois de Boulogne. He talked of divine love in words which were somewhat disconcerting, of present-day vices with piquant details, and of society in society language. Occasionally, expressions which were in vogue and which had only recently been invented, expressions only known among worldly people, would slip into his spiritual consultations and had the same effect as extracts from a newspaper in an ascetic book. There was a pleasant odour of the century about him. His priestly robe seemed to be impregnated with all the pretty little sins which had approached it. He was very well up and always to the point with regard to subtle temptations, admirably shrewd, keen, and tactful in his discussions on sensuality. Women doted on him.

His first step, his *début* in the ecclesiastical career, had been distinguished by a veritable seduction and capturing of souls, by a success which had been a perfect triumph and indeed almost a scandal. After taking the catechism classes for a year in the parish of B— —, the archbishop had appointed him to other work, putting another priest in his place. The result of this was a rebellion, as all the girls who had attended the catechism classes refused to speak or listen to the newcomer. They had lost their young hearts and heads, and there were tears shed by all the flock, a regular riot of wailing and sorrow, which before long changed into revolt. The elder girls, the chief members of the society, kept up the struggle several months. They agreed together not to go to the classes, and they went so far as to refuse to hand over to the curé the cash-box which had been intrusted to them. It was with the greatest difficulty that they were appeased.

The success which all this augured to the Abbé Blampoix had not failed him. His fame had quickly spread. That great force, Fashion, which in Paris affects everything, even a priest's cassock, had taken him up and launched him. People came to him from all parts. The ordinary, commonplace confessions were heard by other priests; but all the choice sins were brought to him. Around him was always to be heard a hubbub of great names, of large fortunes, of pretty contritions, and the rustling of beautiful dresses. Mothers consulted him about taking their daughters out, and the daughters were instructed by him before going into society. He was appealed to for permission to wear low-necked dresses, and he was the man who regulated the modesty of ball costumes and the propriety of reading certain books. He was also asked for titles of novels and lists of moral plays. He prepared candidates for confirmation and led them on to marriage. He baptized children and listened to the confession of the adulterous in thought. Wives who considered themselves slighted or misunderstood came to him to lament over the materiality of their husbands, and he supplied them with a little idealism to take back to their homes. All who were in trouble or despair had recourse to him, and he ordered a trip to Italy for them, with music and painting for diversions and a good confession in Rome.

Wives who were separated from their husbands addressed themselves to him when they wanted to return quietly to their home. His conciliations came between the love of wives and the jealousy of mothers-in-law. He found governesses for the mothers and lady's maids of forty years of age for young wives. Newly married wives learned from him to secure their happiness and to keep their husband's affection by their discreet and dainty toilettes, by cleanliness and care, by the spotlessness and elegance of their linen. "My dear child," he would say sometimes, "a wife should have just a faint perfume of the *lorette* about her." His experience intervened in questions of the hygiene of marriage. He was consulted on such matters as maternity and pregnancy. He would decide whether a wife should become a mother and whether a mother should suckle her child.

This vogue and rôle, the dealings that he had with women and the possession of all their secrets, so many confidences and so much knowledge on all subjects, his intercourse of all kinds with the dignitaries and lady-treasurers of various societies, and the acquaintance he had, thanks to the steps he was obliged to take in the interests of charity, with all the important personages of Paris, all the influence that, as a clever, discreet, and obliging priest, he had succeeded in obtaining, had given to the Abbé Blampoix an immense power and authority which radiated silently and unseen. Worldly interests and social ambitions were confessed to him. Nearly all the marriageable individuals in society were recommended to this priest, who professed no political preferences, who mixed with every one, and who was admirably placed for bringing families together, for uniting houses, arranging matches of expediency or balancing social positions, pairing off money with money, or joining an ancient title to a newly made fortune. It was as though marriages in Paris had an occult Providence in the person of this rare sort of man in whom were blended the priest and the lawyer, the apostle and the diplomatist—Fénelon and M. de Foy. The Abbé Blampoix had an income of sixteen hundred pounds, the half of which he gave to the poor. He had refused a bishopric for the sake of remaining what he was—a priest.

"To whom have I the honour," began the abbé, who appeared to be searching his memory for a name.

"Mme. Mauperin, the mother of Mme. Davarande."

"Oh, excuse me, madame, excuse me. Your family are not persons whom one could forget. Do sit down, please—let me give you this arm-chair."

And then, taking a seat himself with his back to the light, he continued:

"I like to think of that marriage, which gave me the opportunity of making your acquaintance—the marriage of your daughter with M. Davarande. You and I, madame, you, with the devotion of a mother, and I—well, with just the feeble insight of a humble priest—brought about a truly Christian marriage, a marriage which has satisfied the needs of the dear child as regards her religion and her affection and which was also in accordance with her social position. Mme. Davarande is one of my model penitents; I am thoroughly satisfied with her. M. Davarande is an excellent young man who shares the religious beliefs of his wife, and that is a rare thing nowadays. One's mind is easy about such happy and superior young couples, and I am quite convinced beforehand that you have not come about either of these dear children——"

"You are right. I am quite satisfied as regards them, and their happiness is a great joy in my life. It is such a responsibility to get one's children married. No, monsieur, it is not for them that I have come; it is for myself."

"For yourself—madame?"

And the abbé glanced quickly at her with an expression which softened just as quickly.

"Ah, monsieur, time brings many changes. One has a hundred things to think about before one reaches my age. There are the people one meets, and society ties, and all that is very entertaining. We give ourselves up to such things, enjoy them and count on them. We fancy we shall never need anything beyond. Well, now, monsieur, I have reached the age when one does need something beyond. You will understand me, I am sure. I have begun to feel the emptiness of the world. Nothing interests me, and I should like to come back to what I had given up. I know how indulgent and charitable you are. I need your counsel and your hand to lead me back to duties that I have neglected far too long, although I have always remembered and respected them. You must know how wretched I am, monsieur."

While speaking thus, with that easy flow of words so natural to a woman, and especially to a Parisian woman, and which in Parisian slang is known as *bagou*, Mme. Mauperin, who had avoided meeting the priest's eyes, which she had felt fixed on her, now glanced mechanically at a light which was being stirred by the abbé's hands and which flamed up under a ray of sunshine, shining brightly in the midst of this room—the severe-looking, solemn, cold room of a man of business. This light came from a casket containing some diamonds with which the abbé was idly playing.

"Ah, you are looking at this!" said the abbé, catching Mme. Mauperin's eye and answering her thoughts instead of her phrases. "You are surprised to see it, are you not? Yes, a jewel-case, a case of diamonds—and just look at them—rather good ones, too." He passed her the necklace. "It's odd for that to be here, isn't it? But what was I to do? This is our modern society. We are obliged to see a little of all sorts. Such a pitiful scene! I don't feel myself again yet, after it—such sobs and tears! Perhaps you heard—a poor young wife throwing herself down here at my feet—a mother of a family, madame! Alas! that's how the world is—this is what the love of finery and the fondness of admiration will lead to. People spend and spend, until finally they can only pay the interest of what they owe at the shops. Yes, indeed, madame, that happens constantly. I could mention the shops. People hope to be able to pay the capital some day; they count on a son-in-law to whom they can tell everything and who will only be too happy to pay his mother-in-law's debts. But in the meantime the shops get impatient; and at last they threaten to tell the husband everything. Then—oh, just think of the anguish then! Do you know that this woman talked just now of throwing herself into the river? I had to promise to find her twelve hundred pounds. I beg your pardon, though—a thousand times. Here I am talking of my own affairs. Let us go back to yours. You had another daughter—a charming girl. I prepared her for confirmation. Let me see, now, what was her name?"

"Renée."

"Oh, yes, of course, a very intelligent child, very quick—quite an exceptional character. Tell me now, isn't she married?"

"No, monsieur, and it's a great trouble to me. You've no idea what a head-strong girl she is. She is nothing like her sister. It's very unfortunate for a mother to have a daughter with a character like hers. I would rather she were a little less intelligent. We have found most suitable matches for her, and she refuses them in the most thoughtless, foolish way. There was another one yesterday. And her father spoils her so."

"Ah, that's a pity. You have no idea what a maternal affection we have for these dear children that we have led to Christ. But you don't say anything about your son, a delightful young man, so good-looking—and just the age to marry, it seems to me——"

"Do you know him, monsieur?"

"I had the pleasure of meeting him once at his sister's, at Mme. Davarande's, when I went to see her during her illness; those are the only visits we pay, you know—visits to the sick. Then, too, I have heard all sorts of good reports about him. You are a fortunate mother, madame. Your son goes to church, and at Easter he took communion with the Jesuit Fathers. He has not told you, probably, but he was one of those society men, true Christians, who waited nearly all night to get to the confessional—there was such a crowd. Yes, people do not believe it, but, thank God, it is quite true. Some of the young men waited until five o'clock in the morning to confess. I need not tell you how deeply the Church is touched by such zeal, how thankful she is to those who give her this consolation and who pay her this homage in these sad times of demoralization and incredulity. We are drawn towards young men who set such a good example and who are so willing to do what is right, and we are always ready to give them what help we can and to use any influence that we may have in certain families in their favour."

"Oh, monsieur, you are too good. And our gratitude—mine and my son's—if only you would interest yourself on his behalf. What a happy thought it was to come to you! You see I came to you as a woman, but as a mother too. My son is angelic—and then, monsieur, you can do so much."

The abbé shook his head with a deprecatory smile of mingled modesty and melancholy.

"No, madame, you overestimate our power. We are far from all that you say. We are able to do a little good sometimes, but it is with great difficulty. If only you knew how little a priest can do in these days. People are afraid of our influence; they do not care to meet us outside the church, nor to speak to us except in the con-fessional. You yourself, madame, would be surprised if your confessor ventured to speak to you about your daily conduct. Thanks to the deplorable prejudices of people with regard to us, every one's object is to keep us at a distance and to stand on the defensive."

"Oh, dear, why, it is one o'clock—and I saw that your table was laid when I came. I'm quite ashamed of myself. May I come again in a few days?"

"My luncheon can always wait," said the Abbé Blampoix, and turning to a desk covered with papers at his side, he made a sign to Mme. Mauperin to sit down again. There was a moment's silence, broken only by the rustle of papers which the abbé was turning over. Finally he drew out a visiting-card, turned down at the corner, from under a pile of papers, held it to the light, and read:

"Twelve thousand pounds in deeds and preference shares. Six hundred pounds a year from the day of marriage; father and mother dead. Twenty-four thousand pounds on the death of some uncles and aunts who will never marry. Young girl, nineteen, charming, much prettier than she imagines herself to be. You see," said the abbé, putting the card back among the papers. "Think it over. Anyhow, you will see. I have, too, at this very moment a thousand pounds a year on her marriage—an orphan—Ah, no, that would not do—her guardian wants to find some one who is influential. He is sub-referendary judge on the Board of Finance and he will only marry his ward to a son-in-law who can get him promoted. Ah, wait a minute—this would do, perhaps," and he read aloud from some notes: "Twenty-two years of age, not pretty, accomplished, intelligent, dresses well, father sixty thousand pounds, three children, substantial fortune. He owns the house in the Rue de Provence, where the offices of the *Security* are, an estate in the Orne, eight thousand pounds in the Crédit Foncier. Rather an opinionated sort of man, of Portuguese descent. The mother is a mere cipher in the house. There is no family, and the father would be annoyed if you went to see his relatives. I am not keeping anything back, as you see; a family dinner party once a year and that is all. The father will give twelve thousand pounds for the dowry; he wants his daughter to live in the same house.

"Yes," continued the abbé, looking through his notes, "that's all I see that would do for you just now. Will you talk it over with your son, madame, and consult your husband? I am quite at your service. When I have the pleasure of seeing you here again, will you bring with you just a few figures, a little note that would give me an idea of your intentions with regard to settling your son. And bring your daughter with you. I should be delighted to see the dear child again."

"Would you mind fixing some time when I should not disturb you quite so much as I have done to-day, monsieur?"

"Oh, madame, my time belongs to every one who has need of me, and I am only too much honoured. The thing is that in a fortnight's time—if you came then, I should be in the country, and I only come one day a week to Paris, then. Yes, it's a sheer necessity, and so I have had to make up my mind to it. By the end of the winter I get so worn out; I have so much to attend to, and then these four flights of stairs kill me. But what am I to do? I am obliged to pay in some way for the right of having my chapel, for the precious privilege of being able to have mass in my own home. No one could sleep over a chapel, you see. Ah, an idea has just struck me: why should you not come to see me in the country—at Colombes? It would be a little excursion. I have plenty of fruit, and I take a landowner's pride in my fruit. I could offer you luncheon, a very informal luncheon. Will you come, madame— and your daughter? Would your son give me the pleasure of his company too?"

# VII

A quarter of an hour later a footman in a red coat opened the door of a flat on a first floor in the Rue Taitbout in answer to Mme. Mauperin's ring.

"Good-morning, Georges. Is my son in?"

"Yes, madame, monsieur is there."

Mme. Mauperin had smiled on her son's domestic, and as she walked along she smiled on the rooms, on the furniture, and on everything she saw. When she entered the study her son was writing and smoking at the same time.

"Well, I never!" he exclaimed, taking his cigar out of his mouth and leaning his head against the back of his chair for his mother to kiss him. "It's you, is it, mamma?" he went on, continuing to smoke. "You didn't say a word about coming to Paris to-day. What brings you here?"

"Oh, I had some shopping and some visits to pay—you know I am always behind. How comfortable you are here!"

"Ah, yes, to be sure, you hadn't seen my new arrangements."

"Dear me, how well you do arrange everything! There's no one like you, really. It isn't damp here is it, are you quite sure?" and Mme. Mauperin put her hand against the wall. "Tell Georges to air the room always when you are away, won't you?"

"Yes, yes, mother," said Henri in a bored way, as one answers a child.

"Oh, why do you have those? I don't like your having such things." Mme. Mauperin had just caught sight of two swords above the bookcase. "The very sight of them! When one thinks—" and Mme. Mauperin closed her eyes for an instant and sat down. "You don't know how your dreadful bachelor life makes us poor mothers tremble. If you were married, it seems to me that I should not be so worried about you. I do wish you were married, Henri!"

"I do, too, I can assure you."

"Really? Come, now—mothers, you know—well, secrets ought not to be kept from them. I am so afraid, when I look at you, handsome as you are, and so distinguished and clever and fascinating. You are just the sort of man that any one would fall in love with, and I'm so afraid——"

"Of what?"

"Lest you should have some reason for not——"

"For not marrying, you mean, don't you? A chain—is that what you mean?"

Mme. Mauperin nodded and Henri burst out laughing.

"Oh, my dear mamma, if I had one, make your mind easy, it should be a polished one. A man who has any respect for himself would not wear any other."

"Well, then, tell me about Mlle. Herbault. It was your fault that it all came to nothing."

"Mlle. Herbault? The introduction at the Opéra with father? Oh, no, it wasn't that. Yes, yes, I remember, the dinner at Mme. Marquisat's, wasn't it—the last one? That was a trap you laid for me. I must say you are sweetly innocent! I was announced: '*Môssieu Henri Mauperin,*' in that grand, important sort of way which being interpreted meant: '*Behold the future husband!*' I found all the candles in the drawing-room lighted up. The mistress of the house, whom I had seen just twice in my life, overpowered me with her smiles; her son, whom I did not know at all, shook hands with me. There was a lady with her daughter in the room, they neither of them appeared to see me. My place at dinner was next the young person, of course; a provincial family, their money placed in farms, simple tastes, etc. I discovered all that before the soup was finished. The mother, on the other side of the table, was keeping watch over us; an impossible sort of mother, in such a get-up! I asked the daughter whether she had seen the 'Prophet' at the Opéra. 'Yes, it was superb—and then there was that wonderful effect in the third act. Oh, yes, that effect, that wonderful effect.' She hadn't seen it any more than I had. A fibber to begin with. I entertained myself with keeping her to the subject, and that made her crabby. We went back to the drawing-room and then the hostess began: 'What a pretty dress!' she said to me. 'Did you notice it? Would you believe that Emmeline has had that dress five years. I can remember it. She is so careful—so orderly!' 'All right,' I thought to myself, 'a lot of miserly wretches who mean to take me in.'"

"Do you really think so? And yet, from what we were told about them——"

"A woman who makes her dresses last five years! That speaks for itself, that's quite enough. I can picture the dowry hoarded up in a stocking. The money would be in land at two and a half per cent; repairs, taxes, lawsuits, farmers who don't pay their rent, a father-in-law who makes over to you unsalable property. No, no, I'm not quite young enough. I want to get married, but I mean to marry well. Leave me to manage it, and you'll see. You can make your mind easy; I'm not the sort to be taken in with: '*She has such beautiful hair and she is so devoted to her mother!*' You see, mamma, I've thought a great deal about marriage, although you may not imagine I have. The most difficult thing to get in this world, the thing we pay the most dearly for, snatch from each other, fight for, the thing we only obtain by force of genius or by luck, by meanness, privations, by wild efforts, perseverance, resolution, energy, audacity or work, is money—isn't that so? Now money means happiness and the honour of being rich, it means enjoyment, and it brings with it the respect and esteem of the million. Well, I have discovered that there is a way of getting it, straightforwardly and promptly, without any fatigue, without difficulty and without genius, quite simply, naturally, quickly and honourably; and this way is by marriage. Another thing I have discovered is that there is no need to be remarkably handsome nor astonishingly intelligent in order to make a rich marriage; the only thing necessary is to will it, to will it coolly, calmly and with all one's force of will-power, to stake all one's chances on that card; in fact to look upon getting married as one's object in life, one's future career. I see that in playing that game it is no more difficult to make an extraordinary marriage than an ordinary one, to get a dowry of fifty thousand pounds than one of five thousand; it is merely a question of cool-headedness and luck; the stake is the same in both cases. In our times when a good tenor can marry an income of thirty thousand pounds arithmetic becomes a thing of the past. All this is what I have wanted to explain to you, and I am sure you will understand me."

Henri Mauperin took his mother's hand in his as he spoke. She was fairly aghast with surprise, admiration, and a sentiment very near akin to respect.

"Don't you worry yourself," continued her son. "I shall marry well—better even perhaps than you dream of."

As soon as his mother had gone Henri took up his pen and, continuing the article he had commenced for the *Revue économique*, wrote: "The trajectory of humanity is a spiral and not a circle——"

# VIII

Henri Mauperin's age, like that of so many present-day young men, could not be reckoned by the years of his life; he was of the same age as the times in which he lived. The coldness and absence of enthusiasm in the younger generation, that distinguishing mark of the second half of the nineteenth century, had set its seal on him entirely. He looked grave, and one felt that he was icy cold. One recognised in him those elements, so contrary to the French temperament, which constitute in French history sects without ardour and political parties without enthusiasm, such as the Jansenism of former days and the Doctrinarianism of to-day.

Henri Mauperin was a young Doctrinaire. He had belonged to that generation of children whom nothing astonishes and nothing amuses; who go, without the slightest excitement, to see anything to which they are taken and who come back again perfectly unmoved. When quite young he had always been well behaved and thoughtful. At college it had never happened to him in the midst of his lessons to go off in a dream, his face buried in his hands, his elbows on a dictionary and his eyes looking into the future. He had never been assailed by temptations with regard to the unknown and by those first visions of life which at the age of sixteen fill the minds of young men with trouble and delight, shut up as they are between the four walls of a courtyard with grated windows, against which their balls bounce and over and beyond which their thoughts soar. In his class there were two or three boys who were sons of eminent political men and with them he made friends. While studying classics he was thinking of the club he should join later on. On leaving college Henri's conduct was not like that of a young man of twenty. He was considered very steady, and was never seen in places where drinking and gambling went on and where his reputation might have suffered. He was to be met with in staid drawing-rooms, where he was always extremely attentive and polite to ladies who were no longer young. All that would have gone against him elsewhere served him there in good stead. His reserve was considered an attraction, his seriousness was thought fascinating.

There are fashions with regard to what finds favour in men. The reign of Louis Philippe, with its great wealth of scholars, had just accustomed the political and literary circles of Paris to value in a society man that something which recalls the cap and gown, that a professor takes about with him everywhere, even when he has become a minister.

With women of the upper middle class the taste for gay, lively, frivolous qualities of mind had been succeeded by a taste for conversation which savoured of the lecture-room, for science direct from the professor's chair, for a sort of learned amiability. A pedant did not alarm them, even though he might be old; when young he was made much of, and it was rumoured that Henri Mauperin was a great favourite.

He had a practical mind. He set up for being a believer in all that was useful, in mathematical truths, positive religions and the exact sciences. He had a certain compassion for art, and maintained that Boule furniture had never been made as well as at present. Political economy, that science which leads on to all things, had appealed to him when he went out into the world as a vocation and a career, consequently he had decided to be an economist. He had brought to this dry study a narrow-minded intelligence, but he had been patient and persevering, and now, once a fortnight, he published in important reviews a long article well padded with figures which the women skipped and the men said they had read.

By the interest which it takes in the poorer classes, by its care for their welfare and the algebraic account it keeps of all their misery and needs, political economy had, of course, given to Henri Mauperin a colouring of Liberalism. It was not that he belonged to a very decided Opposition: his opinions were merely a little ahead of Government principles, and his convictions induced him to make overtures to whatever was likely to succeed. He limited his war against the powers that were to the shooting of an arrow or to a veiled allusion, the key and meaning of which he would by means of his friends convey to the various *salons*. As a matter of fact, he was carrying on a flirtation, rather than hostilities, with the Government in power. Drawing-room acquaintances, people whom he met in society, brought him within reach of Government influence and into touch with Government patronage. He would prepare the works and correct the proofs of some high official who was always busy and who had scarcely time to do more than sign his books. He had managed to get on good terms with his Prefect, hoping through him to get into the Council and afterward into the Chamber. He excelled in playing double parts, and was clever at compromises and arrangements which kept him in touch with everything without quarrelling with anybody or anything. Though a liberal and political economist, he had found a way of turning aside the distrust of the Catholics and their enmity against himself and his doctrines. He had won the indulgence and sympathy of some of them, and had managed to make himself agreeable to the clergy and to flatter the church by linking together material progress and spiritual progress, the religion of political economy and that of Catholicism: Quesnay and Saint Augustin, Bastiat and the Gospel, statistics and God. Then besides this programme of his, the alliance of Religion and Political Economy, he had a reserve stock of piety, and he observed most regularly certain religious practices, which won for him the affectionate regard of the Abbé Blampoix and brought him into secret communion with believers and with those who observed their religious duties.

Henri Mauperin had taken his flat in the Rue Taitbout for the purpose of entertaining his friends. These entertainments consisted of solemn parties for young men, where the guests would gather round a table which looked like a desk and talk about Natural Law, Public Charities, Productive Forces, and the *Multiplicabilité* of the Human Species. Henri tried to turn these reunions into something approaching conferences. He was selecting the men and looking for the elements he would require for the famous *salon* he hoped to have in Paris as soon as he was married; he lured to his reunions the great authorities and notabilities of economic science, and invited to a sort of honorary presidency members of the Institute, whom he had pursued with his politeness and his newspaper puffs and who, according to his plans, would some day help him to take his seat among them in the moral and political science section.

It was, however, in turning associations to account that Henri had shown his talent and all his skill. He had from the very first clung to that great means of getting on peculiar to ciphers—that means by which a man is no longer one alone, but a unit joined to a number. He had gained a footing for himself in associations of every kind. He had joined the d'Aguesseau Debating Society and had glided in and taken his place among all those young men who were practising speech-making, educating themselves for the platform, doing their apprenticeship as orators and their probation as statesmen for future parliamentary struggles. Clubs, college reunions and banquets of old boys, barriers' lectures, historical and geographical societies, scientific and benevolent societies, he had neglected nothing. Everywhere, in all centres which give to the individual an opportunity of shining and which bring him any profit by the collective influence of a group, he appeared and was here, there and everywhere, making fresh acquaintances, forming new connections, cultivating friendships and interests which might lead him on to something, thus driving in the landmarks of his various ambitions, marching ahead, from the committee of one society to the committee of another society, to an importance, a sort of veiled notoriety and to one of those names which, thanks to political influence, are suddenly brought to the front when the right time comes.

He certainly was well qualified for the part he was playing. Eloquent and active, he could make all the noise and stir which lead a man on to success in this century of ours. He was commonplace with plenty of show about him. In society he rarely recited his own articles, but he usually posed with one hand in his waistcoat, after the fashion of Guizot in Delaroche's portrait.

# IX

"Well!" exclaimed Renée, entering the dining-room at eleven o'clock, breath-less like a child who had been running, "I thought every one would be down. Where is mamma?"

"Gone to Paris—shopping," answered M. Mauperin.

"Oh!—and where's Denoisel?"

"He's gone to see the man with the sloping ground, who must have kept him to luncheon. We'll begin luncheon."

"Good-morning, papa!" And instead of taking her seat Renée went across to her father and putting her arms round his neck began to kiss him.

"There, there, that's enough—you silly child!" said M. Mauperin, smiling as he endeavoured to free himself.

"Let me kiss you *tong-fashion*—there—like that," and she pinched his cheeks and kissed him again.

"What a child you are, to be sure."

"Now look at me. I want to see whether you care for me."

And Renée, standing up after kissing him once more, moved back from her father, still holding his head between her hands. They gazed at each other lovingly and earnestly, looking into one another's eyes. The French window was open and the light, the scents and the various noises from the garden penetrated into the room. A beam of sunshine darted on to the table, lighted on the china and made the glass glitter. It was bright, cheerful weather and a faint breeze was stirring; the shadows of the leaves trembled slightly on the floor. A vague sound of wings fluttering in the trees and of birds sporting among the flowers could be heard in the distance.

"Only we two; how nice!" exclaimed Renée, unfolding her serviette. "Oh, the table is too large; I am too far away," and taking her knife and fork she went and sat next her father. "As I have my father all to myself to-day I'm going to enjoy my father," and so saying she drew her chair still nearer to him.

"Ah, you remind me of the time when you always wanted to have your dinner in my pocket. But you were eight years old then."

Renée began to laugh.

"I was scolded yesterday," said M. Mauperin, after a minute's silence, putting his knife and fork down on his plate.

"Oh!" remarked Renée, looking up at the ceiling in an innocent way and then letting her eyes fall on her father with a sly look in them such as one sees in the eyes of a cat. "Really, poor papa! Why were you scolded? What had you done?"

"Yes, I should advise *you* to ask me that again; you know better than I do myself why I was scolded. What do you mean, you dreadful child?"

"Oh, if you are going to lecture me, papa, I shall get up and—I shall kiss you."

She half rose as she said this, but M. Mauperin interrupted her, endeavouring to speak in a severe tone:

"Sit down again, Renée, please. You must own, my dear child, that yesterday— —"

"Oh, papa, are you going to talk to me like this on such a beautiful day?"

"Well, but will you explain?" persisted M. Mauperin, trying to remain dignified in face of the rebellious expression, made up of smiles mingled with defiance, in his daughter's eyes. "It was very evident that you behaved in the way you did purposely."

Renée winked mischievously and nodded her head two or three times affirmatively.

"I want to speak to you seriously, Renée."

"But I am quite serious, I assure you. I have told you that I was like that on purpose."

"And why—will you tell me that?"

"Why? Oh, yes, I'll tell you, but on condition that you won't be too conceited. It was because—because— —"

"Because of what?"

"Because I love you much more than that gentleman who was here yesterday—there now—very much more—it's quite true!"

"But, then, we ought not to have allowed him to come if you did not care for this young man. We didn't force you into it. It was you yourself who agreed that he should be invited. On the contrary, your mother and I believed that this match— —"

"Excuse me, papa, but if I had refused M. Reverchon at first sight, point-blank, you would have said I was unreasonable, mad, senseless. I fancy I can hear mamma now on the subject. Whereas, as things were, what is there to reproach me with? I saw M. Reverchon once, and I saw him again, I had plenty of time to judge him and I knew that I disliked him. It is very silly, perhaps, but it is nevertheless— —"

"But why did you not tell us? We could have found a hundred ways of getting out of it."

"You are very ungrateful, papa. I have saved you all that worry. The young man is drawing out of it himself and it is not your fault at all; I alone am responsible. And this is all the gratitude I get for my self-sacrifice! Another time— —"

"Listen to me, my dear. If I speak to you like this it is because it is a question of your marriage. Your marriage—ah, it took me a long time to get reconciled to the idea that—to the idea of being separated from you. Fathers are selfish, you see; they would like it better if you never took to yourself wings. They have the greatest difficulty in making up their minds to it all. They think they cannot be happy without your smiles, and that the house will be very different when your dress is not flitting about. But we have to submit to what must be, and now it seems to me that I shall like my son-in-law. I am getting old, you know, my dear little Renée," and M. Mauperin took his daughter's hands in his. "Your father is sixty-eight, my child, he has only just time enough left to see you settled and happy. Your future, if only you knew it, is my one thought, my one torment. Your mother loves you dearly, too, I know, but your character and hers are different; and then, if anything happened to me. You know we must face things; and at my age. You see the thought of leaving you without a husband—and children—without any love which would make up to you for your old father's when he is no longer with you— —"

M. Mauperin could not finish; his daughter had thrown her arms round him, stifling down her sobs, and her tears were flowing freely on his waistcoat.

"Oh, it's dreadful of you, dreadful!" she said in a choking voice. "Why do you talk about it? Never—never!" and with a gesture she waved back the dark shadow called up by her imagination.

M. Mauperin had taken her on his knee. He put his arms round her, kissed her forehead and said, "Don't cry, Renée, don't cry!"

"How dreadful! Never!" she repeated once more, as though she were just rousing herself from some bad dream, and then, wiping her eyes with the back of her hand, she said to her father: "I must go away and have my cry out," and with that she escaped.

"That Dardouillet is certainly mad," remarked Denoisel, as he entered the room. "Just fancy, I could not possibly get rid of him. Ah, you are alone?"

"Yes, my wife is in Paris, and Renée has just gone upstairs."

"Why, what's the matter, M. Mauperin? You look— —"

"Oh, it's nothing—a little scene with Renée that I've just had—about this marriage—this Reverchon. I was silly enough to tell her that I am in a hurry to see my grandchildren, that fathers of my age are not immortal, and thereupon—the child is so sensitive, you know. She is up in her room now, crying. Don't go up; it will take her a little time to recover. I'll go and look after my work people."

Denoisel, left to himself, lighted a cigar, picked up a book and went out to one of the garden seats to read. He had been there about two hours when he saw Renée coming towards him. She had her hat on and her animated face shone with joy and a sort of serene excitement.

"Well, have you been out? Where have you come from?"

"Where have I come from?" repeated Renée, unfastening her hat. "Well, I'll tell you, as you are my friend," and she took her hat off and threw her head back with that pretty gesture women have for shaking their hair into place. "I've come from church, and if you want to know what I've been doing there, why, I've been asking God to let me die before papa. I was in front of a large statue of the Virgin—you are not to laugh—it would make me unhappy if you laughed. Perhaps it was the sun or the effect of gazing at her all the time, I don't know, but it seemed to me all in a minute that she did like this—" and Renée nodded her head. "Anyhow, I am very happy and my knees ache, too, I can tell you; for all the time I was praying I was on my knees, and not on a chair or a cushion either—but on the stone floor. Ah, I prayed in earnest; God can't surely refuse me that!"

# X

A few days after this M. and Mme. Mauperin, Henri, Renée, and Denoisel were sitting together after dinner in the little garden which stretched out at the back of the house, between the walls of the refinery and its outbuildings. The largest tree in the garden was a fir, and the rose-trees had been allowed to climb up to its lowest branches, so that its green arms stirred the roses. Under the tree was a swing, and at the back of it a sort of thicket of lilacs and witch-elms; there was a round plot of grass, with a garden bench and a very small pool with a white curb-stone round it and a fountain that did not play. The pool was full of aquatic plants and a few black newts were swimming in it.

"You don't intend to have any theatricals, then, Renée?" Henri was saying to his sister. "You've quite given up that idea?"

"Given up—no; but what can I do? It isn't my fault, for I would act anything—I'd stand on my head. But I can't find any one else, so that, unless I give a monologue—Denoisel has refused, and as for you, a sober man like you—well, I suppose it's no use asking."

"I, why, I would act right enough," answered Henri.

"You, Henri?" exclaimed Mme. Mauperin in astonishment.

"And then, too, we are not short of men," continued Renée, "there are always men to act. It's for the women's parts. Ah, that's the difficulty—to find ladies. I don't see who is to act with me."

"Oh," said Henri, "if we look about among all the people we know, I'll wager——"

"Well, let's see: there's M. Durand's daughter. Why, yes—what do you think? M. Durand's daughter? They are at Saint-Denis; that will be convenient for the rehearsals. She's rather a simpleton, but I should think for the rôle of Mme. de Chavigny——"

"Ah," put in Denoisel, "you still want to act 'The Caprice'?"

"Now for a lecture, I suppose? But as I'm going to act with my brother——"

"And the performance will be for the benefit of the poor, I hope?" continued Denoisel.

"Why?"

"It would make the audience more disposed to be charitable."

"We'll see about that, sir, we'll see about it. Well, Emma Durand—will that do?

What do you think, mamma?"

"They are not our sort of people, my dear," answered Mme. Mauperin quickly; "they are all very well at a distance, people like that, but every one knows where they sprang from—the Rue St. Honoré. Mme. Durand used to go and receive the ladies at their carriage-door, and M. Durand would slip out at the back and take the servant-men to have a glass at the wine-shop round the corner. That's how the Durands made their fortune."

Although at bottom Mme. Mauperin was an excellent sort of woman she rarely lost an opportunity of depreciating, in this way and with the most superb contempt and disgust, the wealth, birth and position of all the people she knew. It was not out of spite, nor was it for the pleasure of slandering and backbiting, nor yet because she was envious. She would refuse to believe in the respectability and uprightness of people, or even in the wealth they were said to have, simply from a prodigious *bourgeois* pride, from a conviction that outside her own family there could be no good blood, and no integrity; that, with the exception of her own people, every one was an upstart; that nothing was substantial except what she possessed, and that what she had not was not worth having.

"And to think that my wife has tales like that to tell about all the people we know!" said M. Mauperin.

"Come now, papa—shall we have the pretty little Remoli girl—shall we?"

"Ask your mother. Say on, Mme. Mauperin."

"The Remoli girl? But, my dear, you know—"

"I know nothing."

"Oh! do you mean to say that you don't know her father's history? A poor Italian stucco worker. He came to Paris without a sou and bought a bit of ground with a wretched little house at Montparnasse. I don't know where he got the money from to buy it. Well, this land turned out to be a regular Montfaucon! He sold thirty thousand pounds' worth of his precious stuff—and then he's been mixed up with Stock Exchange affairs. Disgusting!"

"Oh, well," put in Henri, "I fancy you are going out of your way to find folks. Why don't you ask Mlle. Bourjot? They happen to be at Sannois now."

"Mlle. Bourjot?" repeated Mme. Mauperin.

"Noémi?" said Renée quickly, "I should just think I should like to ask her. But this winter I thought her so distant with me. She has something or other—I don't know——"

"She has, or rather she will have, twelve thousand pounds a year," interrupted Denoisel, "and mothers are apt to watch over their daughters when such is the case. They will not allow them to get too intimate with a sister who has a brother. They have made her understand this; that's about the long and short of it."

"Then, too, they are so high and mighty, those folks are; they might have descended from—And yet," continued Mme. Mauperin, breaking off and turning to her son, "they have always been very pleasant with you, Henri, haven't they? Mme. Bourjot is always very nice to you?"

"Yes, and she has complained several times of your not going to her soirées; she says you don't take Renée often enough to see her daughter."

"Really?" exclaimed Renée, very delighted.

"My dear," said Mme. Mauperin, "what do you think of what Henri says — Mlle. Bourjot?"

"What objection do you want me to make?"

"Well, then," said Mme. Mauperin, "Henri's idea shall be carried out. We'll go on Saturday, shall we, my dear? And you'll come with us, Henri?"

A few hours later every one was in bed with the exception of Henri Mauperin. He was walking up and down in his room puffing on a cigar that had gone out, and every now and then he appeared to be smiling at his own thoughts.

# XI

Renée often went during the day to paint in a little studio, built out of an old green-house at the bottom of the garden. It was very rustic-looking, half hidden with verdure and walled with ivy, something between an old ruin and a nest.

On a table covered with an Algerian cloth there were, on this particular day in the little studio, a Japanese box with a blue design, a lemon, an old red almanac with the French coat of arms, and two or three other bright-coloured objects grouped together as naturally as possible to make a picture, with the light from the glass roof falling on them. Seated in front of the table, Renée was painting all this with brushes as fine as pins on a canvas which already had something on the under side. The skirt of her white piqué dress hung in ample folds on each side of the stool on which she was seated. She had gathered a white rose as she came through the garden and had fastened it in her loosely arranged hair just above her ear. Her foot, visible below her dress, in a low shoe which showed her white stocking, was resting on the cross-bar of the easel. Denoisel was seated near her, watching her work and making a bad sketch of her profile in an album he had picked up in the studio.

"Oh, you do pose well," he remarked, as he sharpened his pencil again; "I would just as soon try to catch an omnibus as your expression. You never cease. If you always move like that— —"

"Ah, now, Denoisel, no nonsense with your portrait. I hope you'll flatter me a little."

"No more than the sun does. I am as conscientious as a photograph."

"Let me look," she said, leaning back towards Denoisel and holding her maulstick and palette out in front of her. "Oh! I am not beautiful. Truly, now," she continued, as she went on with her painting, "am I like that?"

"Something. Come, Renée—honestly now—what do you think you are like yourself—beautiful?"

"No."

"Pretty?"

"No—no— —"

"Ah, you took the trouble to think the matter over this time."

"Yes, but I said it twice."

"Good! If you think you are neither beautiful nor pretty, you don't fancy either that you are— —"

"Ugly? No, that's quite true. It's very difficult to explain. Sometimes, now, when I look at myself, I think—how am I to explain? Well, I like my looks; it isn't my face, I know, it's just a sort of expression I have at such times, a something that is within me and which I can feel passing over my features. I don't know what it is—happiness, pleasure, a sort of emotion or whatever you like to call it. I get moments like that when it seems to me as though I am taking all my people in finely. All the same, though, I should have liked to be beautiful."

"Really!"

"It must be very pleasant for one's own sake, it seems to me. Now, for instance, I should have liked to be tall, with very black hair. It's stupid to be almost blonde. It's the same with white skin; I should have chosen a skin—well, like Mme. Stavelot, rather orange-coloured. I like that, but it's a matter of taste. And then I should have enjoyed looking in my glass. It's like when I get up in the morning and walk about the carpet with bare feet. I should love to have feet like a statue I once saw—it's just an idea!"

"If that's how you feel you wouldn't care about being beautiful for the sake of other people?"

"Yes and no. Not for every one—only for those I care for. We ought to be ugly for people about whom we are indifferent, for all the people we don't love—don't you think so? They would have just what they deserved then."

Denoisel began sketching again.

"How odd it is, your ideal, to wish to be dark!" he said, after a moment's silence.

"What should you like to be?"

"If I were a woman? I should like to be small and neither very fair nor very dark— —"

"Auburn then?"

"And plump—Oh, as plump as a quail."

"Plump? Ah, I can breathe again. Just for a moment I was afraid of a declaration—If the light had not shown up your hair I should have forgotten you were forty."

"Oh, you don't make me out any older than I am, Renée; that is exactly my age. But do you know what yours is for me?"

"No— —"

"Twelve—and you will always be that age to me."

"Thanks—I am very glad," said Renée. "If that's it I shall always be able to tell you all the nonsense that comes into my head. Denoisel," she continued, after a short silence, "have you ever been in love?" She had drawn back slightly from her canvas and was looking at it sideways, her head leaning over her shoulder to see the effect of the colour she had just put on.

"Oh, well! that's a good start," answered Denoisel. "What a question!"

"What's the matter with my question? I'm asking you that just as I might ask you anything else. I don't see anything in it. Would there be any harm in asking such a thing in society? Come now, Denoisel! you say I am twelve years old and I agree to be twelve; but I'm twenty all the same. I'm a *young person*, that's true, but if you imagine that *young persons* of my age have never read any novels nor sung any love-songs—why, it's all humbug—it's just posing as sweet innocents. After all, just as you like. If you think I am not old enough I'll take back my question. I thought we were to consider ourselves men when we talked about things together."

"Well, since you want to know, yes—I have been in love."

"Ah! And what effect did it have on you—being in love?"

"You have only to read over again the novels you have read, my dear, and you will find the effect described on every page."

"There, now, that's just what puzzles me; all the books one reads are full of love—there's nothing but that! And then in real life one sees nothing of it—at least I don't see anything of it; on the contrary, I see every one doing without it, and quite easily, too. Sometimes I wonder whether it is not just invented for books, whether it is not all imagined by authors—really."

Denoisel laughed at the young girl's words.

"Tell me, Renée," he said, "since we are men for the time being, as you just said and as we talk to each other of what we feel, quite frankly like two old friends, I should like to ask you in my turn whether you have ever—well, not been in love with any one, but whether you have ever cared for any one?"

"No, never," answered Renée, after a moment's reflection, "but then I am not a fair example. I fancy that such things happen to people who have an empty heart, no one to think about; people who are not taken up, absorbed, possessed and, as it were, protected by one of those affections which take hold of you wholly and entirely—the affection one has for one's father, for instance."

Denoisel did not answer.

"You don't believe that that does preserve you?" said Renée. "Well, but I can assure you I have tried in vain to remember. Oh, I'm examining my conscience thoroughly, I promise you. Well, from my very childhood, I cannot remember anything—no, nothing at all. And yet some of my little friends, who were no older than I was, would kiss the inside of the caps of the little boys who used to play with us; and they would collect the peach-stones from the plates the little boys had used and put them into a box and then take the box to bed with them. Yes, I remember all that. Noémi, for instance, Mlle. Bourjot, was very great at all that. But as for me, I simply went on with my games."

"And later on when you were no longer a child?"

"Later on? I have always been a child as regards all that. No, there is nothing at all—I cannot remember a single impression. I mean—well, I'm going to be quite frank with you—I had just a slight, a very slight commencement of what you were talking about—just a sensation of that feeling that I recognised later on in novels—and can you guess for whom?"

"No."

"For you. Oh, it was only for an instant. I soon liked you in quite a different way—and better, too. I respected you and was grateful to you. I liked you for correcting my faults as a spoiled child, for enlarging my mind, for teaching me to appreciate all that is beautiful, elevated and noble; and all, too, in a joking way by making fun of everything that is ugly and worthless and of everything that is dull or mean and cowardly. You taught me how to play ball and how to endure being bored to death with imbeciles. I have to thank you for much of what I think about, for much of what I am and for a little of any good there is in me. I wanted to pay my debt with a true and lasting friendship, and by giving you cordially, as a comrade, some of the affection I have for father."

As Renée said these last words she raised her voice slightly and spoke in a graver tone.

"What in the world is that?" exclaimed M. Mauperin, who had just entered and had caught sight of Denoisel's sketch. "Is that intended for my daughter! Why, it's a frightful libel," and M. Mauperin picked up the album and began to tear the page up.

"Oh, papa!" exclaimed Renée, "and I wanted it—for a keepsake!"

# XII

A light carriage, drawn by one horse, was conveying the Mauperin family along the Sannois road. Renée had taken the reins and the whip from her brother, who was seated at her side smoking. Animated by the drive, the air, and the movement, M. Mauperin was joking about the people they met and bowing gaily to any acquaintances they passed. Mme. Mauperin was silent and absorbed. She was buried in herself, thinking out and preparing her amiability for the approaching visit.

"Why, mamma," remarked Renée, "you don't say a word. Are you not well?"

"Oh, yes, very well, quite well," answered Mme. Mauperin; "but the fact is I'm worrying rather about this visit—and if it had not been for Henri—There's something so stiff and cold about Mme. Bourjot—they are all so high and mighty. Oh, it isn't that they impress me at all—their money indeed! I know too well where they had it from. They made their money from some invention they bought from an unfortunate working-man for a mere nothing—a few coppers."

"Come, come, Mme. Mauperin," put in her husband, "they must have bought more than——"

"Well, anyhow, I don't feel at ease with these people."

"You are very foolish to trouble yourself——"

"We can tell them we don't care a hang for their fine airs!" said Mlle. Mauperin, whipping up the horse so that her slang was lost in the sound of the animal's gallop.

There was some reason for Mme. Mauperin's uneasiness. Her feeling of constraint was certainly justified. Everything in the house to which she was going was calculated to intimidate people, to set them down, crush them, penetrate and overwhelm them with a sense of their own inferiority. There was an ostentatious and studied show of money, a clever display of wealth. Opulence aimed at the humiliation of less fortunate beings, by all possible means of intimidation, by outrageous or refined forms of luxury, by the height of the ceilings, by the impertinent airs of the lackeys, by the footman with his silver chain, stationed in the entrance-hall, by the silver plate on which everything was served, by all kinds of princely ways and customs, such as the strict observance of evening dress, even when mother and daughter were dining alone, by an etiquette as rigid as that of a small German court. The master and mistress were in harmony with and maintained the style of their house. The spirit of their home and life was as it were incarnate in them.

The man, with all that he had copied from the English gentry, his manners, his dress, his curled whiskers, his outward distinction; the woman, with her grand manners, her supreme elegance, all the stiffness and formality of the upper middle class, represented admirably the pride of money. Their disdainful politeness, their haughty amiability, seemed to come down to people. There was a kind of insolence which was visible in their tastes even. M. Bourjot had neither any pictures nor any objects of art; his collection was a collection of precious stones, among which he pointed out a ruby worth a thousand pounds, one of the finest in Europe.

People had overlooked all this display of wealth, and the Bourjot's *salon* was now very much in vogue and conspicuous on account of its pronounced tendencies in favour of the Opposition party. It had become, in fact, one of the three or four important *salons* of Paris. It had been peopled after two or three winters which Mme. Bourjot had spent in Nice under pretext of benefitting her health. She had converted her house there into a kind of hotel on the road to Italy, open to all who passed by provided they were great, wealthy, celebrated, or that they had a name. At her musical evenings, when Mme. Bourjot gave every one an opportunity for admiring her beautiful voice and her great musical talent, the celebrities of Europe and Parisians of repute met in her drawing-room. Scientists, great philosophers and æsthetes mingled with politicians. The latter were represented by a compact group of Orleanists and a band of Liberals not pledged to any party, in whose ranks Henri Mauperin had figured most assiduously for the past year. A few Legitimists whom the husband brought to his wife's *salon* were also to be seen, M. Bourjot himself being a Legitimist.

Under the Restoration he had been a Carbonaro. He was the son of a draper, and his birth and name of Bourjot had from his earliest childhood exasperated him against the nobility, grand houses, and the Bourbons. He had been in various conspiracies, and had met with M. Mauperin at Carbonari reunions. He had figured in all the tumults, and had been fond of quoting Berville, Saint-Just, and Dupin the elder. After 1830 he had calmed down and had contented himself with sulking with royalty for having cheated him of his republic. He read the *National*, pitied the people of all lands, despised the Chambers, railed at M. Guizot, and was eloquent about the Pritchard affair.

The events of 1848 came upon him suddenly, and the landowner then woke up alarmed and rose erect in the person of the Carbonaro of the Restoration, the Liberal of Louis Philippe's reign. The fall in stocks, the unproductiveness of houses, socialism, the proposed taxes, the dangers to which State creditors were exposed, the eventful days of June, and indeed everything which is calculated to strike terror to the heart of a moneyed man during a revolution, disturbed M. Bourjot's equanimity, and at the same time enlightened him. His ideas suddenly underwent a change, and his political conscience veered completely round. He hastened to adopt the doctrines of order, and turned to the Church as he might have done to the police authorities, to the Divine right as the supreme power and a providential security for his bills.

Unfortunately, in M. Bourjot's brusque but sincere conversion, his education, his youth, his past, his whole life rose in revolt. He had returned to the Bourbons, but he had not been able to come back to Jesus Christ, and, old man as he now was, he would make all kinds of slips and give utterance to the attacks and refrains to which he had been accustomed. One felt, the nearer one came to him, that he was still quite a Voltairean on certain points, and Beranger was constantly taking the place of de Maistre with him.

"Give the reins to your brother, Renée," said Mme. Mauperin. "I shouldn't like them to see you driving."

They were in front of a magnificent large gateway, opposite which were two lamps that were always lighted and left burning all night. The carriage turned up a drive, covered with red gravel and planted on each side with huge clumps of rhododendrons, and drew up before a flight of stone steps. Two footmen threw open the glass doors leading into a hall paved with marble and with high windows nearly hidden by the verdure of a wide screen of exotic shrubs.

The Mauperins were then introduced into a drawing-room, the walls of which were covered with crimson silk. A portrait of Mme. Bourjot in evening dress, signed by Ingres, was the only picture in the room. Through the open windows could be seen a pool of water, and near it a stork, the only creature that M. Bourjot would tolerate in his park, and that on account of its heraldic form.

When the Mauperins entered the large drawing-room, Mme. Bourjot, seated by herself on the divan, was listening to her daughter's governess who was reading aloud. M. Bourjot was leaning against the chimney-piece playing with his watch-chain. Mlle. Bourjot, near her governess, was working at some tapestry on a frame.

Mme. Bourjot, with her large, rather hard blue eyes, her arched eye-brows, and the lines of her eye-lids, her haughty and pronounced nose, the supercilious prominence of the lower part of the face, and her imperious grace, reminded one of Georges, when young, in the rôle of Agrippina. Mlle. Bourjot had strongly marked brown eye-brows. Between her long, curly lashes could be seen two blue eyes with an intense, profound, dreamy expression in them. A slight down almost white could be seen when the light was full on her, just above her lip at the two corners. The governess was one of those retiring creatures, one of those elderly women who have been knocked about and worn out in the battle of life, outwardly and inwardly, and who finally have no more effigy left than an old copper coin.

"Why, this is really charming!" said Mme. Bourjot, getting up and advancing as far as a line of the polished floor in the centre of the room. "What kind neighbours—and what a delightful surprise! It seems an age since I had the pleasure of seeing you, dear madame, and if it were not for your son, who is good enough not to forsake us, and who comes to my Monday Evenings, we should not have known what had become of you—of this charming girl—and her mamma——"

As she spoke Mme. Bourjot shook hands with Henri.

"Oh! you are very kind," began Mme. Mauperin, taking a seat at some distance from Mme. Bourjot.

"But please come over here," said Mme. Bourjot, making room at her side.

"We have postponed our visit from day to day," continued Mme. Mauperin, "as we wanted to come together."

"Oh! well, it's very bad of you," continued Mme. Bourjot. "We are not a hundred miles away; and it is cruel to keep these two children apart, when they grew up together. Why, how's this, they haven't kissed each other yet?"

Noémi, who was still standing, presented her cheek coldly to Renée, who kissed her as eagerly, as a child bites into fruit.

"What a long time ago it seems," observed Mme. Bourjot to Mme. Mauperin, as she looked at the two girls, "since we used to take them to the Rue de la Chaussée d'Antin to those lectures, that bored us as much as they did the poor children. I can see them now, playing together. Yours was just like quicksilver, a regular little turk, and mine—Oh, they were like night and day! But yours always led mine on. Oh, dear, what a rage they had at one time for charades—do you remember? They used to carry off all the towels in the house to dress up with."

"Oh, yes," exclaimed Renée, laughing and turning to Noémi, "our finest one was when we did *Marabout*; with *Marat* in a bath that was too hot, calling out, '*Je bous, je bous!*' Do you remember?"

"Yes, indeed," answered Noémi, trying to keep back a smile, "but it was your idea."

"I am so glad, madame, to find you quite inclined beforehand for what I wanted to ask you—for my visit is a selfish one. It was chiefly with the idea of letting our daughters see something of each other that I came. Renée wants to get up a play, and she naturally thought of her old school-friend. If you would allow your daughter to take part in a piece with my daughter—it would be just a little family affair—quite informal."

As Mme. Mauperin made this request, Noémi, who had been talking to Renée and had put her hand in her friend's, drew it away again abruptly.

"Thank you so much for the idea," answered Mme. Bourjot, "thanks, too, to Renée. You could not have asked me anything that would have suited me better and given me so much pleasure. I think it would be very good for Noémi—the poor child is so shy that I am in despair! It would make her talk and come out of herself. For her mind, too, it would be an excellent stimulant——"

"Oh! but, mother, you know very well—why, I've no memory. And then, too—why, the very idea of acting frightens me. Oh, no—I can't act——"

Mme. Bourjot glanced coldly at her daughter.

"But, mother, if I could—No, I should spoil the whole play, I'm sure."

"You will act—I wish you to do so."

Noémi looked down, and Mme. Mauperin, slightly embarrassed and by way of changing the subject, glanced at a Review that was lying open on a work-table at her side.

"Ah!" said Mme. Bourjot, turning to her again, "you've found something you know there—that is your son's last article. And when do you intend having this play?"

"Oh, but I should be so sorry to be the cause—to oblige your daughter——"

"Oh! don't mention it. My daughter is always afraid of undertaking anything."

"Well, but if Noémi really dislikes it," put in M. Bourjot, who had been talking to M. Mauperin and Henri on the other side of the room.

"On the contrary she will be grateful to you," said Mme. Bourjot, addressing Mme. Mauperin without answering M. Bourjot. "We are always obliged to insist on her doing anything for her own enjoyment. Well, when is this play?"

"Renée, when do you think?" asked Mme. Mauperin.

"Why, I should think about—well, we should want a month for the rehearsals, with two a week. We could fix the days and the time that would suit Noémi."

Renée turned towards Noémi, who remained silent.

"Very well, then," said Mme. Bourjot, "let us say Monday and Friday at two o'clock, if that will suit you—shall we?" And turning to the governess she continued: "Mlle. Gogois, you will accompany Noémi. M. Bourjot—you hear—will you give orders for the horses and carriage and the footman to take them to Briche? You can keep Terror for me, and Jean. There, that's all settled. Now, then, you will stay and dine with us, won't you?"

"Oh! we should like to very much; but it is quite impossible. We have some people coming to us to-day," answered Mme. Mauperin.

"Oh, dear, how tiresome of them to come to-day! But I don't think you have seen my husband's new conservatories. I'll make you a bouquet, Renée. We have a flower—there are only two of them anywhere, and the other is at Ferrières—it's a—it's very ugly anyhow—this way."

"Suppose we were to go in here," said M. Bourjot, pointing to the billiard-room, which could be seen through the glass door. "M. Henri, we'll leave you with the ladies. We can smoke here," added M. Bourjot, offering a *cabanas* to M. Mauperin. "Shall we have cannoning?"

"Yes," replied M. Mauperin.

M. Bourjot closed the pockets of the billiard-table.

"Twenty-four?"

"Yes, twenty-four."

"Have you billiards at home, M. Mauperin?"

"No, I haven't. My son doesn't play."

"Are you looking for the chalk?"

"Thanks. And as my wife doesn't think it a suitable game for girls——"

"It's your turn."

"Oh! I'm quite out of practice—I always was a duffer at it though."

"Well, but you are not giving me the game at all. There, it's all up with my play—I was used to that cue," and M. Bourjot gave vent to his feelings in an oath.

"These rascals of workmen—they haven't any conscience at all. There's no getting anything well made in these days. Well, you *are* scoring: three, I'll mark it. The fact is we are at their service. The other day, now, I wanted some chandeliers put up. Well, would you believe it, M. Mauperin, I couldn't get a man? It was a holiday—I forget what holiday it was—and they would not come—they are the lords of creation, nowadays. Do you imagine that they ever bring us anything of what they shoot or fish? Oh, no, when they get anything dainty they eat it themselves. I know what it is in Paris—four? Oh, come now! Every penny they earn is spent at the wine-shop. On Sundays they spend at least a sovereign. The locksmith here has a Lefaucheux gun and takes out a shooting license. Ah, two for me at last! And the money they ask now for their work! Why, they want four shillings a day for mowing! I have vineyards in Burgundy, and they proposed to see to them for me for three years, and then the third year they would be their own. This is what we are coming to! Luckily for me I'm an old man, so that it won't be in my time; but in a hundred years from now there will be no such thing as being waited on—there'll be no servants. I often say to my wife and daughter: 'You'll see—the day will come when you will have to make your own beds. Five?—six?—- you *do* know how to play. The Revolution has done for us, you know." And M. Bourjot began to hum:

> "'Et zonzon, zonzon, zonzon,
> Zonzon, zonzon—— '"

"These were not exactly your ideas some thirty years ago, when we met for the first time; do you remember?" said M. Mauperin with a smile.

"That's true. I had some fine ideas in those days—too fine!" replied M. Bourjot, resting his left hand on his cue. "Ah, we were young—I should just think I do remember. It was at Lallemand's funeral.—By Jove! that was the best blow I ever gave in my life—a regular knock-you-down. I can see the nails in that police inspector's boots now, when I had landed him on the ground so that I could cross the boulevards. At the corner of the Rue Poissonnière I came upon a patrol—they set about me with a vengeance. I was with Caminade—you knew Caminade, didn't you? He was a lively one. He was the man who used to go and smoke his pipe at the mission service belonging to the Church of the Petits-Pères. He went with his meerschaum pipe that cost nearly sixty pounds, and he took a girl from the Palais-Royal. He was lucky, for he managed to escape, but they took me to the police station, belabouring me with the butt-end of their guns. Fortunately Dulaurens caught sight of me——"

"Ah—Dulaurens!" said M. Mauperin. "We were in the same Carbonari society. He had a shawl shop, it seems to me."

"Yes, and do you know what became of him?"

"No. I lost sight of him."

"Well, one fine day—it was after all this business—his partner went off to Belgium, taking with him eight thousand pounds. They put the police on his track, but they could hear nothing of him. Our friend Dulaurens goes into a church and makes a vow to get converted if he finds his money again. They find his money for him and now his piety is simply sickening. I never see him now; but in the old days he was a lively one, I can tell you. Well, when I saw him I gave him a look and he understood. You see, I had twenty-five guns in my house and five hundred cartridges. When the police went there to search he had cleared them away. All the same I was kept three months shut up in the new building, and two or three times was fetched up in the night to be cross-examined, and I always went with a vague idea in my mind that I was going to be shot. You've gone through it all, and you know what it is.—And all that was for the sake of Socialism! And yet I heard a few words that ought to have enlightened me. When I was free again one of my prison friends came to see me at Sedan. 'Why, what's this,' he said, 'that I am told at the hotel? It seems that your father has land and money, and yet you have joined us! Why, I thought you hadn't anything!' Just fancy now, M. Mauperin—and when I think that even that did not open my eyes! You see I was convinced in those days that all those with whom I was in league wanted simply what I wanted: laws for rich and poor alike, the abolition of privileges, the end of the Revolution of '89 against the nobility—I thought we should stop there—eleven? Did I mark your last? I don't think I did—let us say twelve. But, good heavens! when I saw my republic I was disgusted with it, when I heard two men, who had just come down from the barricades in February, say, 'We ought not to have left them until we had made sure of two hundred a year!' And then the system of taxes according to the income; it's an iniquity—the hypocrisy of communism. But with taxes regulated by the income," continued M. Bourjot, eloquently breaking off in the midst of his own phrase, "I challenge them to find any one who will care to take the trouble of making a large fortune—thirteen, fourteen, fifteen—very good! Oh, you are too strong a player. All that has made me turn round—you understand?"

"Perfectly," replied M. Mauperin.

"Where's my ball—there? Yes, it has made me turn completely round; it has positively made a Legitimist of me. There—a bad cue again! But——"

"But what?"

"Well, there is one thing—Oh, on that subject, now, I have the same opinions still. I don't mind telling you. Anything approaching a parson—eighteen?—Oh, come, I'm done for! We invite the one here in this place—he's a very decent fellow; but as to priests—when you've known one as I have, who broke his leg getting over the college wall at night—they are a pack of Jesuits, you know, M. Mauperin!

"'Hommes noirs, d'où sortez-vous?
Nous sortons de dessous, terre.'"

"Ah, that's my man! The god of simple folks!

"'Mes amis, parlons plus bas:
Je vois Judas, je vois Judas!'"

"Twenty-one! You've only three more. Now, at the place where my iron-works are, there's a bishop who is very easy-going. Well, all the bigots detest him. Now, if he pretended to be a bigot, if he were a hypocrite and spent all his time at church——"

"I never saw Mme. Bourjot so amiable," remarked Mme. Mauperin, when she and her family were all back in the carriage.

"An odd chap, that Bourjot," observed M. Mauperin. "It isn't much good having a billiard-table of his own either—I could have given him a start of twelve."

"I think Noémi is very strange," said Renée. "Did you see, Henri, how she wanted to get out of acting?"

Henri did not answer.

# XIII

Noémi had just entered Mme. Mauperin's drawing-room followed by her governess. She looked uncomfortable and ill at ease, almost shy, in fact, but on glancing round she appeared to be somewhat reassured. She advanced to speak to Mme. Mauperin, who kissed her. Renée then embraced her, and, joking and laughing all the time, proceeded to take off her friend's cape and hat.

"Ah, I'm forgetting," she exclaimed, turning the dainty white hat trimmed with pink flowers round on her hand, "let me introduce M. Denoisel again. You have met him before in the old days—that sounds as though we were quite aged, doesn't it?—and he is our theatrical manager, our professor of elocution, our prompter—scene shifter—everything."

"I have not forgotten how kind M. Denoisel used to be to me when I was a little girl," and Noémi, flushing with emotion as her thoughts went back to her childhood, held out her hand somewhat awkwardly and with such timidity that her fingers all clung together.

"Oh, but what a pretty costume!" continued Renée, walking round her. "You look sweet," and then patting her own taffeta dress, which was rather the worse for wear, she held out her skirt and made a low reverence. "You'll make a rather pretty Mathilde—I shall be jealous, you know.—But look, mamma," she continued, drawing herself up to her full height. "I told you so—she makes me quite small.—Now, then—you see you are much taller than I am." As she spoke she placed herself side by side with Noémi and, putting her arm round her waist, led her to the glass and put her shoulder against her friend's. "There, now!" she exclaimed.

The governess was keeping in the background at the other end of the *salon*. She was looking at some pictures in a book that she had only dared to half open.

"Come, my dears, shall we begin to read the play?" said Mme. Mauperin. "It's no use waiting for Henri; he will only come to the last rehearsals when the actresses are well on."

"Oh, just now, mamma, let us talk first. Come and sit here, Noémi. There—we have a lot of little secrets, so many things that have happened since we last met to tell each other about—it is ages ago."

And Renée began prattling and chirping away with Noémi. Their conversation sounded like the fresh, clear, never-ending babbling of a brook, breaking off now and again in a peal of laughter and dying away in a whisper. Noémi, who was very guarded at first, soon gave herself up to the delight of confiding in her friend and of listening to this voice which brought back so many memories of the past. They asked each other, as one does after a long absence, about all that had happened and what they had each been doing. At the end of half an hour, to judge by their conversation, one would have said they were two young women who had suddenly become children again together.

"I go in for painting," said Renée, "what do you do? You used to have a beautiful voice."

"Oh, don't mention that," said Noémi. "They make me sing. Mamma insists on my singing at her big parties—and you've no idea how dreadful it is. When I see every one looking at me, a shiver runs through me. Oh, I'm so frightened—the first few times I burst out crying——"

"Well, we'll have a little refreshment now. I've saved a green apple for you that I was going to eat myself. I hope you still like green apples?"

"No, thanks, Renée dear, I'm not hungry, really."

"I say, Denoisel, what can you see that is so interesting—through that window?"

Denoisel was watching the Bourjot's footman in the garden. He had seen him dust the bench with a fine cambric handkerchief, spread the handkerchief over the green laths, sit down on it in a gingerly way in his red velvet breeches, cross his legs, take a cigar out of his pocket and light it. He was now looking at this man as he sat there smoking in an insolent, majestic way, glancing round at this small estate with the supercilious expression of a servant whose master lives in a mansion and owns a park.

"Why, nothing at all," said Denoisel, coming away from the window; "I was afraid of intruding."

"We have told each other all our secrets now; so you can come and talk to us."

"You know what time it is, Renée?" put in Mme. Mauperin. "If you want to begin the rehearsal to-day——"

"Oh, mamma, please—it's so warm to-day—and then, too, it's Friday."

"And the year began on a 13th," remarked Denoisel gravely.

"Ah!" said Noémi, looking at him with her trustful eyes.

"Don't listen to him—he's taking you in. He plays jokes of that kind on you all day long—Denoisel does. We'll rehearse next time you come, shall we?—there's plenty of time."

"As you like," answered Noémi.

"Very well, then; we'll take a holiday. Denoisel, be funny—at once. And if you are very funny—very, very funny—I'll give you a picture—one of my own——"

"Another?"

"Oh, well, you are polite—I work myself to death——"

"Mademoiselle," said Denoisel to Noémi, "you shall judge of the situation. I have now a picture of a mad-apple and a parsnip, and then to hang with that a slice of pumpkin and a piece of Brie cheese. There's a great deal of feeling, I know, of course, in such subjects; but all the same from the look of my room any one would take me for a private fruiterer."

"That's how men are, you see," said Renée gaily to Noémi. "They are all ungrateful, my dear—and to think that some day we shall have to marry. Do you know that we are quite old maids—what do you think of that? Twenty years old— oh, how quickly time goes, to be sure! We think we shall never be eighteen, and then, no sooner are we really eighteen than it's all over and we can't stay at that age. Well, it can't be helped. Oh, next time you come, bring some music with you and we'll play duets. I don't know whether I could now."

"And we shall rehearse—*quand*?" asked Denoisel.

"In Normandy!" answered Renée, indulging in that kind of joke which for the last few years has been in favour with society people, and which had its origin in the workshop and the theatre. Noémi looked perplexed, as though she had not caught the sense of the word she had just heard.

"Yes," said Renée, "Caen is in Normandy. Ah, you don't go in for word-endings? I used to have a mania for them some time ago. I was quite unbearable with it—wasn't I, Denoisel? And so you go out a great deal. Tell me about your balls."

Noémi did as she was requested, speaking freely and getting gradually more and more animated. She smiled as she spoke, and as her restraint wore off her movements and gestures were graceful. It seemed as if she had expanded under the influence of this air of liberty, here with Renée in this gay, cheerful drawing-room.

At four o'clock the governess rose as if moved by machinery.

"It is time we started, mademoiselle," she said. "There is a dinner-party, you know, at Sannois, and you will want time to dress."

# XIV

"This time you must not expect to enjoy yourself; we are going to rehearse in good earnest," said Denoisel. "Mlle. Noémi, come and sit down there—that's it. We are ready now, are we not? One—two—three," he continued, clapping his hands, "begin."

"The fact is—the first scene," said Noémi, hesitatingly, "I am not quite sure of it—I know the other better."

"The second, then? We'll begin with the second—I'll take Henri's part: '*Good evening, my dear——* '"

Denoisel was interrupted by a peal of laughter from Renée.

"Oh, dear!" she said to Noémi, "how funnily you are sitting! You look like a piece of sugar held in the sugar-tongs."

"Do I?" said Noémi, quite confused and trying to find a better pose.

"If only you would be kind enough not to interrupt the actors, Renée," said Denoisel. "'*Good evening, my dear,*'" he repeated, continuing his rôle, "'*do I disturb you?*'"

"Oh! and where are the purses?" exclaimed Renée.

"Why, I thought you were to see to them."

"I?—not at all. You were to see to them. You are a nice one to count on for the stage properties! I say, Noémi, if you were married, would it ever dawn upon you to give your husband a purse? It's rather shoppy, isn't it? Why not a smoking-cap, at once?"

"Are we going to rehearse?" asked Denoisel.

"Oh, Denoisel, you said that just like a man who really wants to go and have a smoke!"

"I always do want to smoke, Renée," answered Denoisel, "and especially when I ought not to."

"Why, it's quite a vice, then, with you."

"I should just think it is; and so I keep it."

"Well, but what pleasure can you find in smoking?"

"The pleasure of a bad habit—that is the explanation of many passions. '*Good evening, my dear,*'" he repeated, once more going back to M. de Chavigny's arrival on the scene, "'*do I disturb you?*'"

*"Disturb me, Henri—what a question!"* replied Noémi.

And the rehearsal continued.

# XV

"Three o'clock," said Renée, looking up at the time-piece from the little woollen stocking she was knitting. "Really, I begin to think Noémi will not come to-day. She'll spoil the rehearsal. We shall have to fine her."

"Noémi?" put in Mme. Mauperin, as though she had just woke up. "Why, she isn't coming. Oh, I never told you! I don't know what's the matter with me—I forget everything lately. She told me last time that very probably she would not be able to come to-day. They are expecting some people—I fancy—I forget——"

"Well, that's pleasant! There is nothing more tiresome than that—to expect people who don't come after all. And this morning when I woke I said to myself, 'It's Noémi's day.' I was looking forward to having her. Oh, it's quite certain she won't come now. It's funny how I miss her now—Noémi, when she isn't here—ever since she began to take me on again. I miss her just as though she were one of the family. I don't think her amusing, she isn't lively, she isn't at all gay, and then as regards intelligence, why, she's rather feeble—you can take her in so easily. And yet—how is it now?—in spite of all that there is a fascination about her. There is something so sweet, so very sweet about her, and it seems to penetrate you. She calms your nerves, positively, and then the effect she has on you—why, she seems to warm your heart for you, and only by being there, near you. I've known lots of girls who had really more in them, but they haven't what she has. I've always felt as cold as steel with all of them."

"Oh, well, it's very simple," said Denoisel. "Mlle. Bourjot is of a very affectionate, loving disposition. There is a sort of current of affection between such natures and others."

"When she was quite little, I can remember, she was just the same—and so sensitive. How she used to cry, and how fond she was of kissing me; it was amazing—she did nothing else, in fact. And her face tells you just what she is, doesn't it? Her beauty seems to be made up of all the affection she feels, and of all that she has left of her childhood about her. And above all it is her expression. You often feel rather wicked and spiteful, but when she looks at you with that expression of hers it is as though everything of that kind disappears—as though something is melting away. Would you believe that I never ventured to play a single trick on her, and yet I was a terrible tease in the old days!"

"Nevertheless, it's very extraordinary to be as affectionate as all that," said Mme. Mauperin.

"Oh, no, it's quite natural," answered Denoisel. "Imagine a girl, who is born with the instinct of loving, just as we have the instinct of breathing. She is repelled by the coldness of a mother, who feels herself humiliated by her daughter, and who is ashamed of her; she is repelled also by the selfishness of a father, who has no other pride, no other love, and no other child but his wealth; well, a girl like this would be just like Mlle. Bourjot, and in return for any trifling interest you might take in her, she would repay you by the affection and the effusions of which you speak. Her heart would simply overflow with gratitude and love, and you would see in her eyes the expression Renée has noticed, an expression which seems to shine out through tears."

# XVI

The rehearsals had been going on a fortnight, when one day Mme. Bourjot herself brought her daughter to the Mauperins. After the first greetings she expressed her surprise at not seeing the chief actor.

"Oh, Henri has such a wonderful memory," said Mme. Mauperin; "he will only need a couple of rehearsals."

"And how is it getting on?" asked Mme. Bourjot. "I must own that I tremble for my poor Noémi. Is it going fairly well? I came to-day, in the first place, to have the pleasure of seeing you, and then I thought I should like to judge for myself— —"

"Oh, you can be quite at your ease," said Mme. Mauperin. "You will see how perfectly natural your daughter is. She is quite charming."

The actors went to their places and began the first scene of *The Caprice.*

"Oh, you flattered her," said Mme. Bourjot to Mme. Mauperin after the first two or three scenes. "My dear child," she continued, turning to her daughter, "you don't act as though you felt it; you are merely reciting."

"Oh, madame," exclaimed Renée, "you will frighten all the company. We need plenty of indulgence."

"You are not speaking for yourself," answered Mme. Bourjot. "If only my poor child acted as you do."

"Well, then," said Denoisel to Mme. Bourjot, "let us go on to the sixth scene, mademoiselle. We'll hear what they have to say about that, for I think you do it very well indeed; and as my vanity as professor is at stake, Mme. Bourjot will perhaps allow me— —"

"Oh, monsieur," said Mme. Bourjot, "I do not think it has anything to do with the professor in this case; you are not responsible at all."

The scene was given and Mme. Bourjot continued, "Yes, oh yes, that wasn't bad; that might pass. It's a namby-pamby sort of scene, and that suits her. Then, too, she does her utmost; there's nothing to be said on that score."

"Oh, you are severe!" exclaimed Mme. Mauperin.

"You see, I'm her mother," murmured Mme. Bourjot, with a kind of sigh. "And then you'll have a crowd of people here— —"

"Oh, you know one always gets more people than one wants on such occasions," said Mme. Mauperin. "There is always a certain amount of curiosity. I suppose there will be about a hundred and fifty people."

"Suppose I were to make the list, mamma?" suggested Renée, who was anxious to spare Noémi the rest of the rehearsal, as she saw how ill at ease her friend was. "It would be a good way of introducing our guests to Mme. Bourjot. You will make the acquaintance of our acquaintances, madame."

"I shall be very pleased," replied Mme. Bourjot.

"It will be rather a mixed dish, I warn you. It always seems to me that the people one visits are rather like folks one comes across in a stage-coach."

"Oh, that's a delightful idea—and so true too," said Mme. Bourjot.

Renée took her seat at the table and began to write down with a pencil the names of the people, talking herself all the time.

"First comes the family—we'll leave that. Now, then, who is there? Mme. and Mlle. Chanut, a girl with teeth like the pieces of broken glass people put on their walls—you know what I mean. M. and Mme. de Bélizard—people say that they feed their horses with visiting-cards."

"Renée, Renée, come, what will every one think of you?"

"Oh, my reputation's made. I needn't trouble any more about that. Then, too, if you imagine that people don't say quite as much about me as I say——"

"Oh, let her alone, please, let her alone," said Mme. Bourjot to Mme. Mauperin, and turning to Renée she asked with a smile, "And who comes next?"

"Mme. Jobleau. Ah, she's such a bore with her story about her introduction to Louis Philippe at the Tuileries. '*Yes, sire; yes, sire; yes, sire;*' that was all she found to say. M. Harambourg, who can't stand any dust—it makes him faint—every summer he leaves his man-servant in Paris to get the dust from between the cracks of the floors. Mlle. de la Boise, surnamed the Grammar Dragoon; she used to be a governess, and she will correct you during a conversation if you make a slip with the subjunctive mood. M. Loriot, President of the Society for the Destruction of Vipers. The Cloquemins, father, mother, and children, a family—well, like Pan's pipes. Ah! to be sure, the Vineux are in Paris; but it's no use inviting them; they only go to see people who live on the omnibus route. Why, I was forgetting the Méchin trio—three sisters—the Three Graces of Batignolles. One of them is an idiot, one——"

Renée stopped short as she saw Noémi's scared eyes and horrified expression. She looked like some poor, loving creature, who scarcely understood, but who had suddenly been troubled and stirred to the depth of her soul by all this backbiting. Getting up from her seat Renée ran across and kissed her. "Silly girl!" she said gently, "why, these people I am talking about are not people that I like."

# XVII

Henri only came to the last rehearsals. He knew the play and was ready with his part in a week. *The Caprice* was a very short piece for the *soirée*, and it was decided to finish up with something comic. Two or three short plays given at the Palais Royal were tried, but given up as there were not enough actors, and finally a very nonsensical thing was chosen that was just then having a great run in one of the smaller theatres, and which Henri had insisted on in spite of Mlle. Bourjot's apparently groundless objection to it. Considering her usual timidity, every one was surprised at her obstinacy on this point; but it seemed, since Henri had been there, as if she were not quite herself. Renée fancied at times that Noémi was not the same with her now, and that her friendship had cooled. She was surprised to see a spirit of contradiction in her which she had never known before, and she was quite hurt at Noémi's manner to her brother. She was very cool with him, and treated him with a shade of disdain which bordered on contempt. Henri was always polite, attentive, and ready to oblige, but nothing more. In all the scenes in which he and Noémi acted together he was so reserved, so correct, and indeed so circumspect, that Renée, who feared that the coldness of his acting would spoil the play, joked him about it.

"Pooh!" he answered, "I'm like the great actors. I'm keeping my effects for the first night."

# XVIII

A small stage had been put up at the end of Mme. Mauperin's drawing-room, and a leafy screen, made of branches of pine and flowering shrubs, hid the footlights from view. Renée, with the help of her drawing-master, had painted the drop-scene, which looked something like the banks of the Seine. On each side of the stage was a hand-painted poster which read as follows:

**BRICHE THEATRE**
**TO-DAY**
**THE CAPRICE**
**AND**
**PIERROT, BIGAMIST**

The names of the actors were at the end of the bill. All the chairs in the house were placed closely together in rows in front of the stage, and the ladies, in evening dress, were seated, their skirts, their laces, the flashing of their diamonds, and their white shoulders all mingling together. The two doors at the other end of the room leading into the dining-room and the small *salon* had been taken off their hinges, and the masculine part of the audience, in white neckties, were grouped together there and standing on tip-toe.

The curtain rose on the first scene of *The Caprice*. Renée was very lively as Mme. de Léry; Henri, in the rôle of husband, proved himself a talented amateur actor, as so many young men of a cold temperament, and grave society men, often do. Noémi, well sustained by Henri, admirably prompted by Denoisel, and slightly carried away by seeing the large audience, played her touching part as the neglected wife very passably. This was a great relief to Mme. Bourjot, who was seated in the front row anxiously watching her daughter. Her vanity had been alarmed by the thought of a fiasco. The curtain fell, and amid the applause were heard shouts for "*All the actors!*" Her daughter had not made herself ridiculous, and the mother was delighted with this great success and gave herself up complacently to listening to that Babel of voices, opinions, and criticisms, which at amateur dramatic performances succeeds the applause and continues it, as it were, in a sort of murmur. In the midst of it all she heard vaguely one phrase, spoken near her, that came to her distinctly and seemed to rise above the general hubbub.

"Yes, it's his sister, I know," some one was saying; "but for the rôle he takes I don't think he is sufficiently in love with her; he is really far too much in love with his wife—didn't you notice?"

The lady who was speaking saw that Mme. Bourjot was listening, and, leaning towards her neighbour, whispered something to her. This little incident made

Mme. Bourjot turn very serious.

After an interval the curtain was once more raised, and Henri Mauperin appeared as Pierrot, but not arrayed in the traditional calico blouse and black cap. He was an Italian Pierrot, with a straight felt hat, and was entirely clothed in satin from his coat to his slippers. There was a movement among the ladies, which meant that they thought both the man and the costume charming, and then the buffoonery began.

It was the silly story of Pierrot married to one woman and wishing to marry another; a farce mingled with passion, which had been discovered by a vaudeville-writer, aided by a poet, among the stock-pieces of the old Italian theatre. Renée took the part of the deserted wife, this time, appearing in various disguises when her husband was love-making elsewhere. Noémi was the woman with whom he was in love, and Henri delighted the house in his love scenes with her. He acted well, putting plenty of youthful ardour, enthusiasm, and warmth into his part. In the scene where he confessed his love, there was something in his voice and expression that seemed like a real declaration, which had escaped him, and which he could not keep back. Noémi certainly had made up as the prettiest Colombine imaginable. She looked perfectly adorable, dressed as a bride in a Louis XVI costume copied exactly from the *Bride's Minuet*, an engraving by Debucourt lent by M. Barousse. All around Mme. Bourjot it seemed as if every one were bewitched, the sympathetic public appeared to be helping and encouraging the handsome young couple to love each other. The piece continued, and every now and then it was as though Henri's eyes were seeking, beyond the footlights, the eyes of Mme. Bourjot. Meanwhile Renée arrived, disguised as a village bailiff: there was only the contract to be signed now, and Pierrot, taking the hand of the girl he loved, began to speak of all the happiness he should have with her.

The lady who was seated next Mme. Bourjot felt her leaning slightly on her shoulder. Henri finished his speech, the plot came to the climax, and the piece ended. Mme. Bourjot's neighbour suddenly saw something sink down at her side; it was Mme. Bourjot, who had fainted.

# XIX

"Oh, do go in again, please," said Mme. Bourjot to the people who were standing round her in the garden, to which she had been carried for air. "It's all over; there's nothing the matter with me now; it was the heat." She was very pale, but she smiled as she spoke. "I shall be quite right again when I have had a little more air. M. Henri will perhaps stay with me."

Every one returned to the house, and the sound of the footsteps had scarcely died away, when Mme. Bourjot seized Henri's arm in a firm grip with her feverish fingers.

"You love her!" she exclaimed. "You love her!"

"Madame," said Henri.

"Be quiet; you won't tell me the truth!" she exclaimed, pushing his arm away.

Henri merely bowed without attempting to speak.

"I know all. I saw everything. Look at me!" she went on, and she gazed into his eyes. He kept his head bent and was silent. "Say something, anyhow—speak. Ah, you can only act comedy with her!"

"The fact is I have nothing to say, Laure," replied Henri, speaking in his gentlest and clearest voice. Mme. Bourjot drew back when he called her Laure as if he had touched her. "I have been struggling against it for the last year, madame," he continued. "I will not attempt to make any excuse; but everything has drawn me to her. We have known each other from childhood, and the fascination has increased lately day by day. I am very sorry, madame, to have to tell you the truth; but it is quite true that I love your daughter."

"But you never can have talked to her, surely? Why, I blush for her when we are out—you surely have not even looked at her. What in the world possesses you men, tell me! Do you think she is beautiful? What nonsense! why, I am better looking than she is. You are so foolish, all of you. And then, I have spoiled you. You'll see whether she will pamper your pride, let you revel in your vanity, and flatter and help you in your ambitions. Oh, I know you thoroughly. Ah, M. Mauperin, all this is only met with once in a lifetime. And women of my age—old women, you understand—are the only ones who care about the future of those they love. You were not my lover; you were like a dear son to me!" As she said this, Mme. Bourjot's voice changed and she spoke with the deepest feeling. "That's enough, though; we won't talk about that," she continued in a different tone. "I tell you that you don't love my daughter—it is not true—but she is rich——"

"Oh, madame!"

"Well, there are men like that—I have had them pointed out to me. Sometimes it succeeds to begin with the mother in order to finish with the dowry. And for the sake of a million, you know, one can put up with being bored."

"Speak more quietly, I beg you—for your own sake. They have just opened one of the windows."

"It's very fine to be so calm and collected, M. Mauperin, very fine—very fine indeed," said Mme. Bourjot, and her low, hissing voice sounded choked.

Some clouds that were moving quickly along in the sky passed like the wings of night-birds over the moon, and Mme. Bourjot gazed blankly into the darkness in front of her. With her elbows resting on her knees and supported by her high heels, she remained silent, tapping the gravel path with her satin slippers. After a few minutes she sat up, moved her arms about in an unconscious way as though she were scarcely awake, then quickly, and in a jerky way, she put her hand between her dress and waistband, pressing the back of her hand against the ribbon as though she were going to burst it. Finally she rose and began to walk, followed by Henri.

"I count on our never seeing each other again, monsieur," she said, without turning round.

As she passed by the fountain she handed him her handkerchief, saying, "Will you dip that in the water for me?"

Henri obeyed, kneeling down on the curbstone. He handed her the damp handkerchief, and she pressed it to her forehead and her eyes.

"We will go in now," she said; "give me your arm."

"Oh, madame, how courageous you are!" said Mme. Mauperin, advancing to meet Mme. Bourjot when she entered the room. "It is not wise of you, though, at all. I will have your carriage ordered."

"No, please don't, thank you," replied Mme. Bourjot quickly. "I think I promised you that I would sing; I am quite ready now," and she went across to the piano, gracious and valiant once more, with that heroic smile beneath which society actors conceal from the public the tears they are weeping within themselves, and the wounds which discharge themselves into their hearts.

# XX

Mme. Bourjot had married in order that two important business houses should be united; for the sake of amalgamating various interests she had been wedded to a man whom she did not know, and at the end of a week of married life she had felt all the contempt that a wife can possibly feel for a husband. It was not that she had expected anything very ideal, nor that she had looked on marriage as a romantic and imaginative girl so often does. She was remarkably intelligent herself, and seriously inclined, her mind had been formed and nurtured by reading, study, and acquirements which were almost more suitable for a man. All that she asked from the companion of her life was that he should be intellectual and intelligent, a being in whom she could place all her ambitions and her pride as a married woman, a man with a brilliant future before him, capable of winning for himself one of those immense fortunes to which money nowadays leads, and who should prove himself able to leap over the gaps of modern society to a high place in the Ministry, the Public Works, or the Exchequer.

All her castles in the air crumbled away with this husband, whom she found day by day more and more hopelessly shallow, more and more incapable, devoid of all that should have been in him, and which was in her instead, more narrow-minded, more mean and petty as time went on, and all this mingled with and contradicted by all the violences and weaknesses of a childish disposition.

It was her pride that had preserved Mme. Bourjot from adultery, a pride which, it may be said, was aided by circumstances. When she was young, Mme. Bourjot, who was of a spare build and southern type, had features which were too pronounced to be pleasing or beautiful. When she was about thirty-four she began to get rather more plump, and it seemed then that another woman had evolved from the one she had been. Her features, though still strongly pronounced, became softer and more pleasing; the hardness of her expression appeared to have melted away, and her whole face smiled. It was one of those autumn beauties such as age brings to certain women, making one wish to have seen them as they were at twenty; a beauty which makes one imagine for them a youthfulness they never had. As a matter of fact, then, so far Mme. Bourjot had not run any great danger, nor had she known any very great temptations. The society, which on account of her tastes she had chosen, her surroundings, the men who frequented her *salon* and whom she met elsewhere, had scarcely made it necessary for her to stand seriously on the defensive. They were, for the most part, academicians, savants, elderly literary men, and politicians, all of them unassuming and calm, men who seemed old, some of them from stirring up the past and the others the present. Satisfied with very little, they were happy with a mere nothing—the presence of a woman, a flattering speech, or the expression of eyes that were drinking in their words. Accustomed to their academic adoration, Mme. Bourjot had, without much risk, allowed it free scope and had treated it with jests like an Egeria: it had been a flame which did not scorch, and with which she had been able to play.

But the time of maturity arrived for Mme. Bourjot. A great transformation in her face and figure took place. Tormented, as it were, by health which was too robust and an excess of vitality, she seemed to lose the strength morally which she was gaining physically. She had a great admiration for her past, and she felt now that she was less strong-minded, and that there was less assurance in her pride than formerly.

It was just at this time that Henri Mauperin had made his appearance in her drawing-room. He seemed to her young, intelligent, serious, and thorough, equipped for the victories of life with all those dispassionate and unwavering qualities that she had dreamed before her marriage of finding in a husband. Henri had seized the situation at a glance, and, divining his own chances, he made his plans and swooped down on this woman as his prey. He began to make love to her, and this woman, who had a husband and daughter, who had been a faithful wife for twenty years, and who held a high position in Parisian society, scarcely waited for him to tempt her. She yielded to him at their first interview, conducting herself like a mere cocotte. Her love became a mad passion with her, as it so frequently does with women of her age, and Henri proved himself a genius in the art of attaching her to himself and of chaining her, as it were, to her sin. He never betrayed himself, and never for an instant allowed her to see a sign of the weariness, the indifference, or the contempt that a man feels after a too easy conquest, or of that sort of disgust with which certain situations of a woman in love inspire him. He was always affectionate, and always appeared to be deeply moved. He had for Mme. Bourjot those transports of love and jealousy, all those scruples, little attentions, and thoughtfulness which a woman, after a certain age, no longer expects from her lover. He treated her as if she were a young girl, and begged her to give him a ring which she always wore, and which had been one of her confirmation presents. He put up with all the childishness and coquetry which was so ridiculous in the passion of this mother of a family, and he encouraged it all without a sign of impatience on his face or a shade of mockery in his voice. At the same time he made himself entirely master of her, accustoming her to be docile and obedient to him, revealing to her such passionate love that Mme. Bourjot was both grateful to him and proud of her victory over this apparently cold and reserved young man. When he was thus completely master of her, Henri worked her up still more by impressing her with the danger of their meetings and the risks there were in their *liaison*, while by all the emotions of a criminal passion he excited her imagination to such a pitch of fear that her love increased with the very thought of all she had to lose.

She finally reached that stage when she only lived through him and for him, by his presence, his thoughts, his future, his portrait, all that remained to her of him after she had seen him. Before leaving him she would stroke his hair with her hands and then put her gloves on quickly. And all day afterward, when she was at home again with her husband and her daughter, she would put the palms of her hands, which she had not washed since, to her face and inhale the perfume of her lover's hair.

This *soirée*, and this treason and rupture at the end of a year, completely crushed Mme. Bourjot. She felt at first as if she had received a blow, and her life seemed to be ebbing away through the wound. She fancied she was really dying, and there was a certain sweetness in this thought. The following day she hoped Henri would come. She was vanquished and quite prepared to beg his pardon, to tell him that she had been in the wrong, to beg him to forgive her, to entreat him to be kind to her, and to allow her to gather up the crumbs of his love. She waited a week, but Henri did not come. She asked him for an interview that he might return her letters, and he sent them to her. She wrote and begged to see him for the last time that she might bid him farewell. Henri did not answer her letter, but, through his friends and through the newspaper and society gossip, he contrived to let Mme. Bourjot hear the rumour of an action that had been taken against him for one of his articles on the misery of the poor. For a whole week he managed to keep her mind occupied with the ideas of police and police courts, prison, and all that the dramatic imagination of a woman pictures to itself as the consequence of a lawsuit.

When the Attorney-General assured Mme. Bourjot that the action would not be taken, she felt quite a coward after all the terror she had gone through, and weak and helpless from emotion, she could not endure any more, and so wrote in desperation to Henri:

"To-morrow at two o'clock. If you are not there I shall wait on the staircase. I shall sit down on one of the stairs till you come."

# XXI

Henri was ready, and had taken great pains to dress for the occasion in an apparently careless style. He was wearing one of those morning suits in which a young man nearly always looks well.

At the time appointed in the letter there was a ring at the door. Henri opened it and Mme. Bourjot entered. She passed by and walked on in front of him as though she knew the way, until she reached the study. She took a seat on the divan, and neither of them spoke a word. There was plenty of room by her on the divan, but Henri drew up a smoking-chair, which he turned round, and, sitting down astride on it, folded his arms over the back.

Mme. Bourjot lifted her double lace veil and turned it back over her hat. Holding her head slightly aside, and with one hand pulling the glove slowly off the other, she gazed at the things on the wall and on the mantel-shelf. She gave a little sigh as if she were alone, and then, glancing at Henri, she said:

"There is some of my life here—something of me—in all that." She held out her ungloved hand to him, and Henri kissed the tips of her fingers respectfully.

"Forgive me," she went on, "I did not intend speaking of myself; I have not come here for that. Oh, you need not be afraid, I am quite sensible to-day, I assure you. The first moment—well, the first moment was hard! I won't deny that I had to pull myself together," she continued, with a tearful smile, "but it's all over now. I scarcely suffer any more, and I am quite myself again, I assure you. Of course everything cannot be forgotten all in a minute, and I won't say that you are nothing to me now—for you would not believe me. But this I can assure you, and you must believe me, Henri, there is no more love for you in my heart. I am no longer weak; the woman within me is dead—quite dead, and the affection I have for you now is quite pure."

The light seemed to annoy her as she spoke, as if it were some one gazing at her. "Will you put the blind down, dear?" she said. "The sun—my eyes have rather hurt me the last few days."

While Henri was at the window she arranged her hat and let the cloak she was wearing drop from her shoulders. When the light was not so strong in the room she began again:

"Yes, Henri, after struggling a long time, and enduring such anguish as you will never know, after passing nights such as I hope you may never have, and after crying and praying, I have conquered myself. I have won the victory, and I can now think of my daughter's happiness without being jealous, and of yours as the only happiness now left for me on earth."

"You are an angel, Laure," said Henri, getting up and walking up and down the room as though he were greatly agitated. "But you must look at things as they are. You were quite right the other day when you said that we must separate forever—never see each other again. The idea of our constantly meeting! You know we could not. It would take so little to open wounds as slightly closed as ours are. Then, too, even if you are sure of yourself, how do you know that I am as sure of myself? How can I tell—if we were meeting at all times—with such constant temptation—if I were always near you," he said, speaking very tenderly, "why, some day, unexpectedly—how can I tell—and I am an honourable man."

"No, Henri," she answered, taking his hands in hers and drawing him to the seat at her side, "I am not afraid of you, and I am not afraid of myself. It is all over. How can I make you believe me? And you will not refuse me? No, you cannot refuse me the only happiness which remains for me—my only happiness. It is all I have left in the world now—it is to see you, only to see you—" and throwing her arms round Henri's neck she drew him to her closely.

"Ah, no, it is quite impossible," said Henri, when the embrace had lasted a few seconds. "Don't say any more about it," he continued, brusquely, getting up as he spoke.

"I will be brave," said Mme. Bourjot very seriously.

When they had played out their comedy of renunciation they both felt more at ease.

"Now, then, listen to me," began Mme. Bourjot once more, "my husband will give you his daughter."

"How foolish you are, really, Laure."

"Don't interrupt me—my husband will give you his daughter. I fancy he intends asking his son-in-law to live in the same house. Of course you would be quite free—your suite of rooms, your carriage, meals, and everything quite apart—you know what our style of living is. Unless M. Bourjot has changed his mind, she will have a dowry of forty thousand pounds, and unless he should lose his money, which I do not think is very probable, you will have, at our death, four or five times that amount."

"And how can you seriously imagine that Mlle. Bourjot, who has forty thousand pounds, and who will have four or five times that much, would marry——"

"I am her mother," answered Mme. Bourjot in a decisive tone. "And then—don't you love her? Why, it would merely be a kind of marriage of expediency," and Mme. Bourjot smiled. "You provide her with happiness."

"But what will the world say?"

"The world? My dear boy, we should close the world's mouth with truffles," and she gave her shoulders a little shrug.

"And M. Bourjot?"

"That's my part. He will like you very much before the end of two months. The only thing is, as you know, he will want a title; he has always intended his daughter to marry a count. All I can do is to get him to consent to a name tacked on to yours. Nothing is simpler, nowadays, than to get permission to add to one's name the name of some estate, or forest, or even the name of a meadow, or a bit of land of any sort. Didn't I hear some one talking to your mother about a farm called Villacourt that you have in the Haute-Marne? *Mauperin de Villacourt*; that would do very well. You know, as far as I am concerned, how little I care about such things."

"Oh, but it would be so ridiculous, with my principles, and a Liberal, too, bound as I am. And then, you know — —"

"Oh, you can say it is a whim of your wife's. Every one goes about with names like that now; it's a sort of cross people have to bear. Shall I say a word for you to any one in authority?"

"Oh, no; no, please don't! I didn't think I had said anything which could make you imagine I should be inclined to accept. I don't really know, frankly. You understand that I should have to think it over, I should have to collect myself and consider what my duty is; to be more myself, in fact, and less influenced by you, before I could give you an answer."

"I shall call on your mother this week," said Mme. Bourjot, getting up and pressing his hand. "Good-bye," she said sadly; "life *is* a sacrifice!"

# XXII

"Renée," said Mme. Mauperin one evening to her daughter, "shall we go and see Lord Mansbury's collection of pictures to-morrow? It appears that it is very curious; people say that one of the pictures would fetch four thousand pounds. M. Barousse thought it would interest you, and he has sent me the catalogue and an invitation. Should you like to go?"

"Rather. I should just think I should like to go," replied Renée.

The following morning she was very much surprised to see her mother come into the room while she was dressing, busy herself with her toilette, and insist on her putting on her newest hat.

"There are always so many people at these exhibitions," said Mme. Mauperin, arranging the bows on the hat, "and you must be dressed as well as every one else."

Although it was a private exhibition there were crowds of people in the room on the first floor of the Auction Buildings, where Lord Mansbury's collection was on view. The fame of the pictures, and the scandal of such a sale, which it was said had been necessitated by Lord Mansbury's folly in connection with a Palais Royal actress, had attracted all the *habitués* of the Hôtel Drouot; those people whom of late years the fashion for collecting has brought there—all that immense crowd of bric-à-brac buyers, art worshippers, amateurs of repute, and nearly all the idlers of Paris. It had been found necessary to hang the three or four valuable pictures for sale in the hall out of reach of the crowd. In the room one could hear that muffled sound which one always hears at wealthy peoples' sales, the murmur of prices going up, of whims and fancies, of follies which lead on to further follies, of competitions between bankers, and of all kinds of vanities connected with money matters. Bidding, too, could be heard, being quietly carried on among the groups. "The foam was rising," as the dealers say.

When they entered the room, Mme. Mauperin and her daughter saw Barousse, arm-in-arm with a young man of about thirty years of age. The young man had large, soft eyes, which would have been handsome if they had had more expression in them. His figure, which was slightly corpulent, was a little puffy, and this gave him a rather common appearance.

"At last, ladies!" said Barousse, addressing Mme. Mauperin; "allow me to introduce my young friend, M. Lemeunier. He knows the collection thoroughly, and if you want a guide he will take you to the best things. I must ask to be excused, as I want to go and push something in No. 3 room."

M. Lemeunier took Mme. Mauperin and her daughter round the room, stopping at the canvases signed by the most celebrated names. He merely explained the subjects of the pictures, and did not talk art. Renée was grateful to him for this from the bottom of her heart, without knowing why. When they had seen everything, Mme. Mauperin thanked M. Lemeunier, and they bowed and parted company.

Renée wanted to see one of the side-rooms. The first thing she caught sight of on entering was M. Barousse's back, the back of an amateur in the very height of the excitement of the sale. He was seated on the nearest chair to the auctioneer, next to a picture-dealing woman wearing a cap. He was nudging her, knocking her knee, whispering eagerly his bid, which he imagined he was concealing from the auctioneer and his clerk, from the expert, and from all the room.

"There, come, you have seen enough," said Mme. Mauperin, after a short time. "It's your sister's 'At Home' day, and it is not too late. We have not been once this year to it, and she will be delighted to see us."

Renée's sister, Mme. Mauperin's elder daughter, Mme. Davarande, was the type *par excellence* of a society woman. Society filled her whole life and her brain. As a child she had dreamed of it; from the time she had been confirmed she had longed for it. She had married very young, and had accepted the first "good-looking and suitable" man who had been introduced to her, without any hesitation or trouble and entirely of her own accord. It was not M. Davarande, but a position she had married. Marriage for her meant a carriage and servants in livery, diamonds, invitations, acquaintances, drives in the Bois. She had all that, did very well without children, loved dress, and was happy. To go to three balls in an evening, to leave forty cards before dinner, to run about from one reception to another, and to have her own "At Home" day—she could not conceive of any happiness beyond this. Devoting herself entirely to society, Mme. Davarande borrowed everything from it herself, its ideas, its opinions, its way of giving charity, its stock phrases in affairs of the heart, and its sentiments. She had the same opinions as the women whose hair was dressed by the famous coiffeur, Laure. She thought exactly what it was correct to think, just as she wore exactly what it was correct to wear. Everything, from her very gestures to the furniture in her drawing-room, from the game she played to the alms she gave away, from the newspaper she read to the dish she ordered from her cook, aimed at being in good style—good style being her law and her religion. She followed the fashion of the moment in everything and everywhere, even to the theatre of the *Bouffes Parisiens*. She had, when driving in the Bois, been told the names of certain women of doubtful reputation, and could point them out to her friends, and that made an effect. She spelt her name with a small "d," an apostrophe, and a capital A, and this converted it into d'Avarande. Mme. Davarande was pious. It seemed to her that God was *chic*. It would have seemed almost as improper to her to have no parish as to have no gloves. She had adopted one of those churches where grand marriages are celebrated, where people with great names are to be met, where the chairs have armorial bearings, where the beadle glitters with gold lace, where the incense is perfumed with patchouli, and where the porch after high mass on Sundays resembles the corridor of the Opera House when a great artiste has been singing.

She went to hear all the preachers that people were supposed to hear. She confessed her sins, not in the confessional, but in a community. The name and the individuality of the priest played an important part so far as she was concerned in the sacraments of the Church: she would not have felt that she was really married if any one but the Abbé Blampoix had officiated at her wedding, and she would not have considered a baptism valid if a ten-pound note had not been sent to the curé inside the traditional box of sugar-plums. This woman, whose mind was always fixed on worldly things, even when at church and during the benediction, was naturally, thoroughly, and absolutely virtuous, but her virtue was not the result of any effort, merit, or even consciousness. In the midst of this whirlwind, this artificial air and warm atmosphere, exposed to all the opportunities and temptations of society life, she had neither the heart which a woman must have who is given to dreaming nor enough intelligence to be bored by such an existence. She had neither the curiosity nor the inclination which might have led her astray. Hers was one of those happy, narrow-minded dispositions which have not enough in them to go wrong. She had that unassailable virtue, common to many Parisian women who are not even touched by the temptations which pass over them: she was virtuous just in the same way as marble is cold. Physically, even, as it happens sometimes with lymphatic and delicate natures, the effect of society life on her had been to free her from all other desires by using up her strength, her nervous activity, and the movement of the little blood she had in her body, in the rushing about on visits and shopping, the effort of making herself agreeable, the fatigue of evening parties, resulting in utter weariness at night, and enervation the next day.

There are society women in Paris who, by the amount of vitality and vigour they expend, and by the intense application of their energy and grace, remind one of circus-riders and tight-rope dancers, whose temperament suffers from the fatigue of their exercises.

Mme. Mauperin and her daughter met Mme. Davarande in her dining-room, accompanying a smooth-faced gentleman with blue spectacles to the door. She was extremely amiable to him, and when she had seen him out she returned to her mother and sister.

"Excuse my leaving you," she said, as she kissed them, "but it was M. Lordonnot, the architect of the Sacred Heart Convent. I cultivate him for the sake of my collections. Thanks to him I had forty-eight pounds you know last time. That's very good: Mme. de Berthival has never reached thirty-two pounds. I'm so glad to see you; it's very nice of you to have come. We'll go into the other room—there's no one here to-day. Mme. de Thésigny, Mme. de Champromard, and Mme. de Saint-Sauveur, and then two young men, young de Lorsac—you know him I think, mamma, and his friend de Maisoncelles? Wait a minute," she said to Renée, patting her hair down a little, "your hair looks like a little dog's," and then advancing and opening the drawing-room door, she announced her mother and sister.

Every one rose, shook hands, or bowed, and then sat down again and looked at each other. Mme. Davarande's three lady friends were leaning back in their easy chairs in that languid attitude due to cushioned seats. They looked very dainty in their wide skirts, their lovely hats, and gloves about large enough for the hands of a doll. They were dressed perfectly, their gowns had evidently been cut by an artiste, their whole toilette with the hundred little nothings which set it off, their graceful attitudes, their bearing, their gestures, the movement of their bodies, the *frou-frou* of their silk skirts—everything was there which goes to make the charm of the Parisian woman; and, although they were not beautiful, they had discovered the secret of appearing almost pretty, with just a smile, a glance, certain little details and semblances, flashes of wit, animation, and a smart look generally.

The two friends, Lorsac and Maisoncelles, in the prime of their twenty years, with pink-and-white complexions, brilliant health, beardless faces and curled hair, were delighted at being invited to a young married lady's "At Home" day, and were sitting respectfully on the edge of their chairs. They were young men who had been very well brought up. They had just left a *pension* kept by an abbé who gave little parties every evening, at which his sister presided, and which finished up with tea handed round in the billiard-room.

"Henriette," said Mme. de Thésigny to Mme. Davarande, when the conversation had commenced again, "are we going to see Mlle. de Bussan's wedding to-morrow? I hear that every one will be there. It's made such a stir, this marriage."

"Will you call for me, then? What's the bride-groom like—does any one know? Do you know him, Mme. de Saint-Sauveur?"

"No, not at all."

"Is she making a good match?"

"An awful match!" put in Mme. de Champromard, "he hasn't anything—six hundred pounds a year all told."

"But," said Mme. Mauperin, "it seems to me, madame, that six hundred——"

"Oh, madame," continued Mme. de Champromard, "why, nowadays, that isn't enough to pay for having one's jewellery reset."

"M. de Lorsac, are you coming to this wedding?" asked Mme. Davarande.

"I will come if you wish it."

"Well then, I do wish it. Will you keep two chairs for us? One spoils one's dress quite enough without that. I can wear pearl grey, can't I?"

"Oh, certainly," answered Mme. de Thésigny, "it's a moiré antique wedding. M. de Maisoncelles, will you keep two chairs for me? Don't forget."

De Maisoncelles bowed.

"And if you are very good you shall be my cotillon partner on Wednesday."

De Lorsac blushed for de Maisoncelles.

"You don't go out much, do you, mademoiselle?" said Mme. de Sauveur to Renée, who was seated next her.

"No, madame, I don't care about going out," answered Mlle. Mauperin rather curtly.

"Julia," said Mme. de Thésigny to Mme. de Champromard, "tell us again about your famous bride's bed-room—Mme. Davarande wasn't there. Just listen, my dear."

"Oh, it was my sewing-woman who told me. Only fancy, the walls are draped with white satin, finished with applications of lace, and ruches of satin to outline the panels. The sheets—I've seen the pattern—they are of cambric—spider-web. The mattresses are of white satin, caught down with knots of pale blue silk that show through the sheet. And you will be surprised to hear that all that is for a woman who is quite *comme il faut*."

"Oh, yes," said Mme. de Saint-Sauveur, "that is most astonishing, for everything, nowadays, is for the other kind of women. What do you think happened to me in the country—a most disagreeable affair! There is a woman, who is not all she ought to be, living near us. We came across her at church, for she has sittings there—just fancy! Well, ever since she has arrived in our part of the world, everything has gone up in price. We positively cannot get a sewing-girl now in the house for less than seven-pence halfpenny an hour. Money is nothing to creatures of that kind, of course. And then every one adores her—she is such a schemer. She goes to see the peasants when they are ill, she finds situations for their children, and she gives them money—a sovereign at a time. Before she came we used to be able to do things for the poor without much expense, but that isn't possible now. It's outrageous! I told the curé so—it really is quite scandalous! And we owe all this to one of your relatives, M. de Lorsac, to your cousin, M. d'Orambeau. My compliments to him when you see him."

The two young men threw themselves back on their chairs and laughed heartily, and then both of them instinctively bit their canes with delight.

"Where have you just come from?" Mme. Davarande asked her mother and sister.

"From the auction-room," answered Mme. Mauperin. "M. Barousse persuaded us to go to an exhibition of pictures."

"Lord Mansbury's collection," put in Renée.

"Ah, we must go to those auction-rooms, Henriette," said Mme. de Thésigny; "we'll go and *rococoter*—it's great fun."

"Have you seen Petrucci's pictures, my dear?" asked Mme. de Saint-Sauveur.

"Is she selling them?" asked Mme. de Thésigny.

"I did so want to go," said Mme. Davarande. "If I had only known that you were going——"

"We were all there," interrupted Mme. de Saint-Sauveur. "It was so curious. There was a glass-case of jewellery, a necklace of black pearls among other things—if only you had seen it—three rows. There isn't a husband in the world who could give you a thing like that; it would take a national subscription."

"Shall we not see your husband?" asked Mme. Mauperin, turning to Mme. Davarande.

"Oh, he's never here on my day—my husband—thank goodness!" Mme. Davarande looked round as she heard some one coming in by the door behind her chair. It was M. Barousse, followed by the young man who had been with him at the auction-room.

"Ah, we meet again," he said to Mme. Mauperin, as he put down on a chair the little portfolio which never left him.

Renée smiled and the chattering began again.

"Have you read that novel—that novel?"

"The one in the *Constitutional*?"

"No."

"By—I can't think of the name. It's called—wait a minute."

"Every one's talking about it."

"Do read it."

"My husband will get it me from his club."

"Is that play amusing?"

"I only like dramas."

"Shall we go?"

"Let's take a box."

"Friday?"

"No, Saturday."

"Shall we go to supper after?"

"Yes—agreed."

"It's at the *Provençaux*."

"Will your husband come?"

"Oh, he does what I want him to do, always."

They were all talking and answering each other's questions without really listening to anything, as every one was chattering at the same time. Words, questions, and voices were all mingled together in the Babel: it was like the chirping of so many birds in a cage. The door opened, and a tall, thin woman dressed in black, entered.

"Don't disturb yourselves, any of you; I have only just come in as I am passing. I have only one minute."

She bowed to the ladies and took up her position in front of the chimney-piece, with her elbow on the marble and her hands in her muff. She glanced at herself in the glass, and then, lifting her dress skirt, held out the thin sole of her dainty little boot to the fire.

"Henriette," she began, "I have come to ask you a favour—a great favour. You absolutely must undertake the invitations for the ball that the Brodmers are giving—you know, those Americans, who have just come; they have a flat in the Rue de la Paix, and the rent is sixteen hundred a year."

"Oh, the Brodmers—yes," put in Mme. de Thésigny.

"But, my dear," said Mme. Davarande, "it's a very delicate matter—I don't know them. Have you any idea what these people are?"

"Why, they are Americans. They've made their fortune out of cotton, candles, indigo, or negroes—or—I don't know what; but what in the world does that matter to us? Americans, you know, are accepted nowadays. As far as I am concerned—with people who give balls, there's only one thing I care about, and that is that they shouldn't belong to the police and should give good suppers. It's all superb at their house, it seems. The wife is astonishing. She talks the French of the backwoods; and people say she was tattooed when she was a child. That's why she can't wear low dresses. It's most amusing, and she is so entertaining. They want to get plenty of people, you see. You *will* do it for me, won't you? I can assure you that if I were not in mourning I should have had great pleasure in putting on the invitation cards, 'With the Baronne de Lermont's compliments.' And then, too, they are people who will do things properly. Oh, as to that I'm convinced of it. They are sure to make you a present— —"

"Oh no, if I undertake the invitations I don't want a present for it."

"How queer you are! Why, that sort of thing's done every day—it's the custom. It would be like refusing a box of sweets from these gentlemen here on New Year's day. And now I must go. I shall bring them to see you to-morrow—my savages. Good-bye! Oh dear, I'm nearly dead!" and with these words she disappeared.

"Is it really true?" Renée asked her sister.

"What?"

"That guests are supplied for balls in this way?"

"Well, didn't you know that?"

"I was in the same state of ignorance," said the young man M. Barousse had brought.

"It's very convenient for foreigners," remarked Mme. Davarande.

"Yes, but it seems to me that it's rather humiliating for Parisians. Don't you think so, mademoiselle?" said the young man, turning to Mlle. Mauperin.

"Oh, it's an accepted thing, anyhow," said Mme. Davarande.

# XXIII

Mme. Bourjot had just arrived with her daughter at the Mauperins'. She kissed Renée and sat down by Mme. Mauperin on the sofa near the fire.

"My dears," she said, turning to the two girls, who were chattering together on the other side of the room, "suppose you were to let your mothers have a little talk together. Will you take Noémi out in the garden a little, Renée? I give her over to you."

Renée put her arm round Noémi and pulled her along with her, skipping as she went. In the hall she caught up a Pyrenees hood that was lying on a chair and threw it over her head, put on some little overshoes, and ran out into the garden, rushing along like a child, and keeping her arm round her friend all the time.

"There's a secret—a secret. Do you know what the secret is?" she exclaimed, stopping suddenly short and quite out of breath.

Noémi looked at her with her large, sad eyes and did not answer.

"You silly girl!" said Renée, kissing her. "I've guessed it—I caught a few words—mamma lets everything out. It's about his lordship, my brother. There now!"

"Let's sit down—shall we? I'm so tired." And Noémi took her seat on the garden bench, just where her mother had sat on the night of the theatricals.

"Why, you are crying! What's the matter?" exclaimed Renée, sitting down by her. Noémi let her head fall on her friend's shoulder and burst into tears, that were quite hot as they fell on Renée's hand.

"What is it, tell me—answer me—speak, Noémi—come now, Noémi dear!"

"Oh, you don't know!" answered Noémi, in broken words, which seemed to choke her. "I won't—no, I cannot tell you—if only you knew. Oh, do help me!" and she flung her arms round Renée in despair. "I love you dearly—you——"

"Come, come, Noémi; I don't understand anything. Is it this marriage—is it my brother? You must answer me—come!"

"Ah, yes; you are his sister—I had forgotten that. Oh, dear, I wish I could die——"

"Die, but why?"

"Why? Because your brother——"

She stopped short, in horror at the thought of uttering the words she was just going to say, and then, suddenly finishing her sentence in a murmur in Renée's ear, she hid her face on her friend's shoulder to conceal her blushing cheeks and the shame she felt in her inmost soul.

"My brother! You say—no, it's a lie!" exclaimed Renée, pushing her away and springing up with a bound in front of her.

"Should *I* tell a lie about it?" and Noémi looked up sadly at Renée, who read the truth clearly in her eyes.

Renée folded her arms and gazed at her friend. She stood there a few minutes deep in thought, erect and silent, her whole attitude resolute and energetic. She felt within herself the strength of a woman, and something of the responsibility of a mother with this child.

"But how can your father—" she began, "my brother has no name but ours."

"He is to take another one."

"Ah, he is going to give our name up? And quite right that he should!"

# XXIV

"Oh, it's you, is it; you are not in bed yet?" said Henri to Renée, as she went into his room one evening. He was smoking, and it was that blissful moment in a man's life when, with slippers on and his feet on the marble of the chimney-piece, buried in an arm-chair, he gives himself up to day-dreams, while puffing up languidly to the ceiling the smoke of his last cigar. He was thinking of all that had happened during the past few months, and congratulating himself on having manœuvred so well. He was turning everything over in his mind: that suggestion about the theatricals, which he had thrown out with such apparent indifference when they were all sitting in the garden; then his absence from the first rehearsals, and the coolness with which he had treated Noémi in order to reassure her, to take her off her guard, and to prevent her refusing point-blank to act. He was thinking of that master-stroke, of his love suddenly rousing the mother's jealousy in the midst of the play, and it had all appeared to be so spontaneous, as though the rôle he was filling had torn from him the secret of his soul. He thought of all that had followed: how he had worked that other love up to the last extremity of despair, then his behaviour in that last interview; all this came back to him, and he felt a certain pride in recalling so many circumstances that he had foreseen, planned, and arranged beforehand, and which he had so skilfully introduced into the midst of the love-affairs of a woman of forty.

"No, I am not sleepy to-night," said Renée, drawing up a little stool to the fire and sitting down. "I feel inclined for a little chat like we used to have before you had your flat in Paris, do you remember? I got used to cigars, and pipes, and everything here. Didn't we gossip when every one had gone to bed! What nonsense we have talked by this fire! And now, my respected brother is such a very serious sort of man."

"Very serious indeed," put in Henri, smiling. "I'm going to be married."

"Oh," she said, "but you are not married yet. Oh, please Henri!" and throwing herself on her knees she took his hands in hers. "Come now, for my sake. Oh, you won't do it—just for money—I'm begging you on my knees! And then, too, it will bring bad luck to give up your father's name. It has belonged to our family for generations—this name, Henri. Think what a man father is. Oh, do give up this marriage—I beseech you—if you love me—if you love us all! Oh, I beseech you, Henri!"

"What's this all mean; have you gone mad? What are you making such a scene about? Come, that's enough, thank you; get up."

Renée rose to her feet, and looking straight into her brother's eyes she said:

"Noémi has told me everything!"

The colour had mounted to her cheeks. Henri was as pale as if some one had just spat in his face.

"You cannot, anyhow, marry her daughter!" exclaimed Renée.

"My dear girl," answered Henri coldly, in a voice that trembled, "it seems to me that you are interfering in things that don't concern you. And you will allow me to say that for a young girl— —"

"Ah, you mean this is dirt that I ought to know nothing of; that is quite true, and I should never have known of it but for you."

"Renée!" Henri approached his sister. He was in one of those white rages which are terrible to witness, and Renée was alarmed and stepped back. He took her by the arm and pointed to the door. "Go!" he said, and a moment later he saw her in the corridor, putting her hand against the wall for support.

# XXV

"Go up, Henri," said M. Mauperin to his son, and then as Henri wanted his father to pass first M. Mauperin repeated, "No, go on up."

Half an hour later father and son were coming downstairs again from the office of the Keeper of the Seals.

"Well, you ought to be satisfied with me, Henri," observed M. Mauperin, whose face was very red. "I have done as you and your mother wished. You will have this name."

"Father— —"

"All right, don't let us talk about it. Are you coming home with me?" he asked, buttoning his frock-coat with that military gesture with which old soldiers gird up their emotions.

"No, father, I must ask you to let me leave you now. I have so many things to do to-day. I'll come to dinner to-morrow."

"Good-bye, then, till to-morrow. You'd better come; your sister is not well."

When the carriage had driven away with his father Henri drew himself up, looked at his watch, and with the brisk, easy step of a man who feels the wind of fortune behind him blowing him along, walked briskly towards the Rue de la Paix.

At the corner of the Chaussée d'Antin he went into the Café Bignon, where some heavy-looking young men, suggestive of money and the provinces, were waiting for him. During luncheon the conversation turned on provincial cattle shows and competitions, and afterward, while smoking their cigars on the boulevards, the questions of the varied succession of crops, of drainage, and of liming were brought up, and there was a discussion on elections, the opinions of the various departments, and on the candidatures which had been planned, thought of, or attempted at the agricultural meetings.

At two o'clock Henri left these gentlemen, after promising one of them an article on his model farm; he then went into his club, looked at the papers, and wrote down something in his note-book which appeared to give him a great deal of trouble to get to his mind. He next hurried off to an insurance company to read a report, as he had managed to get on to the committee, thanks to the commercial fame and high repute of his father. At four o'clock he sprang into a carriage and paid a round of visits to ladies who had either a *salon* or any influence and acquaintances at the service of a man with a career. He remembered, too, that he had not paid his subscription to the "Society for the Right Employment of the Sabbath among the Working Classes," and he called and paid it.

At seven o'clock, with cordial phrases on the tip of his tongue and ready to shake hands with every one, he went upstairs at Lemardelay's, where the "Friendly Association" of his old college friends held its annual banquet. At dessert, when it was his turn to speak, he recited the speech he had composed at his club, talked of this fraternal love-feast, of coming back to his family, of the bonds between the past and the future, of help to old comrades who had been afflicted with undeserved misfortunes, etc.

There were bursts of applause, but the orator had already gone. He put in an appearance at the d'Aguesseau lecture, left there, pulled a white necktie out of his pocket, put it on in the carriage, and showed up at three or four society gatherings.

# XXVI

The shock which Renée had had on leaving her brother's room, and which had made her totter for a moment, had brought on palpitation of the heart, and for a week afterward she had not been well. She had been kept quiet and had taken medicines, but she did not recover her gaiety, and time did not appear to bring it back to her. On seeing her ill, Henri knew very well what was the matter, and he had done all in his power to make things up with her again. He had been most affectionate, attentive, and considerate, and had endeavoured to show his repentance. He had tried to get into her good graces once more, to appease her conscience, and to calm her indignation; but his efforts were all in vain. He was always conscious of a certain coolness in her manner, of a repugnance for him, and of a sort of quiet resolution which caused him a vague dread. He understood perfectly well that she had only forgotten the insult of his brutality; she had forgiven her brother, but she had not forgiven him as a man.

Her mother had arranged to take her to Paris one day for a little change, and at the last moment had not felt well enough to go. Henri had some business to do, and he offered to accompany his sister. They started, and on reaching Paris drove to the Rue Richelieu. As they were passing the library Henri told the cabman to draw up.

"Will you wait here for me a moment?" he said to his sister, "I want to ask one of the librarians a question. Why not come in with me, though," he added as an after-thought. "You have always wanted to see the manuscript scroll-work and that is in the same room. You would find it interesting, and I could get my information at the same time."

Renée went up with her brother to the manuscript-room, and Henri took her to the end of a table, waited until the prayer-book he had asked for was brought, and then went to speak to a librarian in one of the window recesses.

Renée turned over the leaves of her book slowly. Just behind her one of the employees was warming himself at the hot-air grating. Presently he was joined by another, who had just taken some volumes and some title-deeds to the desk near which Henri was talking, and Renée heard the following conversation just behind her:

"I say, Chamerot, you see that little chap?"

"Yes, at M. Reisard's desk."

"Well, he can flatter himself that he's got hold of some information which isn't quite correct. He's come to ask whether there used to be a family named Villacourt, and whether the name has died out. They've told him that it has. Now if he'd asked me, I could have told him that some folks of that name must be living. I don't know whether it's the same family; but there was one of them there before I left that part of the world, and a strong, healthy fellow too—the eldest, M. Bois-jorand—the proof is that we had a fight once, and that he knew how to give hard blows. Their place was quite near to where we lived. One of the turrets of their house could be seen above Saint-Mihiel, and from a good distance too; but it didn't belong to them in my time. They were a spendthrift lot, that family. Oh, they were queer ones for nobility; they lived with the charcoal-burners in the Croix-du-Sol-dat woods, at Motte-Noire, like regular satyrs."

Saint-Mihiel, the Croix-du-Soldat woods, and Motte-Noire—all these names fixed themselves on Renée's memory and haunted her.

"There, now I have what I wanted," said Henri, gaily, when he came back to her to take her away.

# XXVII

Denoisel had left Renée at her piano, and had gone out into the garden. As he came back towards the house he was surprised to hear her playing something that was not the piece she was learning; then all at once the music broke off and all was silent. He went to the drawing-room, pushed the door open, and discovered Renée seated on the music-stool, her face buried in her hands, weeping bitterly.

"Renée, good heavens! What in the world is the matter?"

Two or three sobs prevented Renée's answering at first, and then, wiping her eyes with the backs of her hands, as children do, she said in a voice choked with tears:

"It's—it's—too stupid. It's this thing of Chopin's, for his funeral, you know—his funeral mass, that he composed. Papa always tells me not to play it. As there was no one in the house to-day—I thought you were at the bottom of the garden—oh, I knew very well what would happen, but I wanted to make myself cry with it, and you see it has answered to my heart's content. Isn't it silly of me—and for me, too, when I'm naturally so fond of fun!"

"Don't you feel well, Renée? Come, tell me; there's something the matter. You wouldn't cry like that."

"No, there's nothing the matter, I assure you. I'm as strong as a horse; there's nothing at all the matter, really and truly. If there were anything I should tell you, shouldn't I? It all came about through that dreadful, stupid music. And to-day, too—to-day, when papa has promised to take me to see *The Straw Hat.*"

A faint smile lighted up her wet eyes as she spoke, and she continued in the same strain:

"Only fancy, *The Straw Hat*—at the Palais Royal. It will be fun, I'm sure; I only like pieces of that kind. As for the others, dramas and sentimental things—well, I think we have enough to stir us up with our own affairs; it isn't worth while going in search of trouble. Then, too, crying with other people; why, it's like weeping into some one else's handkerchief. We are going to take you with us, you know—a regular bachelor's outing it's to be. Papa said we should dine at a restaurant; and I promise you that I'll be as nonsensical, and laugh as I used to when I was a little girl—when I had my English governess—you remember her? She used to wear orange-coloured ribbons, and drink eau de Cologne that she kept in a cupboard until it got in her head. She was a nice old thing."

And as she uttered these words her fingers flew over the keyboard, and she attacked an arrangement with variations of the *Carnival of Venice.*

"You've been to Venice, haven't you?" she said suddenly, stopping short.

"Yes."

"Isn't it odd that there should be a spot like that on earth, that I don't know and yet that attracts me and makes me dream of it? For some people it's one place, and for others it's another. Now, I've never wanted to see any place except Venice. I'm going to say something silly—Venice seems to me like a city where all the musicians should be buried."

She put her fingers on the notes again, but she only skimmed over them without striking them at all, as if she were just caressing the silence of the piano. Her hands then fell on her knees again, and in a pensive manner, giving way to her thoughts, she half turned her head towards Denoisel.

"You see," she said, "it seems as though there is sadness in the very air. I don't know how it is, but there are days when the sun is shining, when I have nothing the matter with me, no worry and no troubles to face; and yet I positively want to be sad, I try to get the blues, and feel as though I *must* cry. Many a time I've said I had a headache and gone to bed, just simply for the sake of having a good cry, of burying my face in the pillow; it did me ever so much good. And at such times I haven't the energy to fight against it or to try to overcome it. It's just the same when I am going off in a faint; there's a certain charm in feeling all my courage leaving me— —"

"There, there, that's enough, Renée dear! I'll have your horse saddled and we'll go for a ride."

"Ah, that's a good idea! But I warn you I shall go like the wind, to-day."

# XXVIII

"What was he to do? poor Montbreton has four children, and none too much money," said M. Mauperin with a sigh, as he folded up the newspaper in which he had just been reading the official appointments and put it at some distance from him on the table.

"Yes, people always say that. As soon as any one ever does anything mean, people always say 'He has children.' One would think that in society people only had children for the sake of that—for the sake of being able to beg, and to do a lot of mean things. It's just as though the fact of being the father of a family gave you the right to be a scoundrel."

"Come, come, Renée," M. Mauperin began.

"No, it's quite true. I only know two kinds of people: the straightforward, honest ones; and then the others. Four children! But that only ought to serve as an excuse for a father when he steals a loaf. *Mère Gigogne* would have had the right to poison hers according to that, then. I'm sure Denoisel thinks as I do."

"I? Not at all; indeed I don't! I vote for indulgence in favour of married folks—fathers of families. I should like to see people more charitable, too, towards any one who has a vice—a vice which may be rather ruinous, but which one cannot give up. As to the others, those who have nothing to use their money for, no vice, no wife, no children, and who sell themselves, ruin themselves, bow down, humiliate, enrich, and degrade themselves—ah! I'd give all such over to you willingly."

"I'm not going to talk to you," said Renée in a piqued tone. "Anyhow, papa," she went on, "I cannot understand how it is that it does not make *you* indignant, you who have always sacrificed everything to your opinions. It's disgusting what he has done, and that's the long and short of it."

"I do not say that it isn't; but you get so excited, child, you get so excited."

"I should think so. Yes, I do get excited—and enough to make me, too. Only fancy, a man who owed everything to the other government, and who said everything bad he could about the present one; and now he joins this one. Why, he's a wretch!—your friend, Montbreton—a wretch!"

"Ah! my dear child, it's very easy to say that. When you have had a little more experience of life you will be more indulgent. One has to be more merciful. You are young."

"No, it's something I've inherited, this is. I'm your daughter, and there's too much of you in me, that's what it is. I shall never be able to swallow things that disgust me. It's the way I'm made—how can I help it? Every time I see any one I know—or even any one I don't know—fail in what you men call points of honour, well, I can't help it at all, but it has the same effect on me as the sight of a toad. I have such a horror of it, and it disgusts me so, that I want to step on it. Come now, do you call a man honourable because he takes care to only do abominable things for which he can't be tried in the law courts? Do you call a man honourable when he has done something for which he must blush when he is alone? Is a man honourable when he has done things for which no one can reproach him and for which he cannot be punished, but which tarnish his conscience? I think there are things that are lower and viler than cheating at the card-table; and the indulgence with which society looks on makes me feel as though society is an accomplice, and I think it is perfectly revolting. There are things that are so disloyal, so dishonest, that when I think of them it makes me quite merciful towards out-and-out scoundrels. You see they do risk something; their life is at stake and their liberty. They go in for things prepared to win or lose: they don't put gloves on to do their infamous deeds. I like that better; it's not so cowardly, anyhow!"

Renée was seated on a sofa at the far side of the drawing-room. Her arms were folded, her hands feverish, and her whole body quivering with emotion. She spoke in jerks, and her voice vibrated with the wrath she felt in her very soul. Her eyes looked like fire lighting up her face, which was in the shade.

"And very interesting, too, he is," she continued, "your M. de Montbreton. He has an income of six hundred or six hundred and fifty pounds. If he did not pay quite such a high house-rent, and if his daughters had not always had their dresses made by Mme. Carpentier——"

"Ah, this requires consideration," put in Denoisel. "A man who has more than two hundred a year, if a bachelor, and more than four hundred if married, can perfectly well remain faithful to a government which is no longer in power. His means allow him to regret——"

"And he will expect you to esteem him, to shake hands with him, and raise your hat to him as usual," continued Renée. "No, it is rather too much! I hope when he comes here, papa—well, I shall promptly go straight out of the room."

"Will you have a glass of water, Renée?" asked M. Mauperin, smiling; "you know orators always do. You were really fine just then. Such eloquence—it flowed like a brook."

"Yes, make fun of me by all means. You know I get carried away, as you tell me. And your Montbreton—but how silly I am, to be sure. He doesn't belong to us, this man, does he? Oh, if it were one of my family who had done such a thing, such a dishonourable thing, such a——"

She stopped short for a second, and then began again:

"I think," she said, speaking with an effort, as though the tears were coming into her eyes, "I think I could never love him again. Yes, it seems to me as though my heart would be perfectly hard as far as he was concerned."

"Good! this is quite touching. We had the young orator just now, and at present it is the little girl's turn. You'd do better to come and look at this caricature album that Davarande has sent your mother."

"Ah yes, let's look at that," said Renée, going quickly across to her father and leaning on his shoulder as he turned over the leaves. She glanced at two or three pages and then looked away.

"There, I've had enough of them, thank you. Goodness, how can people enjoy making things ugly—uglier than nature? What a queer idea. Now in art, in books, and in everything, I'm for all that is beautiful, and not for what is ugly. Then, too, I don't think caricatures are amusing. It's the same with hunchbacks—it never makes me laugh to see a hunchback. Do you like caricatures, Denoisel?"

"Do I? No, they make me want to howl. Yes, it is a kind of comical thing that hurts me," answered Denoisel, picking up a Review that was next the album. "Caricatures are like petrified jokes to me. I can never see one on a table without thinking of a lot of dismal things, such as the wit of the Directory, Carle Vernet's drawings, and the gaiety of middle-class society."

"Thank you," said M. Mauperin laughing, "and in addition to that you are cutting my *Revue des Deux Mondes* with a match. How hopeless he is, to be sure, Denoisel."

"Do you want a knife, Denoisel?" asked Renée, plunging her hand into her pockets and pulling out a whole collection of things, which she threw on the table.

"By Jove!" exclaimed Denoisel, "why, you have a regular museum in your pockets. You'd have enough for a whole sale at the auction-rooms. What in the world are all those things?"

"Presents from a certain person, and they go about with me everywhere. There's the knife for you," and Renée showed it to her father before passing it to Denoisel. "Do you remember where you bought it for me?" she asked. "It was at Langres once when we had stopped for a fresh horse; oh, it's a very old one. This one," she continued, picking up another, "you brought me from Nogent. It has a silver blade, if you please; I gave you a halfpenny for it, do you remember?"

"Ah, if we are to begin making inventories!" said M. Mauperin laughing.

"And what's in that?" asked Denoisel, pointing to a little worn-out pocket-book stuffed full of papers, the dirty crumpled edges of which could be seen at each end.

"That? Oh, those are my secrets," and, picking up all the things she had thrown on the table, she put them quickly back in her pocket with the little book. The next minute, with a burst of laughter and diving once more into her pockets, she pulled the book out again, opened the flap, and scattered all the little papers on the table in front of Denoisel, and without opening them proceeded to explain what they were. "There, this is a prescription that was given for papa when he was ill. That's a song he composed for me two years ago for my birthday——"

"There, that's enough! Pack up your relics; put all that out of sight," said M. Mauperin, sweeping all the little papers from him just as the door opened and M.

Dardouillet entered.

"Oh, you've mixed them all up for me!" exclaimed Renée, looking annoyed as she put them back in her pocket-book.

# XXIX

A month later, in the little studio, Renée said to Denoisel: "Am I really romantic—do you think I am?"

"Romantic—romantic? In the first place, what do you mean by romantic?"

"Oh, you know what I mean; having ideas that are not like every one else's, and fancying a lot of things that can never happen. For instance, a girl is romantic when it would be a great trouble to her to marry, as girls do marry, a man with nothing extraordinary about him, who is introduced to her by papa and mamma, and who has not even so much as saved her life by stopping a horse that has taken fright, or by dragging her out of the water. You don't imagine I'm one of that sort, I hope?"

"No; at least I don't know at all. I'd wager that you yourself don't know, either."

"Nonsense. It may be, in the first place, because I have no imagination; but it has always seemed to me so odd to have an ideal—to dream about some imaginary man. It's just the same with the heroes in novels; they've never turned my head. I always think they are too well-bred, too handsome, too rotten, with all their accomplishments. I get so sick of them in the end. But it isn't that. Tell me now, suppose they wanted to make you live your whole life long with a creature—a creature who— —"

"A creature—what sort of a creature?"

"Let me finish what I am saying. A man, then, who did not answer at all to certain delicate little requirements of your nature, who did not strike you as being poetical—there, that's what I mean—not a scrap poetical, but who on the other hand made up for what was wanting in him, in other ways, by such kindness—well, such kindness as one never meets with— —"

"As much kindness as all that? Oh, I should not hesitate; I should take the kindness blindfold. Dear me, yes, indeed I should. It's so rare."

"You think kindness worth a great deal then?"

"I do, Renée. I value it as one values what one has lost."

"You? Why, you are always very kind."

"I am not downright bad; but that's all. I might perhaps be envious if I had more modesty and less pride. But as for always being kind, oh no, I am not. Life cures you of that just as it cures you of being a child. One gets over one's good-nature, Renée, just as one gets over teething."

"Then you think that a kindly disposition and a good heart——"

"Yes, I mean the goodness that endures in spite of men and in spite of experience—such goodness as I have met with in a primitive state in two or three men in my life. I look upon it as the best and most divine quality a man can have."

"Yes, but if a man who is very good, as good as those you describe—this is just a supposition, you know—suppose he had feet that looked like lumps of cake in his boots. And then, suppose he were corpulent, this good man, this very good man?"

"Well, one need not look at his feet nor at his corpulency—that's all. Oh, I beg your pardon, though, of course, I had completely forgotten."

"What?"

"Oh, nothing; except that you are a woman."

"But that's very insulting to my sex—that remark of yours."

Denoisel did not answer, and the conversation ceased for a few minutes.

"Have you ever wished for wealth?" Renée began again.

"Yes, several times; but absolutely for the sake of treating it as it deserves to be treated—to be disrespectful to it."

"How do you mean?"

"Why, yes, I should like to be rich just to show the contempt I have for money. I remember that two or three times I have fallen asleep with the idea of going to Italy to get married."

"To Italy?"

"Yes, there are more Russian princesses there than anywhere else, and Russian princesses are the only women left in this world who will marry a man without a farthing. Then, too, I was prepared to be contented with a princess who was not very well off. I was not at all exacting, and would have come down without a murmur to thirty thousand pounds a year. That was my very lowest figure though."

"Indeed!" said Renée laughing. "And what should you have done with all that money?"

"I should just have poured it away in streams between my fingers; it would have been something astounding to see; something that I have never seen rich people do with their money. I think all the millionaires ought to be ashamed of themselves. For instance, from the way in which a man lives who has four thousand a year, and the way a man lives who has forty thousand, could you tell their difference of fortune? Now with me you would have known. For a whole year I should have flung away my money in all kinds of caprices, fancies, and follies; I should have dazzled and fairly humiliated Paris; I should have been like a sun-god showering bank-notes down; I should have positively degraded my gold by all kinds of prodigalities; and at the end of a year, day for day, I should have left my wife."

"Nonsense!"

"Certainly; in order to prove to myself that I did not love money. If I had not left her, I should have considered myself dishonoured."

"Well, what extraordinary ideas! I must confess that I haven't arrived at your philosophy yet. A large fortune and all that it gives you, all kinds of enjoyment and luxuries, houses, carriages, and then the pleasure of making the people you don't like envious—of annoying them. Oh, I think it would be most delightful to be rich."

"I told you just now, Renée, that you were a woman—merely a woman."

# XXX

Denoisel had spoken as he really felt. If he had sometimes wished for wealth, he had never envied people who had it. He had a sincere and thorough contempt for money—the contempt of a man who is rich with very little.

Denoisel was a Parisian, or rather he was the true Parisian. Well up in all the experiences of Paris, wonderfully skilled in the great art of living, thanks to the habits and customs of Parisian life, he was the very man for that life; he had all its instincts, its sentiments, and its genius. He represented perfectly that very modern personage, the civilized man, triumphing, day by day, like the inhabitants of a forest of Bondy, over the price of things, over the costly life of capitals, as the savage triumphs over nature in a virgin forest. He had all the show and glitter of wealth. He lived among rich people, frequented their restaurants and clubs, had their habits, and shared in their amusements. He knew some of the wealthiest people, and all that money opened to them was open to him. He was seen at the grand private balls of the Provençaux, at the races, and at first nights at the theatres. In summer he went to the watering-places, to the sea, and to the gambling resorts. He dressed like a man who owns a carriage.

And yet Denoisel only possessed between four and five thousand pounds. Belonging to a family that had been steeped in the ideas of the past with regard to property, attached and devoted to landed wealth, always talking of bankruptcy, and as mistrustful of stocks and shares as peasants formerly were of bank-notes, Denoisel had shaken himself free of all the prejudices of his own people. Without troubling about the advice, the remonstrances, the indignation, and the threats of old and distant relatives, he had sold the small farms which his father and mother had left him. It seemed to him that there was no longer any proportion between the revenue of land and the expenses of modern life. In his opinion landed estate might have been a means of wealth at the time when Paul de Kock's novels said of a young man, "Paul was rich, he had two hundred and fifty a year." But since that time it had, according to him, become an anachronism, a kind of archaic property, a fancy fox which was only permissible in very wealthy people. He therefore realized his land and turned it into a small capital, which he placed, after consulting with a friend of his who frequented the Stock Exchange, in foreign bonds, in shares and securities, thus doubling and tripling his revenue without any risk to his regular income. Having thus converted his capital into a figure which meant nothing, except in the eyes of a notary, and which no longer regulated his current means, Denoisel arranged his life as he had done his money. He organized his expenses. He knew exactly the cost in Paris of vanity, little extras, bargains, and all such ruinous things. He was not ashamed to add up a bill himself before paying it. Away from home he only smoked fourpenny cigars, but at home he smoked pipes. He knew where to buy things, discovered the new shops, which give such good value during the first three months. He knew the wine-cellars at the various restaurants, ordered Chambertin a certain distance up the boulevards, and only ordered it there. If he gave a dinner, his *menu* won the respect of the waiter. And with all that, he knew how to order supper for four shillings at the Café Anglais.

All his expenses were regulated with the same skill. He went to one of the first tailors in Paris, but a friend of his who was in the Foreign Office procured for him from London all the suits he wanted between the seasons. When he had a present to make, or any New Year's gifts to buy, he always knew of a cargo of Indian or Chinese things that had just arrived, or he remembered an old piece of Saxony or Sèvres china that was lying hidden away in some shop in an unfrequented part of Paris, one of those old curiosities, the price of which cannot be discovered by the person for whom it is destined. All this with Denoisel was spontaneous, natural, and instinctive. This never-ending victory of Parisian intelligence over all the extravagance of life had nothing of the meanness and pettiness of sordid calculation about it. It was the happy discovery of a scheme of existence under satisfactory conditions, and not a series of vulgar petty economies, and in the well-organized expenditure of his six hundred pounds a year the man remained liberal and high-minded: he avoided what was too expensive for him, and never attempted to beat prices down. Denoisel had a flat of his own on the first storey of a well-ordered house with a carpeted staircase. He had only three rooms, but the Boulevard des Italiens was at his very door. His little drawing-room, which he had furnished as a smoking-den, was charming. It was one of those snug little rooms which Parisian upholsterers are so clever in arranging. It was all draped and furnished with chintz, and had divans as wide as beds. It had been Denoisel's own wish that the absence of all objects of art should complete the cheerful look of the room. He was waited on in the morning by his hall-porter, who brought him a cup of chocolate and did all the necessary housework. He dined at a club or restaurant or with friends.

The low rent and the simplicity of his household and domestic arrangements left Denoisel more of that money of which wealthy people are so often short, that money for the little luxuries of life, which is more necessary than any other in Paris, and which is known as pocket-money. Occasionally, however, that *force majeure*, the Unforeseen, would suddenly arrive in the midst of this regular existence and disarrange its equilibrium and its budget.

Denoisel would then disappear from Paris for a time. He would ruralize at some little country inn, near a river, on half-a-crown a day, and he would spend no other money than what was necessary for tobacco. Two or three winters, finding himself quite out of funds, he had emigrated, and, on discovering a city like Florence, where happiness costs nothing and where the living is almost as inexpensive as that happiness, he had stayed there six months, lodging in a room with a cupola, dining *à la trattoria* on truffles with Parmesan cheese, passing his evenings in the boxes of society people, going to the Grand Duke's balls, fêted, invited everywhere, with white camellias in his buttonhole—economizing in the happiest way in the world.

Denoisel spent no more for his love-affairs than for other things. It was no longer a question of self-respect with him, so that he only paid what he thought them worth. And yet such things had been his one allurement as a young man. He had, however, always been cool and methodical, even in his love-affairs. He had wanted, in a lordly way, to test for himself what the love of the woman who was the most in vogue in Paris was like. He allowed himself for this experiment about two thousand pounds of the seven thousand he then possessed, and, during the six months that he was the accepted lover of the celebrated Génicot, a woman who would give a five-pound note as a tip to her postillion on returning from the Marche, he lived in the same style as a man with five thousand a year. When the six months were over he left her, and she, for the first time in her life, was in love with a man who had paid for that love.

Tempered by this proof he had had several other experiences afterward, until they had palled on him; and then there had suddenly come to him, not a desire for further love adventures, but a great curiosity about women. He set out to discover all that was unforeseen, unexpected, and unknown to him in woman. All actresses seemed to him very much the same kind of courtesan, and all courtesans very much the same kind of actress. What attracted him now was the unclassed woman, the woman that bewilders the observer and the oldest Parisian. He often went wandering about at night, vaguely and irresistibly led on by one of those creatures who are neither all vice nor all virtue, and who walk so gracefully along in the mire. Sometimes he was dazzled by one of those fine-looking girls, so often seen in Paris, who seem to brighten everything as they pass along, and he would turn round to look at her and stand there even after she had suddenly disappeared in the darkness of some passage. His vocation was to discover tarnished stars. Now and then in some faubourg he would come across one of these marvellous daughters of the people and of Nature, and he would talk to her, watch her, listen to her, and study her; then when she wearied him he would let her go, and it would amuse him later on to raise his hat to her when he met her again driving in a carriage.

Denoisel's wealthy air won for him a welcome in social circles. He soon established himself there and on a superior footing, thanks to his geniality and wit, the services of every kind he was always ready to render, and the need every one had of him. His large circle of acquaintances among foreigners, artists, and theatrical people, his knowledge of the ins and outs of things when small favours were required, made him very valuable on hundreds of occasions. Every one applied to him for a box at a theatre, permission to visit a prison or a picture gallery, an entrance for a lady to the law courts at some trial, or a foreign decoration for some man. In two or three duels in which he had served as seconds, he had shown sound sense, decision, and a manly regard for the honour as well as the life of the man for whom he was answerable. People were under all kinds of obligations to him, and the respect they had for him was not lessened by his reputation as a first-rate swordsman. His character had won for him the esteem of all with whom he came in contact, and he was even held in high consideration by wealthy people, whose millions, nevertheless, were not always respected by him.

# XXXI

"My wife, for instance, wanted to have her portrait painted by Ingres. You've seen it—it isn't like her—but it's by Ingres. Well, do you know what he asked me for it? Four hundred pounds. I paid it him, but I consider that taking advantage; it's the war against capital. Do you mean to say that because a man's name is known he should make me pay just what he likes? because he's an artist, he has no price, no fixed rate, he has a right to fleece me? Why, according to that he might ask me a million for it. It's like the doctors who make you pay according to your fortune. To begin with, how does any one know what I have? I call it an iniquity. Yes, four hundred pounds; what do you think of that?"

M. Bourjot was standing by the chimney-piece talking to Denoisel. He put the other foot, on which he had been standing, to the fire as he spoke.

"Upon my word," said Denoisel, very seriously, "you are quite right: all these folks take advantage of their reputation. You see there's only one way to prevent it, and that would be to decree a legal maximum for talent, a maximum for master-pieces. Why, yes! It would be very easy."

"That's it; that would be the very thing!" exclaimed M. Bourjot, "and it would be quite just, for you see— —"

The Bourjots had dined that evening alone with the Mauperins. The two families had been talking of the wedding, and were only waiting to fix the day, until the expiration of a year from the date of the first insertion of the name of Villacourt in the *Monitor*. It was M. Bourjot who had insisted on this delay. The ladies were talking about the trousseau, jewellery, laces, and wedding-presents, and Mme. Mauperin, who was seated by Mme. Bourjot, was contemplating her as though she were a person who had performed a miracle.

M. Mauperin's face beamed with joy. He had in the end yielded to the fascination of money. This great, upright man, genuine, severe, rigid, and incorruptible as he was, had gradually allowed the vast wealth of the Bourjots to come into his thoughts and into his dreams, to appeal to him and to his instincts as a practical man, as an old man, the father of a family and a manufacturer. He had been won over and disarmed. Ever since his son's success with regard to this marriage, he had felt that respect for Henri which ability or the prospect of a large fortune inspires in people, and, without being aware of it himself, he scarcely blamed him now for having changed his name. Fathers are but men, after all.

Renée, who for some time past had been worried, thoughtful, and low-spirited, was almost cheerful this evening. She was amusing herself with blowing about the fluffy feathers which Noémi was wearing in her hair. The latter, languid and absent-minded, with a dreamy look in her eyes, was replying in monosyllables to Mme. Davarande's ceaseless chatter.

"Nowadays, everything is against money," began M. Bourjot again, sententiously. "There's a league—now, for instance, I made a road for the people at Sannois. Well, do you imagine that they even touch their hats to us? Oh dear no, never. In 1848 we gave them bushels of corn; and what do you think they said? Excuse me, ladies, if I repeat their words. They said: 'That old beast must be afraid of us!' That was all the gratitude I had. I started a model farm, and I applied to the Government for a man to manage it; a red-hot radical was sent to me, a rascal who had spent his life running down the rich. At present I have to do with a Municipal Council with the most detestable opinions. I find work for every one, don't I? Thanks to us, the country round is prosperous. Well, if there were to be a revolution, now, I am convinced that they would set fire to our place. They'd have no compunction about that. You've no idea what enemies you get if you pay as much as three hundred and sixty pounds for taxes. They'd simply burn us out of house and home—they'd have no scruple about it. You see what happened in February. Oh, my ideas with regard to the people have quite changed; and they are preparing a nice future for us, you can count on that. We shall be simply ruined by a lot of penniless wretches. I can see that beforehand. I often think of all these things. If only it were not for one's children—money, as far as I am concerned——"

"What's that you are saying, neighbour?" asked M. Mauperin, approaching.

"I'm saying that I'm afraid the day will come when our children will be short of bread, M. Mauperin; that's what I'm saying."

"You'll make them hesitate about this wedding if you talk like that," said M. Mauperin.

"Oh, if my husband begins with his gloomy ideas, if he's going to talk about the end of the world—" put in Mme. Bourjot.

"I congratulate you that you don't feel the anxiety I do," remarked M. Bourjot, bowing to his wife; "but I can assure you that, without being weak-minded, there is every reason for feeling very uneasy."

"Certainly, certainly," said Denoisel. "I think that money is in danger, in great danger, in very great danger indeed. In the first place, it is threatened by that envy which is at the bottom of nearly all revolutions; and then by progress, which baptizes the revolutions."

"But, sir, such progress would be infamous. Take me, for instance: no one could doubt me. I used to be a Liberal—I am now, in fact. I am a soldier of Liberty, a born Republican; I am for progress of every kind. But a revolution against wealth—why, it would be barbarous! We should be going back to savage times. What we want is justice and common sense. Can you imagine now a society without wealth?"

"No, not any more than a greasy pole without a silver cup."

"What," continued M. Bourjot, who in his excitement had not caught Denoisel's words, "the money that I have earned with hard work, honestly and with the greatest difficulty—the money that is mine, that I have made, and which is for my children—why, there is nothing more sacred! I even look upon the income-tax as a violation of property."

"Why, yes," said Denoisel in the most perfectly good-natured tone, "I am quite of your opinion. And I should be very sorry," he added wickedly, "to make things seem blacker to you than they already do. But you see we have had a revolution against the nobility; we shall have one against wealth. Great names have been abolished by the guillotine, and great fortunes will be done away with next. A man was considered guilty if his name happened to be M. de Montmorency; it will be criminal to be M. Two Thousand Pounds a Year. Things are certainly getting on. I can speak all the more freely as I am absolutely disinterested, myself. I should not have had anything to be guillotined for in the old days, and I haven't enough to be ruined for nowadays. So, you see— —"

"Excuse me," put in M. Bourjot, solemnly, "but your comparison—no one could deplore excesses more than I do, and the event of 1793 was a great crime, sir. The nobility were treated abominably, and all honest people must be of the same opinion as I am."

M. Mauperin smiled as he thought of the Bourjot of 1822.

"But then," continued M. Bourjot, "the situation is not the same at all. Social conditions are entirely changed, the basis of society has been restored. Everything is different. There were reasons—or pretexts, if you prefer that—for this hatred of the nobility. The Revolution of '89 was against privileges, which I am not criticising, but which existed. That is quite different. The fact was people wanted equality. It was more or less legitimate that they should have it, but at least there was some reason in it. At present all that is altered; and where are the privileges? One man is as good as another. Hasn't every man a vote? You may say, 'What about money?' Well, every one can earn money; all trades and professions are open to every one."

"Except those that are not," put in Denoisel.

"In short, all men can now arrive at anything and everything. The only things necessary are hard work, intelligence— —"

"And circumstances," put in Denoisel, once more.

"Circumstances must be made, sir, by each man himself. Just look at what society is. We are all *parvenus*. My father was a cloth merchant—in a wholesale way, certainly—and yet you see—now this is equality, sir, the real and the right kind of equality. There is no such thing as caste now. The upper class springs from the people, and the people rise to the upper class. I could have found a count for my daughter, if I had wanted to. But it is just simply a case of evil instincts, evil passions, and these communist ideas—it is all this which is against wealth. We hear a lot of rant about poverty and misery. Well, I can tell you this, there has never been so much done for the people as at present. There is great progress with regard to comfort and well-being in France. People who never used to eat meat, now eat it twice a week. These are facts; and I am sure that on that subject our young social economist, M. Henri, could tell us— —"

"Yes, yes," said Henri, "that has been proved. In twenty-five years the increase of cattle has been twelve per cent. By dividing the population of France into twelve millions inhabiting the towns, and twenty-four to twenty-five millions inhabiting the country districts, it is reckoned that the former consume about sixty-five kilogrammes a head each year, and the latter twenty kilogrammes twenty-six centigrammes. I can guarantee the figures. What is quite sure is that the most conscientious estimates prove that since 1789 there has been an increase in the average length of life, and this progress is the surest sign of prosperity for a nation. Statistics— —"

"Ah, statistics, the chief of the inexact sciences!" interrupted Denoisel, who delighted in muddling M. Bourjot's brain with paradoxes. "But I grant that," he went on. "I grant that the lives of the people have been prolonged, and that they eat more meat than they have ever eaten. Do you, on that account, believe in the immortality of the present social constitution? There has been a revolution which has brought about the reign of the middle class—that is to say, the reign of money; and now you say: 'Everything is finished; there must be no other; there can be no legitimate revolution now.' That is quite natural; but, between ourselves, I don't know up to what point the supremacy of the middle class can be considered as final. As far as you are concerned, when once political equality is given to all, social equality is complete: that is perhaps quite just; but the thing is to convince people of it, whose interest it is *not* to believe it. One man is as good as another. Certainly he may be in the eyes of God. Every one in this century of ours has a right to wear a black coat—provided he can pay for it. Modern equality—shall I explain briefly what it is? It is the same equality as our conscription; every man draws his number, but if you can pay one hundred and twenty pounds, you have the right of sending another man to be killed instead of you. You spoke of privileges; there are no such things now, that's true. The Bastille was destroyed; but it gave birth to others first. Let us take, for instance, Justice, and I do acknowledge that a man's position, his name, and his money weigh less and are made less of in courts of justice than anywhere else. Well, commit a crime, and be, let us say, a peer of France; you would be allowed poison instead of the scaffold. Take notice that I think it should be so; I am only mentioning it to show you how inequalities spring up again, and, indeed, when I see the ground that they cover now I wonder where the others could have been. Hereditary rights—something else that the Revolution thought it had buried. All that was an abuse of the former Government, about which enough has been said. Well, I should just like to know whether, at present, the son of a politician does not inherit his father's name and all the privileges connected with that name, his father's electors, his connection, his place everywhere, and his chair at the Academy? We are simply overrun with these sons. We come across them everywhere; they take all the good berths and, thanks to these reversions, everything is barred for other people. The fact is that old customs are terrible things for unmaking laws. You are wealthy, and you say money is sacred. But why? Well, you say 'We are not a caste.' No, but you are already an aristocracy, and quite a new aristocracy, the insolence of which has already surpassed all the impertinences of the oldest aristocracies on the globe. There is no court now, you say. There never has been one, I should imagine, in the whole history of the world where people have had to put up with such contempt as in the private office of certain great bankers. You talk of evil instincts and evil passions. Well, the power of the wealthy middle class is not calculated to elevate the mind. When the higher ranks of society are engaged in digesting and placing out money there are no longer any ideas, nothing in fact but appetites, in the class below. Formerly, when by the side of money there was something above it and beyond it, during a revolution instead of asking bluntly for money—clumsy rough coins with which to buy their happiness—the people contented themselves with asking for the change of colours on a flag, or with having a few words written over a guard-house, or even with glorious victories that were quite hollow. But in our times—oh, we all know where the heart of Paris is now. The bank would be besieged instead of the Hôtel de ville. Ah, the *bourgeoisie* has made a great mistake!"

"And what is the mistake, pray?" asked M. Bourjot, astounded by Denoisel's tirade.

"That of not leaving Paradise in heaven—which was certainly its place. The day when the poor could no longer comfort themselves with the thought that the next life would make up to them for this, the day when the people gave up counting on the happiness of the other world—oh, I can tell you, Voltaire did a lot of harm to the wealthy classes——"

"Ah, you are right there!" exclaimed M. Bourjot, impulsively. "That is quite evident. All these wretches ought to go to church regularly——"

# XXXII

There was a grand ball at the Bourjots' in honour of the approaching marriage of their daughter with M. Mauperin de Villacourt.

"You are going in for it to-day. How you are dancing!" said Renée to Noémi, fanning her as she stood talking in a corner of the vast drawing-room.

"I have never danced so much, that's quite true," answered Noémi, taking her friend's arm and leading her away into the small drawing-room. "No, never," she continued, drawing Renée to her and kissing her. "Oh, how lovely it is to be happy," and then kissing her again in a perfect fever of joy, she said: "*She* does not care for him now. Oh, I'm quite sure she doesn't care for him. In the old days I could see she did by the very way she got up when he came; by her eyes, her voice, the very rustle of her dress, everything. Then when he wasn't there, I could tell by her silence she was thinking of him. You are surprised at my noticing, silly thing that I am; but there are some things that I understand with this"—and she drew Renée's hand on to her white moiré dress just where her heart was—"and this never deceives me."

"And you love him now, do you?" asked Renée.

Noémi stopped her saying any more by pressing her bouquet of roses against her friend's lips.

"Mademoiselle, you promised me the first redowa," and a young man took Noémi away. She turned as she reached the door and threw a kiss to Renée with the tips of her fingers.

Noémi's confession had given Renée a thrill of joy, and she had revelled in the smile on her friend's face. She herself felt immensely comforted and relieved. In an instant everything had changed for her, and the thought that Noémi loved her brother chased away all other ideas. She no longer saw the shame and the crime which she had so long seen in this marriage. She kept repeating to herself that Noémi loved him, that they both loved each other. The rest all belonged to the past, and they would each of them forget that past, Noémi by forgiving it, and Henri by redeeming it. Suddenly the remembrance of something came back to her, bringing with it an anxious thought and a vague dread. She was determined, however, just then to see no dark clouds in the horizon and nothing threatening in the future. Chasing all this from her mind, she began to think of her brother and of Noémi once more. She pictured to herself the wedding-day and their future home, and she recalled the voices of some children she had once heard calling "Auntie! Auntie!"

"Will mademoiselle do me the honour of dancing with me?"

It was Denoisel who was bowing in front of her.

"Do we dance together—you and I? We know each other too well. Sit down there, and don't crease my dress. Well, what are you looking at?"

Renée was wearing a dress of white tulle, trimmed with seven narrow flounces and bunches of ivy leaves and red berries. In her bodice and the tulle ruches of her sleeves she wore ivy and berries to match. A long spray of the ivy was twisted round her hair with a few berries here and there and the leaves hung down over her shoulders. She was leaning her head back on the sofa, and her beautiful chestnut hair, which was brought forward, fell slightly over her white forehead. There was a new gleam, a soft intense light in her brown, dreamy eyes, the expression of which could not be seen. A shadow played over her mouth at the corners, and her lips, which were generally closed in a disdainful little pout, were unsealed and half open, partially revealing the gladness which came from her very soul. The light fell on her chin, and a ring of shadow played round her neck each time that she moved her head. She looked charming thus, the outline of her features indistinct under the full light of the chandeliers, and her whole face beaming with childish joy.

"You are very pretty this evening, Renée."

"Ah—this evening?"

"Well, to tell the truth, just lately you've looked so worried and so sad. It suits you much better to enjoy yourself."

"Do you think so? Do you waltz?"

"As though I had just learnt and had been badly taught. But you have only this very minute refused."

"I, refused? What an idea! Why, I want to dance dreadfully. Well, there's plenty of time—oh, don't look at your watch; I don't want to know the time. And so you think I am gay, do you? Well, no, I don't feel gay. I'm happy—I'm very happy—there, now! I say, Denoisel, when you are strolling about in Paris, you know those old women who wear Lorraine caps, and who stand in the doorways selling matches—well, you are to give a sovereign each to the first five you meet; I'll give it you back. I've saved some money—don't forget. Is that waltz still going on? Is it really true that I refused to dance? Well, after this one I'm going to dance everything, and I shall not be particular about my partners. They can be as ugly as they like, they can wear shoes that have been resoled, and talk to me about Royer-Collard if they like, they can be too tall or too short, they can come up to my elbow or I can come up to their waist—it won't matter to me even if their hands perspire—I'll dance with any of them. That's how I feel to-night, and yet people say that I am not charitable."

Just at that moment a man entered the little drawing-room. It was M. Davarande.

"Invite me for this waltz, please," said Renée, and as she passed by Denoisel she whispered:

"You see I'm beginning with the family."

# XXXIII

"What's the matter with your mother this evening?" Denoisel asked Renée. They were alone, as Mme. Mauperin had just gone upstairs to bed, and M. Mauperin to have a look round at the works, which were on late that night.

"What's the matter with her, she seems as— —"

"Surly as a bulldog—say it out."

"Well, but what's it all about?"

"Ah, that's just it," and Renée began to laugh. "The fact is I've just lost a chance of being married—and so here I am still."

"Another? But then that's your speciality!"

"Oh, this is only the fourteenth. That's only an average number; and it's all through you that I've lost this chance."

"Through me? Well, I never! What do you mean?"

Renée got up, put her hands in her pockets, and walked up and down the room from one end to the other. Every now and then she stopped short, turned round on one heel, and gave a sort of whistle.

"Yes, through you!" she said, coming back to Denoisel. "What should you think if I told you that I had refused eighty thousand pounds?"

"They must have been astonished."

"I can't say that I wasn't rather tempted. It's no good setting up for being better than I am; and then, too, with you I don't make any pretences. Well, I'll own that just for a minute I was very nearly caught. It was M. Barousse who arranged it all—very nicely indeed. Then, here at home, they worked me up to it; mamma and Henri besieged me; I was bored to death about it all day long. And then, too, quite exceptionally for me, I began to have fancies, too. Anyhow, it is quite certain that I slept very badly two nights. These big fortunes do keep you awake. Then, too, to be quite just, I must say that I thought a great deal about papa in the midst of it all. Wouldn't he have been proud—wouldn't he, now? Wouldn't he have revelled in my four thousand a year? He has so much vanity always where I am concerned. Do you remember his indignation and wrath that time? 'A son-in-law who would allow my daughter to get in an omnibus!' He was superb, wasn't he? Then I began to think of you—yes, of you—and your ideas, your paradoxes, your theories, of all sorts of things you had said to me; I thought of your contempt for money, and as I thought of it—well, I suppose it is catching, for I felt the same contempt myself.

And so all at once, one fine morning, I just cut it all short. No, you influence me too much, my dear boy, decidedly."

"Well, but I'm—I'm an idiot, Renée. Oh, I'm so sorry. I—I thought that sort of thing was not catching—indeed I did. Come, really now, was it my fault?"

"Yes, yours—in a great measure—and then just a little his fault, too."

"Ah!"

"Yes, it was just a little M. Lemeunier's. When I felt the money getting into my head, when I was seriously thinking of marrying him, why, I just looked at him. And you didn't know you were speaking so truly the other day. I suddenly felt that I was a woman—oh, you've no idea what it was like. Then on the other hand I saw how good he was. Oh, he really is goodness itself. I tried him in every way, I turned him inside out, it worried me to find him so perfect; but it was no use, there was no fault to find in him. He is thoroughly good, that man is. Oh, he's quite different from Reverchon and the others. Only fancy what he said to me: 'Mademoiselle,' he said, 'I know that you don't care for me, but will you let me wait a little and see if you can dislike me less than you do now?' It was quite pathetic. Sometimes I felt inclined to say to him: 'Suppose we were to sit down and cry a little together, shall we?' Fortunately, when he made me feel inclined to cry, papa, on the other hand, made me want to laugh. He looked so funny, my dear old father, half gay and half sad. I never saw such a resigned kind of happiness. The sadness of losing me, and the thought of seeing me make a good match made him feel so mixed up. Well, it's all finished now, thank Heaven! He makes great eyes at me as though he's angry—didn't you notice, when mamma was looking at us? But he is not angry at all in reality. He's very glad in his heart; I can see that."

# XXXIV

Denoisel was at Henri Mauperin's. They were sitting by the fire talking and smoking. Suddenly they heard a noise and a discussion in the hall, and, almost at the same time, the room door was opened violently and a man entered abruptly, pushing aside the domestic who was trying to keep him back.

"M. Mauperin de Villacourt?" he demanded.

"That is my name, monsieur," said Henri, rising.

"Well, my name is Boisjorand de Villacourt," and with the back of his hand he gave Henri a blow which made his face bleed. Henri turned as white as the silk scarf he was wearing as a necktie and, with the blood trickling down his face, he bent forward to return the blow, and then, just as suddenly, drew himself up and stretched his hand out towards Denoisel, who stepped forward, folded his arms, and spoke in his calmest tone:

"I think I understand what you mean, sir," he said; "you consider that there is a Villacourt too many. I think so too."

The visitor was visibly embarrassed before the calmness of this man of the world. He took off his hat, which he had kept on his head hitherto, and began to stammer out a few words.

"Will you kindly leave your address with my servant?" said Henri, interrupting him; "I will send round to you to-morrow."

"A disagreeable affair," began Henri, when he was once more alone with Denoisel. "Where can he have sprung from, this Villacourt? They told me that there were none of them left. Ah, my face is bleeding," he said, wiping it with his handkerchief. "He's a regular buffalo. Georges, bring some water," he called out to his domestic.

"You'll choose the sword, shall you not?" asked Denoisel. "Hand me a stick. Now listen—you must be on guard from the first, and strike out very little. That man's one of the bloodthirsty sort; he'll go straight for you, and you must defend yourself with circular parries. When you are hard pressed and he rushes headlong at you, move aside to the right with the left foot, turn round on tip-toes on your right foot—like that. He'll have nothing in front of him then, and you'll have him from the side and can run him through like a frog."

"No," said Henri, lifting his face from the basin, in which he was sponging it, "not the sword."

"But, my dear fellow, that man is evidently a sportsman; he'll be accustomed to fire-arms."

"My dear fellow, there are certain situations which are most awkward. I've taken another name, and that's always ridiculous. Here's a man who accuses me of having stolen it from him. I have enemies, and a good number of them, too; they'll make a scandal with all this. I must kill this fellow, that's very evident; it's the only way to make my position good. I should put an end to everything by that, law-suits, and all the stories and gossip—everything. The sword would not serve my purpose. With the sword you can kill a man who has been five years at it, who can use it, and who keeps his body in the positions you have been accustomed to. But a man who has had no sword practice, who jumps and dances about, who flourishes it about like a stick; I should wound him, and that would be all. Now with the pistol—I'm a good shot, you know. You must do me the justice of admitting that I was wise in my choice of accomplishments. And my idea is to put it there," he touched Denoisel as he spoke just above the hip, "just there, you see. Higher up, it's no good, the arm is there to ward it off; but here, why there are a lot of very necessary organs; there's the bladder, for instance; now if you are lucky enough to hit that, and if it should happen to be full, why it would be a case of peritonitis. And you'll get the pistol for me. A duel—without a fuss, you understand. I want it kept quite secret, so that no one shall hear of it beforehand. Whom shall you take with you?"

"Suppose I asked Dardouillet? He served in the National Guard, in the cavalry; I shall have to appeal to his military instincts."

"That's the very thing, good! Will you call in and see mother first. Tell her that I cannot come before Thursday. It would be awkward if she happened to drop in on us just the next day or two. I shall not go out; I'll have a bath and get a little more presentable. This mark doesn't show very much now, does it? I shall send out for dinner, and then spend the evening writing two or three necessary letters. By-the-bye, if you see the gentleman to-morrow morning, why not have it out in the afternoon at four o'clock? It's just as well to get it over. To-morrow you'll find me here all the day—or else I shall be at the shooting gallery. Arrange things as you would for yourself, and thanks for all your trouble, old man. Four o'clock, then—if possible."

# XXXV

The name of the farm that Henri Mauperin had added to his surname to make it sound more aristocratic happened, by a strange chance, such as sometimes occurs, to be the name of an estate in Lorraine and of a family, illustrious in former days, but at present so completely forgotten that every one believed it had died out.

The man who had just dealt Henri this blow was the last of those Villacourts who took their name from the domain and château of Villacourt, situated some three leagues from Saint-Mihiel, and owned by them from time immemorial.

In 1303 Ulrich de Villacourt was one of the three lords who set their seal to the will of Ferry, Duke of Lorraine, by order of that prince. Under Charles the Bold, Gantonnet de Villacourt, who had been taken prisoner by the Messinians, only regained his liberty by giving his word never to mount a battle-horse, nor to carry military weapons again. From that time forth he rode a mule, arrayed himself in buffalo-skin, carried a heavy iron bar, and returned to the fight bolder and more terrible than ever. Maheu de Villacourt married Gigonne de Malain and afterward Christine de Gliseneuve. His marble statue, between his two wives, was to be seen before the Revolution in the Church of the Grey Friars at Saint-Mihiel. Duke René allowed him to take eight hundred florins from the town of Ligny for the ransom that he had had to pay after the disastrous battle of Bulgnéville.

Remacle de Villacourt, Maheu's son, was killed in 1476, in the battle waged by Duke René before Nancy against Charles the Daring. Hubert de Villacourt, Remacle's sons, Seneschal of Barrois and Bailiff of Bassigny, followed Duke Antoine as standard-bearer in the Alsatian war, while his brother Bonaventure, a monk of the strict order of Saint-François, was made three times over the triennial Superior of his order, and confessor of Antoine and François, Dukes of Lorraine; and one of his sisters, Salmone, was appointed Abbess of Sainte Glossinde of Metz.

Jean-Marie de Villacourt served in the French army, and after the Landrecies day, the king made him a knight and embraced him. He was afterward captain of three hundred foot soldiers and Equerry of the King's stables, and was then appointed to the captaincy of Vaucouleurs and made Governor of Langres. He had married a sister of Jean de Chaligny, the celebrated gun-founder of Lorraine, who cast the famous culverin, twenty-two feet high. His brother Philibert was a cavalry captain under Charles IX. His brother Gaston made himself famous by his duels. It was he who killed Captain Chambrulard, with two sword-strokes, before four thousand persons assembled at the back of the Chartreux in Paris. Jean-Marie had another brother, Angus, who was Canon of Toul and Archdeacon of Tonnerrois, and a sister, Archange, who was Abbess of Saint-Maur, Verdun.

Then came Guillaume de Villacourt, who fought against Louis XIII. He was obliged to surrender with Charles de Lenoncourt, who was defending the town of Saint-Mihiel, and he shared his four years' captivity in the Bastille. His son, Mathias de Villacourt, married in 1656 Marie Dieudonnée, a daughter of Claude de Jeandelincourt, who opened the salt mine of Château-Salins. Mathias had fourteen children, ten of whom were killed in the service of Louis XIV: Charles, captain of the regiment of the Pont, killed in the siege of Philisbourg; Jean, killed in the battle of Nerwinde; Antoine, captain of the regiment of Normandie, killed in the siege of Fontarabie; Jacques, killed in the siege of Bellegarde, where he had gone by permission of the king; Philippe, captain of the grenadiers in the Dauphin's regiment, killed in the battle of Marsaille; Thibaut, captain in the same regiment, killed in the battle of Hochstett; Pierre-François, commander in the Lyonnais regiment, killed in the battle of Fleurus; Claude-Marie, commander in the Périgord regiment, killed in the passage of the Hogue; Edme, lieutenant in his brother's company, killed at his side in the same affair, and Gerard, Knight of the Order of Saint-Jean of Jerusalem, killed in 1700, in a conflict between four galleys of Christians and a Turkish man-of-war. Of the three daughters of Charles-Mathias, Lydie married the Seigneur de Majastre, Governor of Epinal, and the other two, Berthe and Phœbé, died unmarried.

The eldest of the sons of Charles-Mathias, Louis-Aimé de Villacourt, who served eighteen years and retired from service after the battle of Malplaquet, died in 1702. His son left Villacourt, settled down in Paris, threw himself into the life of the capital, and so got rid of the remainder of a fortune which had already been encroached upon by the loss of a lawsuit between his father and the d'Haraucourts. He endeavoured to recover his losses at the gaming-table, got into debt, and returned to Villacourt with a wife from Carrouge who had kept a gambling house in Paris. He died in 1752, owning very little besides the walls of the château, and leaving a name less famous and less honourable than his father's had been. He had two children by his marriage, a daughter and a son. The daughter became maid of honour to the Empress-Queen, the son remained at Villacourt, leading a low, coarse life as a country gentleman. On the abolition of privileges in 1790 he gave up his rank and lived on a friendly and equal footing with the peasants until he died in 1792. His son Jean, lieutenant in the regiment of the Royal-Liégeois in 1787, was in the Nancy affair. He emigrated, went through the campaigns of 1792 to 1801 in Mirabeau's legion, which was then commanded by Roger de Damas, and in the Bourbon grenadiers in Condé's army. On the thirteenth of August, 1796, he was wounded on the head in the Oberkamlach battle. In 1802 he returned to France, bringing with him a wife he had married in Germany, who died after bearing him four children, four sons. He had become weak in intellect, almost childish in fact, from the result of his wound, and after his wife's death there was no one to regulate the household expenses. Disorder gradually crept in, he kept open table and took to drinking, until at last he was obliged to sell what little land he had round the château. Finally the château itself began to crumble away. He could not have it repaired, as he had no money to pay the workmen. The wind could be felt through the cracks, and the rain came in. The family were obliged to give up one room after another, taking refuge where the roof was still sound. He himself was indifferent to all this; after drinking two or three glasses of brandy he would take his seat in what used to be the kitchen garden, on a stone bench near a meridian, the figures of which had worn away, and there he would get quite cheerful in the sunshine, calling to people over the hedge to come in and drink with him. Decay and poverty, however, made rapid strides in the château. There was nothing left of all the old silver but a salad-bowl, which was used for the food of a horse called Brouska, that the exile had brought with him from Germany, and which was now allowed to roam in liberty through the rooms on the ground-floor.

The four sons grew up as the château went to decay, accustomed to wind, rain, and roughing it. They were entirely neglected and abandoned by their father, and their only education consisted of a few lessons from the parish priest. From living like the peasants, and mixing with them in their work and games, they gradually became regular peasants themselves, and the roughest and strongest in the country round. When their father died the four brothers, by common consent, made over to a land agent the remaining stones of their château in return for a few pounds, with which to pay their most pressing debts, and an annuity of twenty pounds, which was to be paid until the death of the last of the four. They then took up their abode in the forest, which joined their estate, and lived there with the wood-cutters and in the same way as they did, making a regular den of their hut, and living there with their sweethearts or wives, peopling the forest with a half-bred race, in which the Villacourts were crossed with nature, noblemen mated with children of the forest, whose language, even, was no longer French. Some of Jean de Villacourt's old comrades in arms had tried, on his death, to do something for his children. They were interested in this name, which had been so great and had now fallen so low. In 1826 the youngest of the boys, who was scarcely more than sixteen, was brought to Paris. The little savage was clothed and presented to the Duchesse d'Angoulême: he appeared three or four times in the *salons* of the Minister of War, who was related to his family, and who was very anxious to do something for him; but at the end of a week, feeling stifled in these drawing-rooms, and ill at ease in his clothes, he had escaped like a little wolf, gone straight back to his hiding-place, and had not come out of it again for years.

Of these four Villacourts, he was the only one left at the end of twenty years. His three brothers died one after the other, and all by violent deaths; one from drunkenness, the second from illness, and the other from blows he had received in a skirmish. All three had been struck down suddenly, snatched as it were from the midst of life. Living among the bastards they had left, this last of the Villacourts was looked up to in the forest as the chieftain of a clan until 1854, when the game laws came into force. All the regulations and the supervision, the trials, fines, confiscations, and liabilities connected with the chase, which had now become his very life, and the fear of giving way to his anger some day and of putting a bullet into one of the keepers, disgusted him with this part of the world, with France, and with this land which was no longer his own.

It occurred to him to go to America in order to be quite free, and to be able to hunt in untrodden fields where no gun license was necessary. He went to Paris to set sail from Havre, but he had not enough money for the voyage. He then fell back on Africa, but there he found a second France with laws, gendarmes, and forest-keepers. He tried working a grant of land, and then a clearing, but that kind of labour did not suit him. The country and the climate tried him, and the burning heat of the sun and soil began to take effect on his robust health. At the end of two years he returned to France.

On going back to his log-hut at Motte-Noire he found a newspaper there, the only thing which had come for him during his absence. It was a number of the *Moniteur* and was more than a year old. He tore it up to light his pipe, and, just as he was twisting it, caught sight of a red-pencil mark. He opened it out again and read the marked paragraph:

"*M. Mauperin* (*Alfred-Henri*), better known by the name of *Villacourt*, is about to apply to the Keeper of the Seals for permission to add to his name that of Villacourt, and will henceforth be known as *Mauperin de Villacourt.*"

He got up, walked about, fumed, then sat down again, and slowly lighted his pipe.

Three days later he was in Paris.

Just at first on reading the paper he had felt as though some one had struck him across the face with a horsewhip. Then he had said to himself that he was robbed of his name, but that was all, that his name was no longer worth anything, as it was now the name of a beggar. This philosophizing mood did not last long, the thought of the theft of his name gradually came back to him, and it irritated and hurt him, and made him feel bitter. After all he had nothing left but this name, and he could not endure the idea of having it stolen from him, and so started for Paris.

On arriving he was as furious as a mad bull, and his one idea was to go and knock this M. Mauperin down at once. When once he was in the capital, though, with its streets and its crowds, face to face with its people, its shops, its life, all the passers-by, and the noise, he felt dazed, like some wild beast let loose in a huge circus, whose rage is suddenly turned into fright and who stops short after its first leap. He went straight to the law courts, and in the long hall accosted one of those men in black, who are generally leaning against a pillar, and told him what had happened. The man in black informed him that as the year's delay had expired there was nothing to be done but appeal to the high court against the decree authorizing the addition of the name, and he gave him the address of a counsel of the higher court. M. de Villacourt hurried to this counsel. He found a very cold, polite man, wearing a white necktie, who, while leaning back in a green morocco chair, listened with a fixed expression in his eyes all the time to his case, his claims, his rights, his indignation, and to the sound of the parchments he was turning over with a nervous hand.

The expression of the counsel's face never changed, so that when M. de Villacourt had finished he fancied that the other man had not understood, and he began all over again. The lawyer stopped him with a gesture, saying: "I think you will gain your case, monsieur."

"You *think* so? Do you mean to say you are not sure of it?"

"A lawsuit is always a lawsuit, monsieur," answered the lawyer with a faint smile, which was so sceptical that it chilled M. de Villacourt, who was just prepared to burst out in a rage. "The chances are on your side, though, and I am quite willing to undertake your case."

"Here you are then," said M. de Villacourt, putting his roll of title-deeds down on the desk. "Thank you, sir," he added, rising to take his leave.

"Excuse me," said the lawyer on seeing him walk towards the door, "but I must call your attention to the fact that in business of this kind, in an appeal to the higher court, we do not only act as the barrister but as the lawyer of our client. There are certain expenses, for getting information and examining deeds—If I take up your case I shall be obliged to ask you to cover these expenses. Oh, it is only a matter of from twenty to twenty-five pounds. Let us say twenty pounds."

"Twenty to twenty-five pounds! Why, what do you mean!" exclaimed M. de Villacourt, turning red with indignation. "Some one steals my name, and because I have not seen the newspaper in which the man warns me that he intends robbing me, I must pay twenty-five pounds to make this rascal give up my name again. Twenty to twenty-five pounds! But I haven't the money, sir," he said, lowering his head and letting his arms fall down at his sides.

"I am extremely sorry, monsieur, but this little formality is indispensable. Oh, you must be able to find it. I feel sure that among the relatives of the families into which your family has married—in such questions as these, families are always ready to pull together."

"I do not know any one—and the Count de Villacourt will never ask for money. I had just twelve pounds when I arrived. I bought this coat for about two pounds at the Palais Royal on the way here. This hat cost me five and tenpence. I suppose my hotel bill will cost me about a sovereign, and I shall want about a sovereign to get back home. Could you do with what is left?"

"I am very sorry, monsieur——"

M. de Villacourt put his hat on and left the room. At the hall-door he suddenly turned round, passed through the dining-room and opening the office-door again, he said, in a smothered voice which he was doing his utmost to control:

"Can I have the address of M. Henri Mauperin—known as de Villacourt—without paying for it?"

"Certainly; he is a barrister. I shall find his address in this book. Here it is; Rue Taitbout—14."

It was after all this that M. de Villacourt had hurried away to Henri Mauperin's.

# XXXVI

When Denoisel entered the Mauperins' drawing-room that evening he found every one more gay and cheerful than usual. There was a look of happiness on all the faces; M. Mauperin's good-humour could be guessed by the mischievous twinkle in his eyes. Mme. Mauperin was most gracious, she positively beamed and looked blissfully happy. Renée was flitting about the room, and her quick, girlish movements were so bird-like that one could almost imagine the sound of a bird's wings.

"Why, here's Denoisel!" exclaimed M. Mauperin.

"Good-evening, m'sieu," said Renée, in a playful tone.

"You haven't brought Henri with you?" asked Mme. Mauperin.

"He couldn't come. He'll be here the day after to-morrow without fail."

"How nice of you! Oh, isn't he a good boy to have come this evening," said Renée, hovering round and trying to make him laugh as though he had been a child.

"Oh, he's a bad lot! Ah, my dear fellow—" and M. Mauperin shook hands and winked at his wife.

"Yes; just come here, Denoisel," said Mme. Mauperin. "Come and sit down and confess your sins. It appears that you were seen the other day in the Bois—driving——"

She stopped a minute like a cat when it is drinking milk.

"Ah, now your mother's wound up!" said M. Mauperin to Renée. "She's in very good spirits to-day—my wife is. I warn you, Denoisel."

Mme. Mauperin had lowered her voice. Leaning forward towards Denoisel she was telling him a very lively story. The others could only catch a word here and there between smothered bursts of laughter.

"Mamma, it's not allowed; that sort of thing—laughing all to yourselves. Give me back my Denoisel, or I'll tell stories like yours to papa."

"Oh, dear, wasn't it absurd!" said Mme. Mauperin, when she had finished her bit of gossip, laughing heartily as old ladies do over a spicy tale.

"How very lively you all are this evening!" exclaimed Denoisel, chilled by all this gaiety.

"Yes, we are as gay as Pinchon," said Renée, "that's how we all feel! And we shall be like this to-morrow, and the day after, and always; shall we not, papa?" and running across to her father she sat down on his knees like a child.

"My darling!" said M. Mauperin to his daughter. "Well, I never! Just look, my dear, do you remember? This was her knee when she was a little girl."

"Yes," said Mme. Mauperin, "and Henri had the other one."

"Yes, I can see them now," continued M. Mauperin; "Henri was the girl and you were the boy, Renée. Just to fancy that all that was fifteen years ago. It used to amuse you finely when I let you put your little hands on the scars that my wounds had left. What rascals of children they were! How they laughed!" Then turning to his wife he added, "What work you had with them, my dear. It doesn't matter though, Denoisel; it's a good thing to have a family. Instead of only having one heart, it's as though you have several—upon my word it is!"

"Ah, Denoisel, now that you are here, we shall not let you go again," said Renée. "Your room has been waiting for you long enough."

"I'm so sorry, Renée, but really I have some business to attend to this evening in Paris; I have, really."

"Oh, business! You? How important you must feel, to be sure!"

"Do stay, Denoisel," said M. Mauperin. "My wife has a whole collection of stories for you like the one she has just told you."

"Oh yes, do, will you?" pleaded Renée. "We'll have such fun; you'll see. I won't touch the piano at all, and I won't put too much vinegar in the salad. We'll make puns on everything. Come now, Denoisel."

"I accept your invitation for next week."

"Horrid thing!" and Renée turned her back on him.

"And Dardouillet," said Denoisel; "isn't he coming this evening?"

"Oh, he'll come later on," said Mauperin. "By-the-bye, it's just possible he won't come, though. He's very busy—in the very thick of marking out his land. I fancy he's just busy transporting his mountain into his lake and his lake on to the top of his mountain."

"Well, but what about this evening?"

"Oh, this evening—no one knows," said Renée. "He's full of mysteries, M. Dardouillet. But how queer you look to-day, Denoisel!"

"I do?"

"Yes, you; you don't seem at all frolicsome; there's no sparkle about you. What's been ruffling you?"

"Denoisel, there's something the matter," said Mme. Mauperin.

"Nothing whatever, madame," answered Denoisel. "What could be the matter with me? I'm not low-spirited in the least. I'm simply tired; I've had to rush about so much this last week for Henri. He would have my opinion about everything in connection with his furnishing."

"Ah yes," said Mme. Mauperin, her face lighting up with joy; "it's true, the twenty-second is getting near. Oh, if any one had told me this two years ago! I'm afraid I shall be too happy to live on that day. Just think of it, my dear," and she half closed her eyes and revelled in her dreams of the future.

"I shall be simply lovely for the occasion, I can tell you, Denoisel," said Renée. "I have had my dress tried on to-day, and it fits me to perfection. But, papa, what about a dress-coat?"

"My old dress-coat is quite new."

"Oh, but you must have one made, a newer one still, if I'm to take your arm. Oh, how silly I am; you won't take me in, of course. Denoisel, please keep a quadrille for me. We shall give a ball, of course, mamma?"

"A ball and everything that we can give," said Mme. Mauperin. "I expect people will think it is not quite the thing; but I can't help that. I want it to be very festive—as it was for our wedding, do you remember, my dear? We'll dance and eat and drink, and——"

"Yes, that's what we'll do," said Renée, "and we'll let all our work people drink till they are quite merry—Denoisel too. It will liven him up a little to have too much to drink."

"Well, with all this, I don't fancy Dardouillet's coming——"

"What in the world makes you so anxious to see Dardouillet, this evening?" asked M. Mauperin.

"Yes, that's true," put in Renée. "That hasn't been explained. Please explain, Denoisel."

"How inquisitive you are, Renée. It's just a bit of nonsense—nothing that matters. I want him to lend me his bulldog for a rat-fight at my club to-morrow. I've made a bet that he'll kill a hundred in two minutes. And with that I must depart. Good-night, all!"

"Good-night!"

"Then, my boy will be here the day after to-morrow, for sure?" said Mme. Mauperin at the door to Denoisel.

Denoisel nodded without answering.

# XXXVII

On arriving at Dardouillet's little house at the other end of the village, Denoisel rang the bell. An old woman opened the door.

"Has M. Dardouillet gone to bed?"

"Gone to bed? No, indeed! A nice life he leads!" answered the old servant; "he's pottering about in the garden; you'll find him there," and she opened the long window of the dining-room.

The bright moonlight fell on a garden absolutely bare, as square as a handkerchief, and with the soil all turned over like a field. In one corner, standing motionless and with folded arms, on a hillock, was a black figure which looked like a spectre in one of Biard's pictures. It was M. Dardouillet, and he was so deeply absorbed that he did not see his visitor until Denoisel was quite close to him.

"Ah, it's you, M. Denoisel? I'm delighted to see you. Just look now," and he pointed to the loose soil all round. "What do you think of that? Plenty of lines there, I hope; and it's all quite soft and loose, you know," and he put his hand out over the plan of his rising ground as though he were stroking the brow of his ideal hill.

"Excuse me, M. Dardouillet," said Denoisel. "I've come about an affair that——"

"Moonlight—remember that—if ever you have a garden—there's nothing like moonlight for seeing what you have done—exactly as it is. By daylight you can't see the embankments——"

"M. Dardouillet, I want to appeal to a man who has worn a soldier's uniform. You are a friend of the Mauperins. I have come to ask you if you will act for Henri as——"

"A duel?" And Dardouillet fastened up the black coat he wore, winter and summer alike, with all that was left of the button. "Good heavens! Yes, a service of that kind is a duty."

"I shall take you back with me, then," said Denoisel, putting his arm through Dardouillet's. "You can sleep at my place. It must be settled quickly. It will be all over to-morrow, or the day after at the latest."

"Good!" said Dardouillet, looking regretfully at a line of stakes that had been commenced, the shadows of which the moon threw on the ground.

# XXXVIII

On leaving Henri Mauperin's, M. de Villacourt had suddenly recollected that he had no friends, no one at all whom he could ask to serve as seconds. This had not occurred to him before. He remembered two or three names which had been mixed up in his father's family history, and he went along the streets trying to find the houses where he had been taken when he had come to Paris in his boyhood. He rang at several doors, but either the people were no longer living there or they were not at home to him.

At night he returned to his lodging-house. He had never before felt so absolutely alone in the world. When he was taking the key of his bed-room, the landlady asked him if he would not have a glass of beer and, opening a door in a passage, showed him into a café which took up the ground-floor of the house.

Some swords were hanging from the hat-pegs, with cocked hats over them. At the far end, through the tobacco smoke, he could see men dressed in military uniform moving about round a billiard-table. A sickly looking boy with a white apron on was running to and fro, scared and bewildered, giving the *Army Monitor* and the other papers a bath, each time that he put a glass or cup on the table.

Near the counter, a drum-major was playing at backgammon with the landlord of the café in his shirt-sleeves. On every side voices could be heard calling out and answering each other, with the rolling accent peculiar to soldiers.

"To-morrow I'm on duty at the theatre."

"I take my week."

"Gaberiau is beadle at Saint-Sulpice."

"He was proposed and was to be examined."

"Who's on service at the Bourdon ball?"

"What an idea! to blow his brains out when he hadn't a single punishment down on his book!"

It was very evident that they were the Paris Guards from the barracks, just near, waiting until nine o'clock for the roll-call.

"Waiter, a bowl of punch and three glasses," said M. de Villacourt, taking his place at a table where two of the Guards were seated.

When the punch was brought he filled the three glasses, pushed one before each of the Guards, and rose to his feet.

"Your health, gentlemen!" he said, and then lifting his glass he continued:

"You are military men—I have to fight to-morrow, and I haven't any one I can ask. I feel sure that you will act as seconds for me."

One of the Guards looked full at M. de Villacourt, and then turned to his comrade.

"We may as well, Gaillourdot; what do you say?"

The other did not reply, but picking up his glass touched M. de Villacourt's with it.

"Well then, to-morrow morning at ten o'clock. Room 27."

"Right!" answered the Guards.

The following morning, just as Denoisel was starting with Dardouillet to call on M. Boisjorand de Villacourt, his door-bell rang and the two Guards entered. As their mission was to accept everything, terms, weapons, and distances, the arrangements for the duel were soon made. Pistols were decided upon at a distance of thirty-five paces, both adversaries to be allowed to walk ten paces. Denoisel requested, in Henri's name, that the affair should be got over as quickly as possible. This was precisely what M. de Villacourt's seconds were about to ask, as they were supposed to be going to the theatre that evening, and were only free that day until midnight. A meeting was fixed for four o'clock at the Ville-d'Avray Lake. Denoisel next went to one of his friends who was a surgeon, and then to order a carriage for bringing home the wounded man. He called to see Henri, who was out; then went on to the shooting-gallery, where he found him, amusing himself with shooting at small bundles of matches hanging from a piece of string, at which he fired, setting the brimstone alight with the bullet.

"Oh, that's nothing!" he said to Denoisel; "I fancy those matches get set on fire with the wind from the bullet; but look here!" and he showed him a cardboard target, in the first ring of which he had just put a dozen bullets.

"It's to be to-day at four, as you wished," said Denoisel.

"Good!" said Henri, giving his pistol to the man. "Look here," he continued, putting his fingers over two holes on the cardboard which were rather far away from the others; "if it were not for these two flukes this would be fit to frame. Oh, I'm glad it's arranged for to-day." He lifted his arm with the gesture of a man accustomed to shooting and just about to take aim, and then shook his hand about to get the blood into it again.

"Only imagine," he continued, "that it had quite an effect on me—the idea of this affair—when I was in bed this morning. It's that deuced horizontal position; I don't fancy it's good for one's courage."

They all lunched together at Denoisel's and then proceeded to smoke. Henri was cheerful and communicative, talking all the time. The surgeon arrived at the hour appointed, and they all four got into the carriage and drove off.

They had been silent until they were about half way, when Henri suddenly threw his cigar out of the window impatiently.

"Give me a cigar, Denoisel, a good one. It's very important to have a good cigar when you are going to shoot, you know. If you are to shoot properly you mustn't be nervous; that's the principal thing. I took a bath this morning. One must keep calm. Now, driving is the most detestable thing; the reins saw your hand for you. I'd wager you couldn't shoot straight after driving; your fingers would be stiff. Novels are absurd with their duels, where the man arrives and flings his reins to his groom. What should you think if I told you that one ought to go in for a sort of training? It's quite true, though. I never knew such a good shot as an Englishman I once met; he goes to bed at eight o'clock; never drinks stimulants and takes a short walk every evening like my father does. Every time that I have driven in a carriage without springs to the shooting-gallery, my targets have shown it. By-the-bye, this is a very decent carriage, Denoisel. Well, with a cigar it's the same thing. Now a cigar that's difficult to smoke keeps you at work, you have to keep lifting your hand to your mouth, and that makes your hand unsteady; while a good cigar—you ask any good shot, and he'll tell you the same thing—it's soothing, it puts your nerves in order. There's nothing better than the gentle movement of the arm as you take the cigar out of your mouth and put it in again. It's slow and regular."

On arriving, they found M. de Villacourt and his seconds waiting between the two lakes. The ground was white with the snow that had fallen during the morning. In the woods the trees stretched their bare branches towards the sky, and in the distance the red sunset could be seen between the rows of dark trees. They walked as far as the Montalet road. The distances were measured, Denoisel's pistols loaded, and the opponents then took their places opposite each other. Two walking-sticks, laid on the snow, marked the limits of the ten paces they were each allowed. Denoisel walked with Henri to the place which had fallen to his lot, and as he was pushing down a corner of his collar for him which covered his necktie, Henri said in a low voice: "Thanks, old man; my heart's beating a trifle under my armpit, but you'll be satisfied——"

M. de Villacourt took off his frock-coat, tore off his necktie, and threw them both some distance from him. His shirt was open at the neck, showing his strong, broad, hairy chest. The opponents were armed, and the seconds moved back and stood together on one side.

"Ready!" cried a voice.

At this word M. de Villacourt moved forward almost in a straight line. Henri kept quite still and allowed him to walk five paces. At the sixth he fired.

M. de Villacourt fell to the ground, and the witnesses watched him lay down his pistol and press his thumbs with all his strength on the double hole which the bullet had made on entering his body.

"Ah! I'm not done for—Ready, monsieur!" he called out in a loud voice to Henri, who, thinking all was over, was moving away.

M. de Villacourt picked up his pistol and proceeded to do his four remaining paces as far as the walking-stick, dragging himself along on his hands and knees and leaving a track of blood on the snow behind him. On arriving at the stick he rested his elbow on the ground and took aim slowly and steadily.

"Fire! Fire!" called out Dardouillet.

Henri, standing still and covering his face with his pistol, was waiting. He was pale, and there was a proud, haughty look about him. The shot was fired; he staggered a second, then fell flat, with his face on the ground and with outstretched arms, his twitching fingers grasping for a moment at the snow.

# XXXIX

M. Mauperin had gone out into the garden as he usually did on coming down-stairs in the morning, when, to his surprise, he saw Denoisel advancing to meet him.

"You here, at this hour?" he said. "Why, where did you sleep?"

"M. Mauperin," said Denoisel, pressing his hand as he spoke.

"What is it? What's the matter?" asked M. Mauperin, feeling that something had happened.

"Henri is wounded."

"Dangerously? Is it a duel?"

Denoisel nodded.

"Wounded? Ah, he is dead!"

Denoisel took M. Mauperin's two hands in his for a second, without uttering a word.

"Dead!" repeated M. Mauperin mechanically, and he opened his hands as though something had slipped from their grasp. "His poor mother, Henri!" and the tears came with the words. "Oh, God—We don't know how much we love them till this comes—and only thirty years old!" He sank down on a garden-seat, choked with sobs.

"Where is he?" he asked at last.

"There," and Denoisel pointed to the window of Henri's room.

From Ville-d'Avray he had taken the corpse straight to M. Dardouillet's, and during the evening had found a pretext for sending for M. Bernard, who had a key of the Mauperins' house. In the middle of the night, while the family were asleep, the three men had taken off their shoes, carried Henri's dead body upstairs, and laid it on the bed in his own room.

"Thank you," said M. Mauperin, and making a sign to him that he could not talk he got up.

They walked round the garden four or five times in silence. The tears came every now and then into M. Mauperin's eyes, but they did not fall. Words, too, seemed to come to his lips and die away again. Finally, in a deep, crushed voice, breaking the long silence by a desperate effort, and not looking at Denoisel, M. Mauperin asked an abrupt question.

"Was it an honourable death?"

"He was your son," answered Denoisel.

The father lifted his head at these words, as if strength had come to him with which to fight against his grief. "Well, well; I must do my duty now. You have done your part," and he drew Denoisel nearer to him, his tears falling freely at last.

# XL

"Murder is the name for affairs of this kind," M. Barousse was saying to Denoisel as they followed the hearse to the cemetery. "Why didn't you arrange matters between them?"

"After that blow?"

"After or before," said M. Barousse, peremptorily.

"You'd better say that to his father!"

"He's a soldier—but you, hang it all—you've never served in the army, and you let him get killed! I consider you killed him."

"Look here, I've had enough, M. Barousse."

"You see, I reason things out; I've been a magistrate."—Barousse had been a judge on the Board of Trade.—"You have the law courts and you can demand justice. But duels are contrary to all laws, human or divine; remember that. Why, just fancy—a scoundrel comes and gives me a blow in the face; and he must needs kill me as well. Ah, I can promise you one thing: if ever I'm on a jury, and there's a case of a duel—well, I look upon it as murder. Duellists are assassins. In the first place it's a cowardly thing——"

"A cowardly thing that every one hasn't the courage to carry through, M. Barousse; it's like suicide."

"Ah, if you are going to uphold suicide," said Barousse, and leaving the discussion he continued in a softened tone: "Such a fine fellow too, poor Henri! And then Mauperin, and his wife, and his daughter—the whole family plunged into this grief. No, it makes me wild when I think of it. Why, I had known him all his life." Barousse pulled his watch half out of his waistcoat-pocket as he spoke. "There!" he said, breaking off suddenly; "I know it will be sold; I shall have missed *The Concert*, a superb proof, earlier than the one with the dedication."

Denoisel returned to Briche with M. Mauperin, who, on arriving, went straight upstairs to his wife. He found her in bed, with the blinds down and the curtains drawn, overwhelmed and crushed by her terrible sorrow.

Denoisel opened the drawing-room door and saw Renée, seated on an ottoman, sobbing, with her handkerchief up to her mouth.

"Renée," he said, going to her and taking her hands in his, "some one killed him——"

Renée looked at him and then lowered her eyes.

"That man would never have known; he never read anything and he did not see any one; he lived like a regular wolf; he didn't subscribe to the *Moniteur*, of course. Do you understand?"

"No," stammered Renée, trembling all over.

"Well, it must have been an enemy who sent the paper to that man. Ah, you can't understand such cowardly things; but that's how it all came about, though. One of his seconds showed me the paper with the paragraph marked — —"

Renée was standing up, her eyes wide open with terror; her lips moved and she opened her mouth to speak — to cry out: "I sent it!"

Then all at once she put her hand to her heart, as if she had just been wounded there, and fell down unconscious and rigid on the carpet.

# XLI

Denoisel came every day to Briche to inquire about Renée. When she was a little better, he was surprised that she did not ask for him. He had always been accustomed to seeing her when she was not well, even when she was lying down, as though he had been one of the family. And whenever she had been ill, he was always one of the first she had asked for. She expected him to entertain and amuse her, to enliven her during her convalescence and bring back her laughter. He was offended and kept away for a day or two, and then when he came again he still could not see her. One day he was told that she was too tired, another day that the Abbé Blampoix was talking to her. Finally, at the end of a week, he was allowed to see her.

He expected an effusive welcome, such as invalids give their friends when they see them again for the first time. He thought that after an illness she would, in her impulsive way, be almost ready to embrace him. Renée held out her hand to him and just let her fingers lie in his for a second; she said a few words such as she might have said to any one, and after about a quarter of an hour closed her eyes as though she were sleepy. This coldness, which he could not understand in the least, irritated Denoisel and made him feel bitter. He was deeply hurt and humiliated, as his affection for Renée was pure and sincere and of such long standing. He tried to imagine what she could possibly have against him, and wondered whether M. Barousse had been instilling his ideas into her. Was she blaming him, as a witness of the duel, for her brother's death? Just about this time one of his friends who had a yacht at Cannes invited him for a cruise in the Mediterranean, and he accepted the invitation and went away at once.

Renée was afraid of Denoisel. She only remembered the commencement of the attack that she had had in his presence, that terrible moment which had been followed by her fall and a fit of hysterics. She had had a sensation of being suffocated by her brother's blood, and she knew that a cry had come to her lips. She did not know whether she had spoken, whether her secret had escaped her while she was unconscious. Had she told Denoisel that she had killed Henri, that it was she who had sent that newspaper? Had she confessed her crime?

When Denoisel entered her room she imagined that he knew all. The embarrassment which he felt and which was the effect of her manner to him, his coldness, which was entirely due to her own, all this confirmed her in her idea, in her certainty that she had spoken and that it was a judge who was there with her.

Before Denoisel's visit was over, her mother got up to go out of the room a minute, but Renée clung to her with a look of terror and insisted on her staying. It occurred to her that she might defend herself by saying that it was a fatality; that by sending the newspaper she had only meant to make the man put in his claim; that she had wanted to prevent her brother from getting this name and to make him break off his engagement; but then she would have been obliged to say why she had wished to do this—why she had wished to ruin her brother's future and prevent him from becoming a rich man. She would have had to confess all; and the bare idea of defending herself in such a way, even in the eyes of the man she respected more than any other, horrified and disgusted her. It seemed to her that the least she could do would be to leave to the one she had killed his fair fame and the silence of death.

She breathed freely when she heard of Denoisel's departure, for it seemed to her, then, as though her secret were her own once more.

# XLII

Renée gradually recovered and in a few months' time seemed to be quite well again. All the outward appearances of health came back to her, and she had no suffering at all. She did not even feel anything of the disturbance which illness leaves in the organs it has touched and in the life it has just attacked.

All at once the trouble began again. When she went upstairs or walked uphill she suddenly felt suffocated. Palpitation became more frequent and more violent, and then just as suddenly all this would stop again, as it happens sometimes with these insidious diseases which at intervals seem to entirely forget their victims.

At the end of a few weeks the doctor from Saint-Denis, who was attending Renée, took M. Mauperin aside.

"I don't feel satisfied about your daughter," he said. "There is something not quite clear to me. I should like to have a consultation with a specialist. These heart affections are very treacherous sometimes."

"Yes, these heart affections—you are quite right," stammered M. Mauperin.

He could not find anything else to say. His former notions of medicine, the desperate doctrines of the old school, Corvisart, the epigraph in his famous book on the subject of heart affections: "*Hæret lateri lethalis arundo*"; all these things came suddenly back to his mind, clearly and distinctly. He could see the pages again of those books so full of terror.

"You see," the doctor went on, "the great danger of these diseases is that they are so often of long standing. People send for us when the disease has made great headway. There are symptoms that the patient has not even noticed. Your daughter must have been very impressionable always, from her very childhood, I should say; isn't that so? Torrents of tears for the least blame, her face on fire for nothing at all, and then her pulse beating a hundred a minute, a constant state of emotion with her, very excitable, tempers like convulsions, always slightly feverish. She would put a certain amount of passion into everything, I should say, into her friendship, her games, her likes and dislikes; am I not right? Oh yes, this is generally the way with children in whom this organ predominates and who have an unfortunate predisposition to hypertrophy. Tell me now, has she lately had any great emotion—any great grief?"

"Yes, oh yes; her brother's death."

"Her brother's death. Ah yes, there was that," said the doctor, not appearing to attach any great importance, nevertheless, to this information. "I meant to ask you, though, whether she had been crossed in love, for instance."

"She? Crossed in love? Oh, good heavens!" and M. Mauperin shrugged his shoulders, and half joining his hands looked up in the air.

"Well, I'm only asking you that for the sake of having my conscience clear. Accidents of this kind only develop the germ that is already there and hasten on the disease. The physical influence of the passions on the heart is a theory—It has been studied a great deal the last twenty years; and quite right, too, in my opinion. The thesis that the heart is lacerated in a burst of temper, in any great moral——"

M. Mauperin interrupted him:

"Then, a consultation—you fancy—you think—don't you?"

"Yes, M. Mauperin, that will be quite the best thing. You see, it will be more satisfactory for every one; for you, and for me. We should call in M. Bouillaud, I suppose. He is considered the first authority."

"Yes—M. Bouillaud," repeated M. Mauperin, mechanically nodding his head in assent.

# XLIII

It was just five minutes past twelve, and M. Mauperin was seated by Renée's bed, holding her two hands in his. Renée glanced at the time-piece.

"He'll be here soon," said M. Mauperin.

Renée answered by closing her eye-lids gently, and her breathing and the beating of her heart could be heard like the ticking of a watch in the silence of the room at night.

Suddenly a peal of the door-bell rang out, clearly and imperiously, vibrating through the house. It seemed to M. Mauperin as though it had been rung within him, and a shudder passed through him to his very finger-tips like a needle-prick. He went to the door and opened it.

"It is some one who rang by mistake, sir," said the servant-man.

"It's very warm," said M. Mauperin to his daughter as he took his seat again, looking very pale.

Five minutes later the servant knocked. The doctor was waiting in the drawing-room.

"Ah!" said M. Mauperin, getting up once more.

"Go to him," murmured Renée, and then calling him back, she asked, looking alarmed: "Is he going to examine me?"

"I don't know; I don't think so. There'll be no need, perhaps," answered M. Mauperin, playing with the knob of the door.

M. Mauperin had fetched the doctor and left him with his daughter. He was in the drawing-room waiting the result. He had walked up and down, taken a seat, and gazed mechanically at a flower on the carpet, and had then gone to the window and was tapping with his fingers on the pane.

It seemed to him as though everything within himself and all round had suddenly stopped. He did not know whether he had been there an hour or a minute. It was one of those moments in life for him, the measure and duration of which cannot be calculated. He felt as though he were living again through his whole existence, and as though all the emotions of a lifetime were crowded into a moment that was eternal.

He turned dizzy, like a man in a dream falling from a height and enduring the anguish of falling. All kinds of indistinct ideas, of confused anxieties and vague terrors, seemed to rise from the pit of his stomach and buzz round his temples.

Yesterday, to-day, to-morrow, the doctor, his daughter, her illness, all this whirled round in his head, perplexing him, mingled as it all was with a physical sensation of uneasiness, anxiety, fear, and dread. Then all at once one idea became distinct. He had one of those clear visions that cross the mind at such times. He saw the doctor with his ear pressed against his daughter's back and he listened with him. He thought he heard the bed creak as it does when any one turns on it. It was over, they would be coming now; but no one came. He began pacing up and down again, as he could not keep still. He grew irritable with impatience and thought the doctor was a very long time, but the next minute he said to himself that it was a good sign, that a great specialist would not relish wasting his time, and that if there had been nothing he could do, he would already have been back. Fresh hope came to him with this thought: his daughter was saved; when the doctor came in he should see by his face that his daughter was saved. He watched the door, but no one came. Then he began to say to himself that they would have to take precautions, that perhaps she would always be delicate, that there were plenty of people who went on living in spite of palpitation of the heart. Then the word, the terrible word, *death*, came to him and haunted him. He tried to drive it away by thinking over and over again the same thoughts about convalescence, getting well, and good health. He went over in his mind all the persons he had known, who had been ill a long time, and who were not dead. And yet in spite of all his efforts the same question kept coming back to him: "What would the doctor tell him?"

He repeated this over and over again to himself. It seemed to him as though this visit were never going to finish and never would finish. And then at times he would shudder at the idea of seeing the door open. He would have liked to remain as he was forever, and *never* know. Finally hope came back to him once more, just as the door opened.

"Well?" said M. Mauperin to the doctor as he entered the room.

"You must be brave," said the doctor.

M. Mauperin looked up, glanced at the doctor, moved his lips without uttering a word—his mouth was dry and parched.

The doctor began to explain in full his daughter's disease, its gravity, the complications that were to be feared: he then wrote out a long prescription, saying to M. Mauperin at each item:

"You understand?"

"Perfectly!" answered M. Mauperin, looking stupefied.

"Ah, my dear little girl, you are going to get well!"

These were M. Mauperin's words to his daughter when he went back to her room.

"Really?" she asked.

"Kiss me."

"What did he tell you?"

"Well, you need only look at my face to know what he said," answered M. Mauperin, smiling at her. He felt as though it would kill him, though, that smile; and turning away under the pretence of looking for his hat, he continued, "I must go to Paris to get the prescription made up."

# XLIV

At the railway station M. Mauperin saw the doctor getting into the train. He got into another compartment, as he did not feel as though he had the strength to speak to him or even look at him.

On arriving in Paris he went to a chemist's and was told that it would take three hours to make up the prescription. "Three hours!" he exclaimed, but at heart he was glad that it would be so long. It would give him some time before returning to the house. When once he was in the street he walked fast. He had no consecutive ideas, but a sort of heavy, ceaseless throbbing in his head like the throb of neuralgia. His sensations were blunted, as though he were in a stupor. He saw nothing but the legs of people walking and the wheels of the carriages turning round. His head felt heavy and at the same time empty. As he saw other people walking, he walked too. The passers-by appeared to be taking him with them, and the crowd to be carrying him along in its stream. Everything looked faint, indistinct, and of a neutral tint, as things do the day after any wild excitement or intoxication. The light and noise of the streets he seemed to see and hear in a dream. He would not have known there was any sun if it had not been for the white trousers the policemen were wearing, which had caught his eye several times.

It was all the same to him whether he went to the right or left. He neither wanted anything nor had he the energy to do anything. He was surprised to see the movement around him—people who were hurrying along, walking quickly, on their way to something. He had had neither aim nor object in life for the last few hours. It seemed to him as though the world had come to an end, as though he were a dead man in the midst of the life and activity of Paris. He tried to think of anything in all that might happen to a man capable of moving him, of touching him in any way, and he could not conceive of anything which could reach to the depths of his despair.

Sometimes, as though he were answering inquiries about his daughter, he would say aloud, "Oh, yes, she is very ill!" and it was as though the words he had uttered had been said by some one else at his side. Often a work-girl without any hat, a pretty young girl with a round waist, gay and healthy with the rude health of her class, would pass by him. He would cross the street that he might not see her again. He was furious just for a minute with all these people who passed him, with all these useless lives. They were not beloved as his daughter was, and there was no need for them to go on living. He went into one of the public gardens and sat down. A child put some of its little sand-pies on to the tails of his coat; other children getting bolder approached him with all the daring of sparrows. Presently, feeling slightly embarrassed, they left their little spades, stopped playing and stood round, looking shyly and sympathetically, like so many men and women in miniature, at this tall gentleman who was so sad. M. Mauperin rose and left the garden.

His tongue was furred and his throat dry. He went into a café, and opposite him was a little girl wearing a white jacket and a straw hat. Her frock was short, showing her little firm, bare legs with their white socks. She was moving about all the time, climbing and jumping on to her father and standing straight up on his knees. She had a little cross round her neck. Every few minutes her father begged her to keep still.

M. Mauperin closed his eyes; he could see his own little daughter just as she had been at six years old. Presently he opened a review, *The Illustration*, and bent over it, trying to make himself look at the pictures, and when he reached the last page he set himself to find out one of the enigmas.

When M. Mauperin lifted his head again he wiped his face with his handkerchief. He had made out the enigma: *"Against death there is no appeal."*

# XLV

The terrible existence of those who have given up hope, and who can only wait, now commenced for M. Mauperin; that life of anguish, fear and trembling, of despair and of constant shocks, when every one is listening and on the watch for death; that life when one is afraid of any noise in the house, and just as afraid of silence, afraid of every movement in the next room, afraid of the sound of voices drawing near, afraid to hear a door close, and afraid of seeing the face of the person who opens the door when one enters the house, and of whom one asks without speaking if the beloved one still lives.

As people frequently do when nursing their sick friends, he began to reproach himself bitterly. He made his sorrow still harder to bear by making himself believe that it was partly his own fault, that everything had not been done which ought to have been, that she might have been saved if only there had been a consultation earlier, if at a certain time, a certain month or day, he had only thought of something or other.

At night his restlessness in bed seemed to make his grief more wild and feverish. In the solitude, the darkness, and the silence, one thought, one vision, was with him all the time—his daughter, always his daughter. His anxiety worked on his imagination, his dread increased, and his wakefulness had all the intensity of the terrible sensation of nightmare. In the morning he was afraid to wake up, and just as a man, when half-awake, will instinctively turn over from the light, so he would do his utmost to fall asleep again, to drive away his first thoughts, not to remember anything and so escape for a moment longer from the full consciousness of the present.

Then the day came again with all its torments, and the father was obliged to control his feelings, to conquer himself, to be gay and cheerful, to reply to the smiles of the suffering girl, to answer her pitiful attempts to be gay, and to keep up her feeble illusions, her clinging to the future, with some of those heart-rending words of comfort with which dying people will delude themselves, asking as they so often do for hope from those who are with them.

She would say to him, sometimes, in that feeble, soft whisper peculiar to invalids and which dies away to a whisper, "How nice it would be to have no pain! I can tell you, I shall enjoy life as soon as I get quite well."

"Yes, indeed," he would answer, choking down his tears.

# XLVI

Sick people are apt to believe that there are places where they would be better, countries which would cure them. There are certain spots and memories which come back to their mind and seem to fascinate them as an exile is fascinated by his native land, and which lull them as a child is lulled to rest in its cradle. Just as a child's fears are calmed in the arms of its nurse, so their hopes fly to a country, a garden, or a village where they were born and where surely they could not die.

Renée began to think of Morimond. She kept saying to herself that if she were once there she should get well. She felt sure, quite sure of it. This Briche house had brought her bad luck. She had been so happy at Morimond! And with this longing for change, the wish to move about which invalids get, this fancy of hers grew, and became more and more persistent. She spoke of it to her father and worried him about it. It would not make any difference to any one, she pleaded, the refinery would go along by itself, and M. Bernard, his manager, was trustworthy and would see to everything, and then they could come back in the autumn.

"When shall we start, father dear?" she kept saying, getting more and more impatient every day.

M. Mauperin gave in at last. His daughter promised him so faithfully that she would get well at Morimond that he began to believe it himself. He imagined that this sick fancy was an inspiration.

"Yes, the country will perhaps do her good," said the doctor, accustomed to these whims of dying people, who fancy that by going farther away they will succeed in throwing death off their track.

M. Mauperin promptly arranged his business matters, and the family started for Morimond.

The pleasure of setting off, the excitement of the journey, the nervous force that all this gives even to people who have no strength at all, the breeze coming in by the open window of the railway carriage kept the invalid up as far as Chaumont. She reached there without being overfatigued. M. Mauperin let her rest a day, and the following morning hired the best carriage he could get in the town and they all set out once more for Morimond. The road was bad and the journey was disagreeable and long. It began to get warm at nine o'clock, and by eleven the sun scorched the leather of the carriage. The horses breathed hard, perspired, and went along with difficulty. Mme. Mauperin was leaning back against the front cushion and dozing. M. Mauperin, seated next his daughter, held a pillow at her back, against which she fell after every little jolt. Every now and then she asked the time, and when she was told she would murmur, "No later than that!"

Towards three o'clock they were getting quite near their destination; the sky was cloudy, there was less dust, and it was cooler altogether. A water-wagtail began to fly in front of the carriage about thirty paces at a time, rising from the little heaps of stones. There were elm-trees all along the road and some of the fields were fenced round. Renée seemed to revive as one does in one's natal air. She sat up and, leaning against the door with her chin on her hand as children do when in a carriage, she looked out at everything. It was as though she were breathing in all she saw. As the carriage rolled along, she said:

"Ah, the big poplar-tree at the Hermitage is broken. The little boys used to fish for leeches in this pool—oh, there are M. Richet's rooks!"

In the little wood near the village her father had to get out and pluck a flower for her, which he could not see and which she pointed out to him growing on the edge of the ditch.

The carriage passed by the little inn, the first houses, the grocer's, the blacksmith's, the large walnut-tree, the church, the watchmaker's, who was also a dealer in curiosities, and the Pigeau farm. The villagers were out in the fields. Some children who were tormenting a wet cat stopped to see the carriage drive past. An old man, seated on a bench in front of his cottage door, with a woollen shawl wrapped round him and shivering in spite of the sun, lifted his cap. Then the horses stopped, the carriage door was opened, and a man who was waiting in front of the lodge lifted Mlle. Mauperin up in his arms.

"Oh, our poor young lady; she's no heavier than a feather!" he said.

"How do you do, Chrétiennot—how do you do, comrade?" said M. Mauperin, shaking hands with the old gardener, who had served under him in his regiment.

# XLVII

The next day and the days which followed, Renée had the most delicious waking moments, when the light which was just breaking, the morning of the earth and sky, mingled—in the dawn of her thoughts—with the morning of her life. Her first memories came back to her with the first songs outdoors. The young birds woke up in their nests, awakening her childhood.

Supported and indeed almost carried by her father, she insisted on seeing everything again—the garden, the fruit-trees on the walls, the meadow in front of the house, the shady canals, the pool with its wide sheet of still water. She remembered all the trees and the garden paths again, and they seemed to her like the things one gradually recalls of a dream. Her feet found the way along paths which she used to know and which were now grown over with trees. The ruins seemed as many years older to her as she was older since she had last seen them. She remembered certain places on the grass where she had seen the shadow of her frock when as a child she had been running there. She found the spot where she had buried a little dog. It was a white one, named *Nicolas Bijou*. She had loved it dearly, and she could remember her father carrying it about in the kitchen garden after it had been washed.

There were hundreds of souvenirs, too, for her in the house. Certain corners in the rooms had the same effect on her as toys that have been stored away in a garret, and that one comes across years after. She loved to hear the sound of the mournful old weather-cock on the house-top, which had always soothed her fears and lulled her to sleep as a child.

She appeared to rouse up and to revive. The change, her natal air, and these souvenirs seemed to do her good. This improvement lasted some weeks.

One morning, her father, who was with her in the garden, was watching her. She was amusing herself with cutting away the old roses in a clump of white rose-bushes. The sunshine made its way through the straw of her large hat, and the brilliancy of the light and the softness of the shade rested on her thin little face. She moved about gaily and briskly from one rose-tree to another, and the thorns caught hold of her dress as though they wanted to play with her. At every clip of her scissors, from a branch covered with small, open roses, with pink hearts all full of life, there fell a dead earth-coloured rose which looked to M. Mauperin like the corpse of a flower.

All at once, leaving everything, Renée flung herself into her father's arms.

"Oh, papa, how I do love you!" she said, bursting into tears.

# XLVIII

From that day the improvement began to disappear again. She gradually lost the healthy colour which life's last kiss had brought to her cheeks. She no longer had that delightful restlessness of the convalescent, that longing to move about which only a short time ago had made her take her father's arm constantly for a stroll. No more gay words sprang from her mind to her lips, as they had done at first when she had forgotten for a time all suffering; there was no more of the happy prattle which had been the result of returning hope. She was too languid to talk or even to answer questions.

"No, there's nothing the matter with me—I am all right;" but the words fell from her lips with an accent of pain, sadness, and resignation.

She suffered from tightness of breath now, and constantly felt a weight on her chest, which her respiration had difficulty in lifting. A sort of constraint and vague discomfort, caused by this, made itself felt throughout her whole system, attacking her nerves, taking from her all vital energy and all inclination to move about, keeping her crushed and submissive, without any strength to fight against it or to do anything.

Her father persuaded her to try the effect of a cupping-glass.

# XLIX

She took off her shawl in that slow way peculiar to invalids, so slow that it seems painful. Her trembling fingers felt about for the buttons that she had to unfasten, her mother helped her to take off the flannel and cotton-wool in which she was wrapped, leaving her poor thin neck and arms bare.

She looked at her father, at the lighted candle, the twisted paper and the wine-glasses, with that dread that one feels on seeing the hot irons or fire being prepared for torturing one's flesh.

"Am I right like this?" she asked, trying to smile.

"No, you want to be in this position," answered M. Mauperin, showing her how to sit.

She turned round on her arm-chair, put her two hands on the back of it and her cheek down on her hand, pulled her legs up, crossed her feet, and, half-kneeling and half-crouching, only showed the profile of her frightened face and her bare shoulders. She looked ready for the coffin with her bony angles. Her hair, which was very loose, glided with the shadow down the hollow of her back. Her shoulder-blades projected, the joints of her spine could be counted, and the point of a poor thin little elbow appeared through the sleeves of her under-linen, which had fallen to the bend of her arm.

"Well, father?"

He was standing there, riveted to the spot, and he did not even know of what he was thinking. At the sound of his daughter's voice he picked up a glass, which he remembered belonged to a set he had bought for a dinner-party in honour of Renée's baptism. He lighted a piece of paper, threw it into the glass, and closed his eyes as he turned the glass over. Renée gave a little hiss of pain, a shudder ran through all the bones down her back, and then she said:

"Oh, well; I thought it would hurt me much more than that."

M. Mauperin took his hand from the glass and it fell to the ground; the cupping had not succeeded.

"Give me another," he said to his wife.

Mme. Mauperin handed it to him in a leisurely way.

"Give it me," he said, almost snatching it from her. His forehead was wet with perspiration, but he no longer trembled. This time the vacuum was made: the skin puckered up all round the glass and rose inside as though it were being drawn by the scrap of blackened paper.

"Oh, father! don't bear on so," said Renée, who had been holding her lips tightly together; "take your hand off."

"Why, I'm not touching it—look," said M. Mauperin, showing her his hands.

Renée's delicate white skin rose higher and higher in the glass, turning red, patchy, and violet. When once the cupping was done the glass had to be taken away again, the skin drawn to the edge on one side of the glass, and then the glass swayed backward and forward from the other side. M. Mauperin was obliged to begin again, two or three times over, and to press firmly on the skin, near as it was to the bones.

# L

Disease does its work silently and makes secret ravages in the constitution. Then come those terrible outward changes which gradually destroy the beauty, efface the personality, and, with the first touches of death, transform those we love into living corpses.

Every day M. Mauperin sought for something in his daughter which he could not find—something which was no longer there. Her eyes, her smile, her gestures, her footstep, her very dress which used proudly to tell of her twenty years, the girlish vivacity which seemed to hover round her and light on others as it passed— everything about her was changing and life itself gradually leaving her. She no longer seemed to animate all that she touched. Her clothes fell loosely round her in folds as they do on old people. Her step dragged along, and the sound of her little heels was no longer heard. When she put her arms round her father's neck, she joined her hands awkwardly, her caresses had lost their pretty gracefulness. All her gestures were stiff, she moved about like a person who feels cold or who is afraid of taking up too much space. Her arms, which were generally hanging down, now looked like the wet wings of a bird. She scarcely even resembled her old self. And when she was walking in front of her father, with her bent back, her shrunken figure, her arms hanging loosely at her sides, and her dress almost falling off her, it seemed to M. Mauperin that this could not be his daughter, and as he looked at her he thought of the Renée of former days.

There was a shadow round her mouth that seemed to go inside when she smiled. The beauty spot on her hand, just by her little finger, had grown larger, and was as black as though mortification had set in.

# LI

"Mother, it's Henri's birthday to-day."

"Yes, I know," said Mme. Mauperin without moving.

"Suppose we were to go to church?"

Mme. Mauperin rose and went out of the room, returning very soon with her bonnet and cape on. Half an hour later M. Mauperin was helping his daughter out of the carriage at the Maricourt church-door. Renée went to the little side-chapel, where the marble altar stood on which was the little miraculous black wooden Virgin to which she had prayed with great awe as a child. She sat down on a bench which was always there and murmured a prayer. Her mother stood near her, looking at the church and not praying at all. Renée then got up and, without taking her father's arm, walked with a step that scarcely faltered right through the church to a little side door leading into the cemetery.

"I wanted to see whether *that* was still there," she said to her father, pointing to an old bouquet of artificial flowers among the crosses and wreaths which were hung on the tomb.

"Come, my child," said M. Mauperin; "don't stand too long. Let us go home again now."

"Oh, there's plenty of time."

There was a stone seat under the porch with a ray of sunshine falling on it.

"It's warm here," she said, laying her hand on the stone. "Put my shawl there so that I can sit down a little. I shall have the sun on my back—there."

"It isn't wise," said M. Mauperin.

"Oh, just to make me happy." When she was seated and leaning against him, she murmured in a voice as soft as a sigh, "How gay it is here."

The lime-trees, buzzing with bees, were stirring gently in the faint wind. A few fowl in the thick grass were running about, pecking and looking for food. At the foot of a wall, by the side of a plough and cart, the wheels of which were white with dry mud, on the stumps of some old trees with the bark peeled off, some little chickens were frolicking about, and some ducks were asleep, looking like balls of feathers. There seemed to be a murmur of hushed voices from the church, and the light played on the blue of the stained-glass windows. Flights of pigeons kept starting up and taking refuge in the niches of sculpture and in the holes between the old grey stones. The river could be seen and its splashing sound heard; a wild white colt bounded along to the water's edge.

"Ah!" said Renée after a few moments, "we ought to have been made of something else. Why did God make us of flesh and blood? It's frightful!"

Her eyes had fallen on some soil turned up in a corner of the cemetery, half hidden by two barrel-hoops crossed over each other and up which wild convolvulus was growing.

# LII

Renée's complaint did not make her cross and capricious, nor did it cause her any of that nervous irritability so common to invalids, and which makes those who are nursing them share their suffering morally. She gave herself entirely up to her fate. Her life was ebbing away without any apparent effort on her part to hold it back or to stop it in its course. She was still affectionate and gentle. Her wishes had none of the unreasonableness of dying fancies. The darkness which was gathering round her brought peace with it. She did not fight against death, but let it come like a beautiful night closing over her white soul.

There were times, however, when Nature asserted itself within her, when her mind faltered from sheer bodily weakness, and when she listened to the stealthy progress of the disease which was gradually detaching her from her hold on life. At such times she would maintain a profound silence and would be terribly calm, remaining for a long time mute and motionless almost like a dead person. She would pass half the day in this way without even hearing the clock strike, gazing before her just beyond her feet with a steady, fixed gaze and seeing nothing at all. Her father could not even catch the expression of her eyes at such times. Her long lashes would quiver two or three times, and she would hide her eyes by letting the lids droop over them, and it seemed to him then as though she were asleep with her eyes half open. He would talk to her, search his brains for something that might interest her, and endeavour to make jokes, so that she should hear him and feel that he was there; but in the middle of his sentence his daughter's attention, her thoughts, and her intelligent look would leave him. He no longer felt the same warmth in her affection, and when he was with her he himself felt chilled now. It seemed as if disease were robbing him day by day of a little more of his daughter's heart.

# LIII

Sometimes, too, Renée would let a few words slip, showing that she was mourning her fate as sick people do, words which sink to the heart and give one a chill like death itself.

One day her father was reading the newspaper to her; she took it from him to look at the marriage announcements.

"Twenty-nine! How old she was, wasn't she?" she said, as though speaking to herself. She had been glancing down the death column. M. Mauperin did not answer; he paced up and down the room for a few minutes and then went away.

When Renée was alone she got up to close the door, which her father had not pulled to, and which kept banging. She fancied she heard a groan in the corridor and looked, but there was no one there; she listened a minute; but as everything was silent again she was just going to close the door, when she thought she heard the same sound again. She went out into the corridor as far as her father's room. It was from there that it came. The key was not in the lock, and Renée stooped down and, through the keyhole, saw her father, who had flung himself on his bed, weeping bitterly and shaken with sobs. His head was buried in the pillow, and he was endeavouring to stifle down his tears and his despair.

# LIV

Renée was determined that her father should weep no more on her account.

"Listen to me, papa," she said, the following morning. "We are going to leave here at the end of September; that's settled, isn't it? We are going everywhere, a month to one place and a fortnight to another—just as we fancy. Well, *I* want you to take me now to all the places where you fought. Do you know, I've heard that you fell in love with a princess? Suppose we were to come across her again, what should you say to that? Wasn't it at Pordenone that you got those great scars?" And, taking her father's face in her two hands, she pressed her lips to the white, hollow places which had been marked by the finger of Glory.

"I want you to tell me all about everything," she continued; "it will be ever so nice to go all through your campaigns again with your daughter. If one winter will not be enough for it all, why, we'll just take two. And when I'm quite myself again—we are quite rich enough surely, Henriette and I; you've worked hard enough for us—well, we'll just sell the refinery, and we'll all come here. We'll go to Paris for two months of the year to enjoy ourselves; that will be quite enough, won't it? Then as you always like to have something to do, you can take your farm again from Têtevuide's son-in-law. We'll have some cows and a nice farm-yard for mamma—do you hear, mamma? I shall be outdoors all day; and the end of it will be that I shall get *too* well—you'll see. And then we'll have people to visit us all the time. In the country we can allow ourselves that little luxury—that won't ruin us—and we shall be as happy, as happy—you'll see."

Travelling and plans of all kinds—she talked of nothing but the future now. She spoke of it as of a promised thing, a certainty. It was she, now, who made every one hopeful, and she concealed the fact that she was dying so skilfully and pretended so well that she wanted to live, that M. Mauperin on seeing her and listening to her dreams, gave himself up to dreaming with her of years which they had before them and which would be full of peace, tranquility, and happiness. Sometimes, even, the illusions that the invalid had invented herself dazzled her too, for an instant, and she would begin to believe in her own fiction, forget herself for a moment and, quite deceived like the others, she would say to herself, "Suppose, after all, that I should get well!" At other times she would delight in going back to the past. She would tell about things that had happened, about her own feelings, funny incidents that she remembered, or she would talk about her childish pleasures. It was as though she had risen from her death-bed to embrace her father for the last time with all she could muster of her youth.

"Oh, my first ball-dress," she said to him one day; "I can see it now—it was a pink tulle one. The dressmaker didn't bring it—- it was raining—and we couldn't get a cab. How you did hurry along! And how queer you looked when you came back carrying a cardboard box! And you were so wet when you kissed me! I remember it all so well."

Renée had only herself and her own courage to depend on, in her task of keeping her father up and herself too. Her mother was there, of course; but ever since Henri's death she had been buried in a sort of silent apathy. She was indifferent to all that went on, mute and absent-minded. She was there with her daughter, night and day, without a murmur, patient and always even-tempered, ready to do anything, as docile and humble as a servant, but her affection seemed almost mechanical. The soul had gone out of her caresses, and all her ministrations were for the body rather than the heart; there was nothing of the mother about her now except the hands.

# LV

Renée could still drag along with her father to the first trees of the little wood near the house. She would then sink down with her back against the moss of an oak-tree on the boundary of the wood. The smell of hay from the fields, an odour of grass and honey came to her there with a delicious warmth from the sunshine, the fresh air from the wood, damp from the cool springs and the unmade paths.

In the midst of the deep silence, an immense, indistinct rustling could be heard, and a hum and buzz of winged creatures, which filled the air with a ceaseless sound like that of a bee-hive and the infinite murmur of the sea. All around Renée, and near to her, there seemed to be a great living peace, in which everything was being swayed—the gnat in the air, the leaf on the branch, the shadows on the bark of the trees, the tops of the trees against the sky, and the wild oats on each side of the paths. Then from this murmur came the sighing sound of a deep respiration, a breeze coming from afar which made the trees tremble as it passed them, while the blue of the heavenly vault above the shaking leaves seemed fixed and immovable. The boughs swayed slowly up and down, a breath passed over Renée's temples and touched her neck, a puff of wind kissed and cheered her. Gradually she began to lose all consciousness of her physical being, the sensation and fatigue of living; an exquisite languor took possession of her, and it seemed to her as though she were partially freed from her material body and were just ready to pass away in the divine sweetness of all these things. Every now and then she nestled closer to her father like a child who is afraid of being carried away by a gust of wind.

There was a stone bench covered with moss in the garden. After dinner, towards seven o'clock, Renée liked to sit there; she would put her feet up, leaning her head against the back of the seat, and with a trail of convolvulus tickling her ear she would stay there, looking up at the sky. It was just at the time of those beautiful summer days which fade away in silvery evenings. Imperceptibly her eyes and her thoughts were fascinated by the infinite whiteness of the sky, just ready to die away. As she watched she seemed to see more brilliancy and light coming from this closing day, a more dazzling brightness and serenity seemed to fall upon her. Gradually some great depths opened in the heavens, and she fancied she could see millions of little starry flames as pale as the light of tapers, trembling with the night breeze. And then, from time to time, weary of gazing into that dazzling brightness which kept receding, blinded by those myriads of suns, she would close her eyes for an instant as though shrinking from that gulf which was hanging over her and drawing her up above.

# LVI

"Mother," she said, "don't you see how nice I look? Just see all the trouble I've taken for you;" and joining her hands over her head, her dress loose at the waist, she sank down on the pillows full length on the sofa in a careless, languid attitude which was both graceful and sad to see. Renée thought that the bed and the white sheets made her look ill. She would not stay there, and gathered together all her remaining strength to get up. She dressed slowly and heroically towards eleven o'clock, taking a long time over it, stopping to get breath, resting her arms over and over again, after holding them up to do her hair. She had thrown a fichu of point-lace over her head, and was wearing a dressing-gown of starched white piqué, with plenty of material in it, falling in wide pleats. Her small feet were incased in low shoes, and instead of rosettes she wore two little bunches of violets which Chrétiennot brought her every morning. In order to look more alive, as invalids do when they are up and dressed, she would stay there all day in this white girlish toilette fragrant with violets.

"Oh, how odd it is when one is ill!" she said, looking down at herself and then all round the room. "I don't like anything that is not pretty now, just fancy! I couldn't wear anything ugly. Do you know I've thought of something I want. You remember the little silver-mounted jug—so pretty it was—we saw it in a jeweller's shop in the Rue Saint Honoré when we had just gone out of the theatre for the interval. If it isn't sold—if he still has it, you might let him send it. Oh, I know I'm getting the most ruinous tastes—I warn you of that. I want to arrange things here. I'm getting very difficult to please; in everything I have the most luxurious ideas. I used not to be at all elegant in my tastes; and now I have eyes for everything I wear, and for everything all round me—oh, such eyes! There are certain colours that positively pain me—just fancy—and others that I had never noticed before. It is being ill that makes me like this—it must be that. It's so ugly to be ill; and so it makes you like everything that is beautiful all the more."

With all this coquetry which the approach of death had brought to her, these fancies and caprices, these little delicacies and elegancies, other senses too seemed to come to Renée. She was becoming, and she felt herself becoming, more of a woman. Under all the languor and indolence caused by illness, her disposition, which had always been affectionate but somewhat masculine and violent, grew gentler, more unbending, and more calm. Gradually the ways, tastes, inclinations, and ideas—all the signs of her sex, in fact—made their appearance to her. Her mind seemed to undergo the same transformation. She gave up her impetuous way of criticising and her daring speech. Occasionally she would use one of her old expressions, and then she would say, smiling, "That is a bit of the old Renée come back." She remembered speeches she had made, bold things she had done, and her familiar manner with young men; she would no longer dare to act and speak as in those old days. She was surprised, and did not know herself in her new character. She had given up reading serious or amusing books; she only cared now for works which set her thinking, books with ideas. When her father talked to her about hunting and the meets to which she had been and of those in store for her, it gave her the sensation of being about to fall, and the very idea of mounting a horse frightened her. All the emotions and weaknesses that she felt were quite new to her. Flowers about which she had never troubled much were now as dear to her as persons. She had never liked needlework, and now that she had started to embroider a skirt, she enjoyed doing it. She quite roused up and lived over again in the memories of her early girlhood. She thought of the children with whom she used to play, of the friends she had had, of different places to which she had been, and of the faces of the girls in the same row with her at her confirmation.

# LVII

As she was looking out of the window one day, she saw a woman sit down in the dust in the middle of the village street, between a stone and a wheel-rut, and unswathe her little baby. The child lay face downward, the upper part of its body in the shade, moving its little legs, crossing its feet, and kicking about, and the sun caressed it lovingly as it does the bare limbs of a child. A few rays that played over it seemed to strew on its little feet some of the rose petals of a Fête-Dieu procession. When the mother and child had gone away Renée still went on gazing out of the window.

# LVIII

"You see," she said to her father, "I never could fall in love; you made me too hard to please. I always knew beforehand that no one could ever love me as you did. I saw so many things come into your face when I was there, such happiness! And when we went anywhere together, weren't you proud of me! Oh! weren't you just proud to have me leaning on your arm! It would have been all no good for any one else to have loved me; I should never have found any one like my own father; you spoiled me too much."

"But all that won't prevent my dear little girl one of these fine days, when she gets well, finding a handsome young man— —"

"Oh, your handsome young man is a long way off yet," said Renée, a smile lighting up her eyes. "It seems strange to you," she went on, "doesn't it, that I have never seemed anxious to marry. Well, I tell you, it is your own fault. Oh, I'm not sorry in the least. What more did I want? Why, I had everything; I could not imagine any other happiness. I never even thought of such a thing. I didn't want any change. I was so well off. What *could* I have had, now, more than I already had? My life was so happy with you; and I was so contented. Yes," she went on, after a minute's silence, "if I had been like so many girls, if I had had parents who were cold and a father not at all like you; oh yes, I should certainly have done as other girls do, I should have wanted to be loved, I should have thought about marriage as they do. Then, too, I may as well tell you all, I should have had hard work to fall in love; it was never much in my way, all that sort of thing, and it always made me laugh. Do you remember before Henriette's marriage, when her husband was making love to her? How I did tease them! *'Bad child!'* do you remember, that was what they used to call me. Oh, I've had my fancies, like every one else; dreamy days when I used to go about building castles in the air. One wouldn't be a woman without all that. But it was only like a little music in my mind; it just gave me a little excitement. It all came and went in my imagination; but I never had any special man in my mind, oh never. And then, too, when once I came out of my room, it was all over. As soon as ever any one was there, I only had my eyes; I thought of nothing but watching everything so that I could laugh afterward—and you know how your dreadful daughter could watch. They would have had to— —"

"Monsieur," said Chrétiennot, opening the door, M. Magu is downstairs; "he wants to know if he can see mademoiselle."

"Oh, father," said Renée, beseechingly, "no doctor to-day, please. I don't feel inclined. I'm very well. And then, too, he snorts so; why does he snort like that, father?"

M. Mauperin could not help laughing.

"I'll tell you," she went on, "it's the effect of driving about in a gig on his rounds in the winter. As both his hands are occupied, one with the reins and the other with the whip, he's got into the way of not using his handkerchief——"

# LIX

"Is the sky blue all over, father? Look out and tell me, will you?" said Renée, one afternoon, as she lay on the sofa.

"Yes, my child," answered M. Mauperin from the window, "it is superb."

"Oh!"

"Why? Are you in pain?"

"No, only it seemed to me that there must be clouds—as though the weather were going to change. It's very odd when one is ill, it seems as if the sky were much nearer. Oh, I'm a capital barometer now." And she went on reading the book she had laid down while she spoke.

"You tire yourself with reading, little girl; let us talk instead. Give it me," and M. Mauperin held out his hand for the book, which she slipped from her fingers into his. On opening it, M. Mauperin noticed some pages that he had doubled down some years before, telling her not to read them, and these forbidden pages were still doubled down.

Renée appeared to be sleepy. The storm which was not yet in the sky had already begun to weigh on her. She felt a most unbearable heaviness which seemed to overwhelm her, and at the same time a nervous uneasiness took possession of her. The electricity in the air was penetrating her and working on her.

A great silence had suddenly come over everything, as though it had been chased from the horizon, and the breath of solemn calm passing over the country filled her with immense anxiety. She looked at the clock, did not speak again, but kept moving her hands about from place to place.

"Ah, yes," said M. Mauperin, "there is a cloud, really, a big cloud over Fresnoy. How it is moving along! Ah, it's coming over on to our side—it's coming. Shall I shut everything up—the window and the shutters, and light up? Like that my big girl won't be so frightened."

"No," said Renée, quickly, "no lights in the daytime—no, no! And then, too," she went on, "I'm not afraid of it now."

"Oh, it is some distance off yet," said M. Mauperin, for the sake of saying something. His daughter's words had called up a vision of lighted tapers in this room.

"Ah, there's the rain," said Renée, in a relieved tone. "It's like dew, that rain is. It's as if we were drinking it, isn't it? Come here—near me."

Some large drops came down, one by one, at first. Then the water poured from the sky, as it does from a vase that has been upset. The storm broke over Morimond and the thunder rolled and burst in peals. The country round was all fire and then all dark. And at every moment in the gloomy room, lighted up with pale gleams, the flashes would suddenly cover the reclining figure of the invalid from head to foot, throwing over her whole body a shroud of light.

There was one last peal of thunder, so loud and which burst so near, that Renée threw her arms round her father's neck and hid her face against him.

"Foolish child, it's over now," said M. Mauperin; and like a bird which lifts its head a little from under its wing, she looked up, keeping her arms round him.

"Ah, I thought we were all dead!" she said, with a smile in which there was something of a regret.

# LX

One morning on going to see Renée, who had had a bad night, M. Mauperin found her in a doze. At the sound of his footstep she half opened her eyes and turned slightly towards him.

"Oh, it's you, papa," she said, and then she murmured something vaguely, of which M. Mauperin only caught the word "journey."

"What are you saying about a journey?" he asked.

"Yes, it's as though I had just come back from far away—from very far away—from countries I can't remember." And opening her eyes wide, with her two hands flat out on the sheet, she seemed to be trying to recall where she had been, and from whence she had just come. A confused recollection, an indistinct memory remained to her of stretches and spaces of country, of vague places, of those worlds and limbos to which sick people go during those last nights which are detaching them from earth, and from whence they return, surprised, with the dizziness and stupor of the Infinite still upon them, as if in the dream they have forgotten they had heard the first flapping of the wings of Death.

"Oh, it's nothing," she said after a minute's silence, "it's just the effect of the opium—they gave me some last night to make me sleep." And moving as though to shake off her thoughts, she said to her father, "Hold the little glass for me, will you, so that I can make myself look nice? Higher up—oh, these men—how awkward they are, to be sure."

She put her thin hands through her hair to fluff it up and pulled her lace into its place again.

"There now," she said, "talk to me. I want to be talked to," and she half closed her eyes while her father talked.

"You are tired, Renée; I'll leave you," said M. Mauperin, seeing that she did not appear to be listening.

"No, I have a touch of pain. Talk to me, though; it makes me forget it."

"But you are not listening to me. Come now, what are you thinking about, my dear little girl?"

"I'm not thinking about anything. I was trying to remember. Dreams, you know—it isn't really like that—it was—I don't remember. Ah!"

She broke off suddenly, with a pang of sharp pain.

"Does it hurt you, Renée?"

She did not answer, and M. Mauperin could not help his lips moving, as he looked up with an expression of revolt.

"Poor father," said Renée, after a few minutes. "You see I'm resigned. No, we ought not to be so angry with pain. It is sent to us for some reason. We are not made to suffer simply for the sake of suffering."

And in a broken voice, stopping continually to get breath, she began talking to him of all the good sides of suffering, of the wells of tenderness it opens up in us, of the delicacy of heart, and the gentleness of character that it gives to those who accept its bitterness without allowing themselves to get soured by it.

She spoke to him of all the meannesses and the pettinesses that go away from us when we suffer; of the tendency to sarcasm which leaves us, and the unkind laughter which we restrain; of the way in which we give up finding pleasure in other people's little miseries, and of the indulgence that we have for every one.

"If you only knew," she said, "what a stupid thing wit seems to me now." And M. Mauperin heard her expressing her gratitude to suffering as a proof of election. She spoke of selfishness and of all the materiality in which robust health wraps us up; of that hardness of heart which is the result of the well-being of the body; and she told him what ease and deliverance come with sickness; how light she felt inwardly and what aspirations it brings with it for something outside ourselves.

She spoke, too, of suffering as an ill which takes our pride away, which reminds us of our infirmity, which makes us humane, causes us to feel with all those who suffer, and which instils charity into us.

"And then, too," she added with a smile, "without it there would be something wanting for us; we should never be sad, you know——"

# LXI

"My dear fellow, we are very unhappy," said M. Mauperin, one evening, a few days later, to Denoisel, who had just jumped down from a hired trap. "I had a presentiment you would come to-day," he went on. "She is asleep now; you'll see her to-morrow. Oh, you'll find her very much changed. But you must be hungry," and he led the way to the dining-room, where supper was being laid for him.

"Oh, M. Mauperin," said Denoisel, "she is young. At her age something can always be done."

M. Mauperin put his elbows on the table and great tears rolled slowly from his eyes.

"Oh, come, come, M. Mauperin; the doctors haven't given her up; there's hope yet."

M. Mauperin shook his head and did not answer, but his tears continued to flow.

"They haven't given her up?"

"Yes, they have," said M. Mauperin, who could not contain himself any longer, "and I didn't want to have to tell you. One is afraid of everything, you see, when it comes to this stage. It seems to me that there are certain words which would bring the very thing about, and to own this, why, I fancied it would kill my child. And then, too, there might be a miracle. Why shouldn't there be? They spoke of miracles—the doctors did. Oh, God! She still gets up, you know; it's a great thing, that she can get up. The last two days there has been an improvement, I think. And then to lose two in a year—it would be too terrible. Oh, that would be too much! But there, eat, man, you are not eating anything," and he put a large piece of meat on Denoisel's plate. "Well, well, we must bear up and be men; that's all we can do. What's the latest news in Paris?"

"There isn't any; at least, I don't know any. I've come straight from the Pyrenees. Mme. Davarande read me one of your letters; but she is far from thinking her so ill."

"Have you no news of Barousse?"

"Oh, yes! I met him on the way to the station. I wanted to bring him with me, but you know what Barousse is; nothing in the world would induce him to leave Paris for a week. He must take his morning walk along the quays. The idea of missing an engraving with its full margin ——"

"And the Bourjots?" asked M. Mauperin with an effort.

"They say that Mlle. Bourjot will never marry."

"Poor child, she loved him."

"As to the mother, it is the saddest thing—it appears it's an awful ending—there are rumours of strange things—madness, in fact. There's some talk of sending her to a private asylum."

# LXII

"Renée," said M. Mauperin, on entering his daughter's room the following day, "there is some one downstairs who wants to see you."

"Some one?" And she looked searchingly at her father. "I know, it's Denoisel. Did you write to him?"

"Not at all. You did not ask to see him, so that I did not know whether it would give you any pleasure. Do you mind?"

"Mother, give me my little red shawl—there, in the drawer," she said, without answering her father. "I mustn't frighten him, you know. Now then, bring him here quickly," she added, as soon as her shawl was tied at the neck like a scarf.

Denoisel came into the room, which was impregnated with that odour peculiar to the young when they are ill, and which reminds one of a faded bouquet and of dying flowers.

"It's very nice of you to have come," said Renée. "Look, I've put this shawl on for your benefit; you used to like me in it."

Denoisel stooped down, took her hands in his and kissed them.

"It's Denoisel," said M. Mauperin to his wife, who was seated at the other end of the room.

Mme. Mauperin did not appear to have heard. A minute later she got up, came across to Denoisel, kissed him in a lifeless sort of way, and then went back to the dark corner where she had been sitting.

"Well, how do you think I look? I haven't changed much, have I?" And then without giving him time to answer, she went on: "I have a dreadful father who will keep saying I don't look well, and who is most obstinate. It's no good telling him I am better; he will have it that I am not. When I am quite well again, you'll see—he'll insist on fancying that I am still an invalid."

Denoisel was looking at her wasted arm, just above the wrist.

"Oh, I'm a little thinner," said Renée, quickly buttoning her sleeve, "but that's nothing; I shall soon pick up again. Do you remember our good story about that, papa? It made us laugh so. It was at a farmer's house at Têtevuide's—that dinner, you remember, don't you? Only imagine it, Denoisel, the good fellow had been keeping some shrimps for us for two years. Just as we were sitting down to table, papa said, 'Oh, but where's your daughter, Têtevuide? She must dine with us. Isn't she here?' 'Oh, yes, sir.' 'Well, fetch her in, then, or I shall not touch the soup.'

Thereupon the father went into the next room, and we heard talking and crying going on for the next quarter of an hour. He came back alone, finally. 'She will not come in,' he said, 'she says she's too thin.' But, papa," Renée went on, suddenly changing the subject, "for the last two days mamma has never been out of this room. Now that I have a new nurse, suppose you take her out for a stroll?"

"Ah, Renée dear," said Denoisel, when they were alone, "you don't know how glad I am to see you like this—to find you so gay and cheerful. That's a good sign, you know; you'll soon be better, I assure you. And with that good father of yours, and your poor mother, and your stupid old Denoisel to look after you—for I'm going to take up my abode here, for a time, with your permission."

"You, too, my dear boy? Now do just look at me!"

And she held out her two hands for him to help her to turn over, so that she could face him and have the daylight full on her.

"Can you see me now?"

The smile had left her eyes and her lips, and all animation had suddenly dropped from her face like a mask.

"Ah, yes," she said, lowering her voice, "it's all over, and I haven't long to live now. Oh, I wish I could die to-morrow. I can't go on, you know, doing as I am doing. I can't go on any longer cheering them all up. I have no strength left. I've come to the end of it, and I want to finish now. He doesn't see me as I am, does he? I can't kill him beforehand, you know. When he sees me laugh, why it doesn't matter about the doctors having given me up—he forgets that—he doesn't see anything, and he doesn't remember anything—so, you see, I am obliged to go on laughing. Ah, for people who can just pass away as they would like to—finish peacefully, die calmly, in a quiet place, with their face to the wall—why, that must be so easy. It's nothing to pass away like that. Well, anyhow, the worst part is over. And now you are here; and you'll help me to be brave. If I were to give way, you would be there to second me. And when—when I go, I count on you—you'll stay with him the first few months. Ah, don't cry," she said; "you'll make me cry, too."

There was a moment's silence.

"Six months already since Henri's funeral," she began again. "We've only seen each other once since that day. What a fearful turn I had, do you remember?"

"Yes, indeed I do remember," said Denoisel. "I've gone through it all again, often enough. I can see you now, my poor child, enduring the most horrible suffering, and your lips moving as though you wanted to cry out, to say something, and you could not utter a single word."

"I could not utter a single word," said Renée, repeating Denoisel's last words.

She closed her eyes, and her lips moved for a second as though they were murmuring a prayer. Then, with such an expression of happiness that Denoisel was surprised, she said:

"Ah, I am so glad to see you! Both of us together—you'll see how brave we shall be. And we'll take them all in finely—poor things!"

# LXIII

It was stiflingly hot. Renée's windows were left open all the evening, and the lamp was not lighted, for fear of attracting the moths, which made her so nervous. They were talking, until as the daylight gradually faded, their words and thoughts were influenced by the solemnity of the long hours of dreamy reverie, without light.

They all three soon ceased speaking at all, and remained there mute, breathing in the air and giving themselves up to the evening calm. M. Mauperin was holding Renée's hand in his, and every now and then he pressed it fondly.

The gloom was gathering fast, and gradually the whole room grew quite dark. Lying full length on the sofa, Renée herself disappeared in the indistinct whiteness of her dressing-gown. Presently nothing at all could be seen, and the room itself seemed all one with the sky.

Renée began to talk then in a low, penetrating voice. She spoke gently and very beautifully; her words were tender, solemn, and touching, sometimes sounding like the chant of a pure conscience, and sometimes falling on the hearts around her with angelic consolation.

Her ideas became more and more elevated, excusing and pardoning all things. At times the things she said fell on the ear as from a voice that was far away from earth, higher than this life, and gradually a sort of sacred awe born of the solemnity of darkness, silence, night, and death, fell on the room where M. and Mme. Mauperin, and Denoisel were listening eagerly to all which seemed to be already fluttering away from the dying girl in this voice.

# LXIV

On the wall-paper were bouquets of corn, cornflowers, and poppies, and the ceiling was painted with clouds, fresh-looking and vapoury. Between the door and window a carved wood praying-chair with a tapestry cushion looked quite at home in its corner; above it, against the light, was a holy-water vessel of brass-work, representing St. John baptizing Christ. In the opposite corner, hanging on the wall with silk cords, was a small bracket with some French books leaning against each other, and a few English works in cloth bindings. In front of the window, which was framed with creeping plants joining each other over the top and with the leaves that hung over bathed in light, was a dressing-table, covered with silk and guipure lace, with a blue velvet mirror and silver-mounted toilet bottles. The shaped mantel-shelf surmounted with a carved panel, had its glass framed with the same light shade of velvet as that on the dressing-table. On each side of the glass were miniatures of Renée's mother, one when quite young and wearing a string of pearls round her neck, and a daguerrotype representing her much older. Above this was a portrait of her father in his uniform, painted by herself, the frame of which, leaning forward, caused the picture to dominate the whole room. On a rosewood dinner-wagon, in front of the chimney-piece, were one or two knick-knacks, the sick girl's latest fancies — the little jug and the Saxony bowl that she had wanted. A little farther away, by the second window, all the souvenirs that Renée had collected in her riding days — her hunting and shooting relics, riding-canes, a Pyrenees whip, and some stags' feet with a card tied with blue ribbon, telling the day and place where the animal had been run to cover. Beyond the window was a little writing-desk which had been her father's at the military school, and on its shelf stood the boxes, baskets, and presents she had received as New Year's gifts. The bed was entirely draped with muslin. At the back of it, and as though under the shelter of its curtains, all the prayer-books Renée had had since her childhood were arranged on an Algerian bracket, from which some chaplets were hanging. Then came a chest of drawers covered with a hundred little nothings: doll's-house furniture, some glass ornaments, halfpenny jewellery, trifles won in lotteries, even little animals made of bread-crumbs cooked in the stove and with matches for legs, a regular museum of childish things, such as young girls hoard up and treasure as reminiscences. The room was bright and warm with the noonday sun. Near the bed was a little table arranged as an altar, covered with a white cloth. Two candles were burning and flickering in the golden daylight.

Through the dead silence, broken only by sobs, could be heard the heavy foot-steps of a country priest going away. Then all was hushed, and the tears which were falling round the dying girl suddenly stopped as though by a miracle. In a few seconds all signs of disease and the anxious look of pain had disappeared from Renée's thin face, and in their place an ecstatic beauty, a look of supreme deliverance had come, at the sight of which her father, her mother, and her friend instinctively fell on their knees. A rapturous joy and peace had descended upon her. Her head sank gently back on the pillow as though she were in a dream. Her eyes, which were wide open and looking upward, seemed to be filled with the infinite, and her expression gradually took the fixity of eternal things. A holy aspiration seemed to rise from her whole face. All that remained of life—one last breath, trembled on her silent lips, which were half open and smiling. Her face had turned white. A silvery pallor lent a dull splendour to her delicate skin and shapely forehead. It was as though her whole face were looking upon another world than ours. Death was drawing near her in the form of a great light.

It was the transfiguration of those heart diseases which enshroud dying girls in all the beauty of their soul and then carry away to Heaven the young faces of their victims.

# LXV

People who travel in far countries may have come across, in various cities or among old ruins—one year in Russia, another perhaps in Egypt—an elderly couple who seem to be always moving about, neither seeing nor even looking at anything. They are the Mauperins, the poor heart-broken father and mother, who are now quite alone in the world, Renée's sister having died after the birth of her first child.

They sold all they possessed and set out to wander round the world. They no longer care for anything, and go about from one country to another, from one hotel to the next, with no interest whatever in life. They are like things which have been uprooted and flung to the four winds of heaven. They wander about like exiles on earth, rushing away from their tombs, but carrying their dead about with them everywhere, endeavouring to weary out their grief with the fatigue of railway journeys, dragging all that is left them of life to the very ends of the earth, in the hope of wearing it out and so finishing with it.

# THE PORTRAITS OF EDMOND AND JULES DE GONCOURT

**EDMOND DE GONCOURT.**
**DRAWN FROM LIFE BY WILL ROTHENSTEIN, 1894.**

Like Dickens, Théophile Gautier, Mérimée, and some other literary celebrities, the brothers Goncourt tried their hands at drawing and engraving before devoting themselves to letters. Sometimes in their hours of leisure they further made essays in water-colour and pastel. Thanks to Philippe Burty, Jules de Goncourt's "Etchings," collected in a volume, and some of Edmond's sepia and washed drawings, allow us to glean certain of the earliest of those records in which the faithful Dioscuri endeavoured to portray each other with a care both affectionate and touching. A very pretty "Portrait of Jules as a child, in the costume of a Garde Française," a drawing heightened with pastel, is described by Burty as one of Edmond's best works, but one, unfortunately, which it was not possible to reproduce. "In the swallow-tail coat of the French Guard," says Burty, "starting for a fancy dress ball, the brilliance of his eyes heightened by the powder, his hand on his sword-guard, at the age of ten, plump and spirited as one of Fragonard's Cupids." Here we have the younger of the Goncourts, delineated with all the subtlety of a delicate mannerism. Edmond was eighteen at the time. Scarcely free of the ferule of his pedagogues, he already looked at life with that air of keen astonishment which was never to leave him, and which was to kindle in his eye the sort of phosphorescent reflection that shone there to his last hour. It was the elder and more observant of the two who first attempted to represent his young brother, the one who was to be the greater artist of the pair, as if the compact had already been entered upon, as if both by tacit consent accepted the prolific life in common, then only at its dawn. A great delight to the two brothers was their meeting with Gavarni, at the offices of *L'Eclair*, a paper founded towards the end of 1851 by the Comte de Villedeuil.

EDMOND DE GONCOURT.
FROM AN ETCHING BY JULES DE GONCOURT, 1860.

From that first meeting dated the strong friendship between the trio, a friendship that verged on worship on the side of the Goncourts, and on tenderness on that of Gavarni. Two years later, on April 15, 1853, in the series called *Messieurs du Feuilleton* which he began in *Paris*, the master draughtsman of the *lorette* and the prodigal gave a delicious sketch of Edmond and Jules de Goncourt. In his *Masques et Visages*, M. Alidor Delzant, a bibliophile very learned in the iconography of the Goncourts, declares these to be the best and most faithful of all the portraits of the two brothers. We give a reproduction of this fine lithograph. Seated in a box at the theatre in profile to the right, an eye-glass in his eye, Jules, apparently intent on the play, leans forward from beside Edmond, who sits in a meditative attitude, his hands on his knees. M. Delzant compares these portraits to those of Alfred and Tony Johannot by Jean Gigoux. And do they not also recall another group of two literary brothers, older, it is true, the delicate faces of Paul and Alfred de Musset in the delicious frame of the Musée Carnavalet? Gavarni's drawing is a perfect master-piece of expression and subtlety.

**EDMOND AND JULES DE GONCOURT.
FROM A LITHOGRAPH BY GAVARNI, 1853.**

**PORTRAIT OF EDMOND DE GONCOURT.**
**FROM AN ETCHING FROM LIFE BY JULES DE GONCOURT, 1861.**

Placed one against the other, like the antique medals on which Castor and Pollux are graved in profile in the same circle, how admirably each of these gentle faces, in which we note more than one analogy, completes the other! And as we admire them, are we not tempted to exclaim: Here indeed are the Frères Zemganno of letters!

**MEDALLION OF EDMOND AND JULES DE GONCOURT.
FROM AN ENGRAVING BY BRACQUEMOND, 1875.**

The reputation of the two brothers increased proportionately with their works—works of the most intense and subtle psychological research. Installed in that apartment of the Rue Saint Georges which they so soon transformed into a veritable museum of prints and trinkets, Edmond and Jules de Goncourt prepared those brilliant monographs of queens and favourites, which have made them the rare and enchanting historians of the most licentious and factious of centuries.

**EDMOND DE GONCOURT.**
**IN 1888.**
**PORTRAIT ON WOOD IN *LA VIE POPULAIRE*.**

In 1857 Edmond made the water-colour drawing of "Jules smoking a Pipe," which was afterward lithographed. His feet on the edge of the mantel-piece in front of him, Jules, seated in an arm-chair, a small pipe in his mouth, gives himself up to the delights of the *far niente*. This contemplative attitude was a favourite one with him, and one in which he was often discovered by visitors. By representing him thus, Edmond gave an additional force to the living memory that all who knew his brother have retained of him.

Three years later (1860) Jules in his turn made a portrait of Edmond, not in the same indolent attitude, but also in profile, and with a pipe in his mouth. This print is one of the best in the Burty album. We know of no further mutual representations by the brothers; with the exception of Jules de Goncourt's etching of Edmond seated across a chair, smoking a cigar, the design of which we reproduce. But there are several fine portraits by other hands of the younger brother, the one who was the first to go, perforce abandoning his sublime and suicidal task.

JULES DE GONCOURT.
FROM A WATER-COLOUR BY EDMOND DE GONCOURT, 1857.

**EDMOND DE GONCOURT.**
**FROM A PHOTOGRAPH BY NADAR, 1892.**

It was in 1870 that Jules de Goncourt died at the age of thirty-nine. "It was impossible," wrote Paul de Saint-Victor in *La Liberté*, "to know and not to love this young man, with his child's face, his pleasant, ready laugh, his eyes sparkling with intellect and purpose.... That blond young head was bent over his work for months at a time...." It was the profile of this "blond young head" that Claudius Popelin traced for the enamel that was set into the binding of the *Nécrologe*, in which Edmond preserved all the articles, letters, and tokens of sympathy called forth by the irreparable loss of his beloved companion and fellow-labourer. This medallion, etched by Abot, was prefixed afterward to the edition of Jules de Goncourt's *Letters*, published by Charpentier. The profile, which is reproduced as the frontispiece to this edition of *Renée Mauperin*, is infinitely gentle; the emaciated contours, the extraordinary delicacy of the features, betray the intellectual dreamer, his mind intent on literary questions, and we understand M. Émile Zola's dictum: "Art killed him."

**EDMOND DE GONCOURT.
FROM AN ETCHING BY BRACQUEMOND, 1882.
(THE ORIGINAL DRAWING IS IN THE LUXEMBOURG MUSEUM.)**

Prince Gabrielli and Princesse Mathilde also made certain furtive sketches of Jules which have since been photographed. Méaulle engraved a portrait of him on wood, and Varin made an etching of him. Henceforth, save in Bracquemond's double medallion, and in one or two papers in which studies of him by different hands appeared, Edmond de Goncourt was no longer represented in company with his gifted brother, but always alone.

**EDMOND DE GONCOURT.**
**FROM A PHOTOGRAPH BY NADAR, 1893.**

On March 15, 1885, the *Journal Illustré* published two portraits of the Goncourts drawn by Franc Lamy, and on November 20, 1886, the *Cri du Peuple* gave two others, in connection with the appearance of *Renée Mauperin* at the Odéon. We may also note that the medallion of the two brothers drawn and engraved by Bracquemond for the title-page of the first edition of *L'Art du XVIIIème Siècle* appeared in 1875. A delicate commemorative fancy caused the artist to surround the profile of Jules with a wreath of laurel.

**PORTRAITS OF THE FRÈRES DE GONCOURT.
PART OF A DESIGN BY WILLETTE, IN *LE COURRIER FRANÇAIS*,
1895.**

Utterly crushed at first by the sense of loneliness and desolation his loss had created, Edmond de Goncourt was long entirely absorbed in memories of the departed. The spiritual presence of Jules filled the house with its mute and mournful sentiment. The heart-broken survivor could find consolation and relief for his pain only in friendship. Théophile Gautier, Paul de Saint-Victor, Jules Vallès, the painter De Nittis, Burty, Flaubert, Renan, Taine, and Théodore de Banville sustained him with their affection. A band of ardent, active, and audacious young men, among whom M. Émile Zola was specially distinguished by the research of his formulæ, began to link him with Flaubert, offering them a common worship. Alphonse Daudet (we have now come to the year 1879) sketched the most faithful portrait of him to whom a whole generation was soon to give the respectful title of "the Marshal of Letters": "Edmond de Goncourt looks about fifty. His hair is gray, a light steel gray; his air is distinguished and genial; he has a tall, straight figure, and the sharp nose of the sporting dog, like a country gentleman keen for the chase, and, on his pale and energetic face, a smile of perpetual sadness, a glance that sometimes kindles, sharp as the graver's needle. What determination in that glance, what pain in that smile!" Many artists attempted to fix that glance and that smile with pencil or burin, but how few were successful!

**EDMOND DE GONCOURT.
BY EUGÈNE CARRIÈRE.
LITHOGRAPHED IN 1895.**

One of these few was the sculptor Alfred Lenoir, in a remarkable work executed quite at the end of Edmond de Goncourt's life. His white marble bust well expresses the patrician of letters, the collector, the worshipper of all kinds of beauty. A voluptuous thrill seems to stir the nostrils, a flash of sympathetic observation to gleam from the deep set eyes.

EDMOND DE GONCOURT.
BY EUGÈNE CARRIÈRE.
FROM THE COVER OF A VELLUM-BOUND BOOK.

The author of this bust, a work elaborated and modelled after the manner of those executed by Pajou, Caffieri, and Falconnet in the eighteenth century (see the reproduction at the beginning of this volume), may congratulate himself on having given to Edmond de Goncourt's friends the most exquisite semblance of their lost comrade. Carrière, on the other hand, in his superb lithograph, where only the eyes are vivid, and Will Rothenstein, in a sketch from nature which represents the master with a high cravat round his throat, his chin resting on a hand of incomparable form and distinction, have reproduced, with great intensity and comprehension, Edmond de Goncourt grown old, but still robust, upright and gallant, a soldier of art in whom the creative faculty is by no means exhausted. Rothenstein's lithograph in particular, with the sort of morbid languor that pervades it, the mournful fixity of the gaze, the aristocratic slenderness of the hands and the features, surprises and startles the spectator. "By nature and by education," says M. Paul Bourget, "M. Ed. de Goncourt possesses an intelligence, the overacuteness of which verges on disease in its comprehension of infinitesimal gradations and of the infinitely subtle creature." Mr. Rothenstein has made this intelligence flash from every line of his drawing.

Frédéric Régamey, Bracquemond (in the fine drawing at the Luxembourg), De Nittis (in pastel), Raffaelli (in an oil painting), Desboutins (in an etching), and finally M. Helleu (in dry point), have striven to penetrate and preserve the subtle psychology of the master's grave, proud, and gentle countenance. With these distinguished names the iconography of the Goncourts concludes. Perhaps, as a light and graceful monument of memory, we might add the fine drawing made by Willette on the occasion of the Edmond de Goncourt banquet, which represents the elder brother standing, leaning against the pedestal of his brother's statue, while at his feet three creatures, symbolizing the principal forms of their inspiration, are grouped, superb and mournful. Who are they? No doubt *Madame de Pompadour*, the *Geisha* of Japanese art, and finally, bestial and degraded, *La Fille Élisa*—types that symbolize the most salient aspects of that genius—historic, æsthetic, and fictional—which will keep green the precious memory of Edmond and Jules de Goncourt.

OCTAVE UZANNE.

**EDMOND DE GONCOURT.**
**UNPUBLISHED PORTRAIT FROM LIFE, BY GEORGES JEANNI-
OT.**

Lector House believes that a society develops through a two-fold approach of continuous learning and adaptation, which is derived from the study of classic literary works spread across the historic timeline of literature records. Therefore, we aim at reviving, repairing and redeveloping all those inaccessible or damaged but historically as well as culturally important literature across subjects so that the future generations may have an opportunity to study and learn from past works to embark upon a journey of creating a better future.

This book is a result of an effort made by Lector House towards making a contribution to the preservation and repair of original ancient works which might hold historical significance to the approach of continuous learning across subjects.

HAPPY READING & LEARNING!

**LECTOR HOUSE LLP**
E-MAIL: lectorpublishing@gmail.com

9 789389 582635